# LOVETOWN

MICHAŁ WITKOWSKI was born in 1975 in Wrocław and now lives in Warsaw. He has written a doctoral dissertation in Polish philology at the University of Wrocław, and published five books, two of which were nominated for Poland's prestigious NIKE Literary Award. *Lovetown* – the first of those nominees – also won both the Literary Prize of the City of Gdynia and the Polish Booksellers Association Prize; it has been translated into over a dozen languages.

W. MARTIN has published translations of work by Natasza Goerke, Marcin Świetlicki, Erich Kästner and Günter Grass. He edited the 'New Polish Writing' issue of the *Chicago Review* and co-edited its 'New Writing in German' issue. He is the recipient of a 2008 NEA Fellowship in Translation, and currently works for the Polish Cultural Institute in New York.

# LOVETOWN

## MICHAŁ WITKOWSKI

Translated from the Polish by W. Martin

Portobello
BOOKS

Published by Portobello Books Ltd 2010

Portobello Books Ltd
Twelve Addison Avenue
London W11 4QR

Copyright © Michał Witkowski 2009
English translation copyright © W. Martin 2010

Published by permission of Wydawnictwo W.A.B., 2010.

Originally published in Polish by Wydawnictwo W.A.B. as
*Lubiewo* in 2009.

The rights of Michał Witkowski to be identified as the author of
this Work and of W. Martin to be identified as the translator
of this Work have been asserted by them in accordance with
the Copyright, Designs and Patents Act 1988.

The publication of this work was supported by a grant from the
Arts Council.

This book has been selected to receive financial assistance from
English PEN's Writers in Translation programme supported by
Bloomberg.

The publication of this book has been subsidized by the Book
Institute – the © POLAND Translation programme

A CIP catalogue record is available from the British Library

9 8 7 6 5 4 3 2 1

ISBN 978 1 84627 087 1

www.portobellobooks.com

Designed by Lindsay Nash
Typeset by Avon DataSet Ltd, Bidford on Avon, Warwickshire

Printed in the UK by CPI William Clowes Beccles NR34 7TL

# PART I
# THE BOOK OF
# THE STREET

Fourth floor, I buzz the entryphone and hear what sounds like squealing, oohs and aahs.

This must be it. I boldly step into the filthy lobby.

Patricia and Lucretia are already old men; whatever lives they once enjoyed are long over and done with. Since 1992, to be precise. Patricia: a heavy-set, run-down man with a huge bald patch and animated, bushy eyebrows. Lucretia: wrong side of fifty, smooth-shaven, cynical, just as fat. Black fingernails eaten away by ringworm, little jokes, blasé airs. Stock phrases: 'If they finish school, they're not real men!' Their whole lives they made ends meet working as hostesses, orderlies, cloakroom attendants. It was a way to get by while giving themselves time for the really important things.

I take a rickety lift up to the fourth floor of a gloomy, socialist apartment block, circa 1960. Stinks of piss. Out in the courtyard little kids are screaming their heads off. I look at the buttons scorched here and there by cigarettes, labels peeling. I read the graffiti: football slogans, a threat to send someone to the ovens. I give the bell a quick poke. The door opens immediately; it's Lucretia. Patricia is in the kitchen, making the tea. They're both excited about the 'reporter man' who's come to visit; they're acting like real celebrities. For now they're living off their pensions, barely scraping by. They don't even have a vegetable patch where they can grow a few cloves of garlic, or share memories of the good old days over the garden fence with the old dear next door. No, their memories aren't things you'd want strangers to hear. Which is exactly why I'm going to hear them today.

Lucretia had once been a German teacher, but he could never keep a job for long; he was always landing himself in trouble by making the moves on his students, until finally he ended up working as a private tutor. In the seventies, he moved from Bydgoszcz to Wrocław. Here, in a park where the queers go, in a dirty public toilet, he met Patricia. Patricia was sprawled out, drunk, his head in a pool of piss, thinking he'd never get back on his feet. But Lucretia helped the little slut out, finding him a job as a cloakroom attendant in a workers' cultural centre. From then on, it was Patricia's job to dispense ping-pong balls to young functionaries who came to play table tennis in the club room. The work was easy, the pay like any other. By day, Patricia drank coffee out of recycled mustard jars and gossiped with the caretaker. Night was when she came alive. Sometimes she stayed out on her shift, as if she were a night porter, until dawn. Then she would fantasise that she was a Baroque lady wearing an enormous crinoline and a tall wig, taking a carriage to see her lover; she imagined she had some completely unpronounceable name and a huge fan to hide her face behind. The roof might be leaking into a bucket, the wind howling outside the window, but Patricia would get up, make coffee or tea with a little heating

4

coil, add a shot of vodka, then return to her carriage, to Versailles, to skirts so wide you could fit a couple of lovers and a bottle of poison under their pleats. She'd light up a Wiarus and go on her rounds, and by the time she returned she had already worked out her next step. All she needed were earplugs, because the nights were never quiet, and the guard dogs outside were always chasing cats. Morning sobered her up like a splash of cold water. She had to clock off, she had to go back; once again people would be making demands of her, and once again she would be lazy and insubordinate in return.

But that was a long time ago, back when the workers at Hydral and Stolbud still had energy at the end of the working day for things like ballet, back before phrases like 'child molesting' had been invented, and newspapers were only interested in their own problems. Television had yet to come to the night shift, so people had to let their imaginations run at full steam, else they would die of boredom.

Today the rooms in Patricia's cultural centre have all been taken over by different companies. The façade is plastered with signs showing which floor houses the pawn shop, the currency exchange, the pool hall, the candle wholesaler. What was once a studio where workers awkwardly learned to dance now has the romantic moniker 'Everything for Five Zlotys'. Nobody wants to give Patricia a job anymore, everyone's just looking out for number one, and building security is handled by a special firm. The world is a bad place because the poetry recitation contests, the girls' calisthenics, the ballet classes, and the corrective gymnastics have given way to filthy dens where wannabe-mafiosi trade unfashionable second-hand mobile phones. And as if that wasn't bad enough, you can't buy earplugs at the kiosks anymore. Patricia gave this all some thought and decided, with no regrets, to take her much-deserved pension.

Poland's Third Republic never got a foot in her door.

* * *

They refer to each other as *she* and *her*, call each other *sister* or *girl*, and it wasn't all that long ago that they were still picking up men – in the park, behind the opera house, and at the train station. Who knows how much is true, how much is legend, and how much is simply taking the piss. But one thing is sure: they're just two of the innumerable legion of sex addicts. Connoisseurs of cock! Even today, pot-bellied pensioners, they have a few tricks up their sleeves. Neither has ever heard of plastic surgery or sex-change operations. They get by with a flourish or two of their plain black satchels, which they call 'handbags'. They make do with what they've got – the quintessence of communist-era mediocrity. All they have to do is hold their cigarettes a little differently, shave every day, and put their words, their language, to use. For their power lies in their words. They have nothing; whatever they do have they've had to make up, lie up, sing up. Today you can buy anything you want: your sex, your eye colour, your hair – there's no place left for the imagination. Which is why they would rather be poor and 'have a bit of fun'.

'Oh *stop*, darling!' Patricia gets 'dramatic' and pours tea into a chipped cup; old and grimy though it may be, it still comes on a saucer and with a serviette. Form, form is all that matters. And words.

'Oh stop! My glory days are long over, my arse is even sagging. O where o where are the snows of yesteryear? Christ, what a fruity-pie! What a crazy dame! Do you mind? Old Villon said it best: it's better to choose boys. And boy could we choose 'em!'

Being 'dramatic', 'camping it up', and 'being swish' mean acting like a woman, whatever they understand by that. Apparently it means flapping their hands and squealing, saying things like 'Oh stop!' and 'Christ, Christina!', or going up to a cute lad, holding their bent wrists in his face, and saying, 'Sit up straight, puppy dog, when you're talking to me!'

They don't want to be women at all; they want to be swishy men. That's how they like it, how they've been their whole lives: pretend femmes. To actually be a woman would be beside the point. What's exciting is the pretending; to actually satisfy their imagination would be... but satisfaction isn't a word in their language. The only words they know are 'hunger,' 'frustration,' 'cold night,' 'wind,' and 'come with me.' A permanent stopover in the upper regions of the depths, between the railway station, where the pickings were slimmest, their miserable jobs and the park, where the public toilet was. The arse-hole of the world.

And as it happens, someone had lined this arsehole with saw-dust and rags especially for them. All comfy and cosy.

No one ever went hungry with that tinned soup, with those pota-toes, the subsidies of socialism. There was always enough to eat and a roof over your head; a lady doesn't need much to get by. Now they're building a great big shopping mall in that park of theirs; they're burying their entire history. Patricia insists she will protest. But she's only kidding. More bitterly and sadly every time.

'What can a bag lady like me do? Lay into Big Capital with my walking stick? Hit it over the head with my handbag? What should I tell them, that it's an historic site? Oh, go and get the ashtray, Lucretia, the gentleman has nowhere to put his (ha! ha!) *aaaassshh!*'

Patricia realises she's called herself a 'bag lady', and she's delighted at her new joke. Somewhere deep down it contains a trickle of indignity, and Patricia is already planning to drink it, to lick it up like a drop of eggnog from the bottom of a glass. Tonight.

'So there I am on my way to the park. First I stop at the kiosk and buy some cigarettes, like I've done for years. They're fine; they're not at all seriously harmful to my health. Then I see this guy I knew way back, made a name for himself, a businessman. And he cuts me this look like I'm a prostitute or something, like I'm a streetwalker down by the station. Well, I suppose I *am* walking the street. But I'm nobody's streetwalker... So I listen to what he says, but none of it has anything to do with me, something about the credit. Can you believe it? He's got the credit, but he's losing his job. And I'm thinking, darling, if all I needed was credit to make me happy... So I'm having all these deep philosophical thoughts, see, and Lucia La Douche, who I share them with, completely agrees. That we're living in the highest regions of the depths, like in paradise. Nothing can threaten us, and...' – Lucretia lazily stretches her entire body – 'life actually has meaning!' She licks herself indecently.

I'm sitting at the wobbly table in the kitchen of their dilapidated flat. Nothing has changed here since the days of communism. All around me are Taiwanese gold watches from the market, barometers from the market, glittery figurines from the market, all of it from Russia. Even their speech is full of Russianisms:

8

'Not much by him in the trousers…'

Grinding poverty. Their laundry dries on a line hung over the stove. Men's underwear, all of it black, and the cheapest brand; darned socks, black too. First, because black is weird, and second, because mourning is the rule in this household, and has been for over a decade.

Lucretia poses like a dowager countess deprived of her fortune by the vicissitudes of war. She crosses her legs (a pale calf, tattooed with a web of veins, appears between her sock and the cuff of her brown trousers), lights a cigarette, holds the smoke in for a moment, then releases it with a deep sigh, a lady lost in revery. They put on their favourite Anna German record. The disc spins round on the turntable:

> *In the café on the corner there's a concert every night*
> *Stay there in the doorway, you dancing Eurydices,*
> *Before the walls are streaked with the day's first light*
> *May your drunken Orpheuses*
> *Hold you in their arms…*

They offer me a cup of sweet, lukewarm tea. Their flat is furnished like the waiting room of a clinic. You can tell how little people need in life when they 'live' by other means, when their flat is nothing more than a waiting room, somewhere to spend the time between nocturnal forays. It's seedy, as the homes of (sex) addicts usually are. The bottom halves of the walls are painted with a yellow, oil-based paint; the top halves are grimy. The windowsills are lined with white plastic pots of grasses and a recently deceased money tree. I wait for the two ladies (gentlemen?) to finally sit down for their tea and cigarettes, to stop running around. But the moment one takes a seat, the other suddenly realises she needs to spray her armpits with deodorant, or brush her hair in front of the cracked mirror. Something is cooking in the kitchen, too, and Lucretia gets up to water the plants from a communist-era milk bottle. Who knows where that came from? They preen and primp themselves the whole time. Guests make rare appearances in this house of mourning.

'Let's begin. First, perhaps you could tell me something about life for homosexuals in Wrocław back then?' I set the Dictaphone on the table, but their loud squeals of laughter make me pause.

'Look who's asking! Patricia, *save me*! Get this little slut away from me! So the Holy Virgin doesn't know? Patricia, what was it they called our reporter man here back at the Fairy and around the opera house? Wasn't it "Snowflake"? Snowflake – because she was always covered with flakes of... Ha! Snow! It's OK, you can edit that part out, you don't have to transcribe everything... Anyway, the park was our cruising ground, you see. But we called it the "picket line" or the "cruising ground". And cruising we called "picketing", or sometimes "pricketing"! You could pick up a trick and do him right there. Service him, you know. Which means sucking him off. There've been parks for as long as I've been blowing whistles, which is since before the war. Time was when the picket line stretched all the way from one end of town to the other, and that's how you should start your novel about us actually. "The Countess left the house at half past nine in the evening" and went to the park, because ten was always the best time for a bit of cock. Do you remember the Countess, Patricia? They killed her in '88,

I think, poor thing. Now, what was it she did for a living?'

'Don't be stupid! It was Cora they killed in '88. She was always taking grunt home, and she finally got what was coming to her. Some rough grunt killed her with her own kitchen knife. Knifed her for one of those stupid Narev radios – she had nothing else for him to steal. Half the Wrocław picket line was in her funeral procession, even a few, umm… priests (can I… can I say that? This isn't for a Catholic paper, is it?). Anyway, priests. You know what I shouted at them? I said, "Have you girls even said your breviary today?! And now you're out cruising?" But they just started walking faster.'

'Do they believe in God?'

'Who, homos? How can they not believe in God? Many gods even. Any minute, out on the street, young gods are coming round every corner…

'But what was it I wanted to say…? Right, so the Countess was killed long before that, in '79. She was a grandfather, and she worked as a toilet lady – so I guess that makes her a grandmother! She worked in the bogs in the underpass, so she never had far to go. And she lived in a basement flat right off the park. All the queens lived near the park. They made it a point to rent flats there so they could go strolling in the summer, and now they wish they hadn't because the cranes are right outside their windows.'

'What exactly is a grunt…?' My question is drowned out by wild squeals.

'What is a grunt? What is a grunt…? Christ, *Christina!* What exactly is a grunt? Fine, let's pretend you don't know. Grunt is what gives our lives meaning. A grunt is a bull, a drunken bull of a man, a macho lowlife, a con man, a top, sometimes a guy walking home through the park, or passed out in a ditch or on a bench at the station or somewhere else completely unexpected. Our drunken Orpheuses! A queen doesn't have to go lezzing around with other queens after all! We need straight meat! Grunt can be homosexual, too, as long as he's simple as an oak and uneducated – because if he finishes school he's not a real man any more, he's just some intellectual. Grunt can't be someone who puts on airs. He has to have a mug like a thigh – a box covered with hide, the last place where anything can be expressed, least of all feelings! Tell me where you'd find that in those queer bars. There are dozens of stories of straight grunt willingly going off with some queen, playing the homosexual in bed, and only afterwards turning violent, stealing, murdering, making off with the goods… Sometimes even before you get back through the door, they go home. You call out, ask them something, and they turn around and punch you in the face. As if they were furious with themselves.

'But a queen won't let that scare her off. Not real queens like us. Maybe one of those falsies from the bars. They all dream of copping off with some drunken Orpheus – the whole time he's having sex he has no idea it's not a woman he's doing. They dream of looking at his face, watching him thinking he's with a woman. But then he'd have to be completely off his face, or… Well, the best grunt is straight, and to pick that up you either have to get him completely shit-faced or…'

'Or what?'

'Anyway, as I was saying about the Countess…' Patricia dodges my question. 'So get this: there I am, it's eleven at night – this was back before those cranes dug everything up, the little hills and ruins, our trees with all those names and messages notched into the bark. So there I am in the middle of the night, having a nostalgic moment, because it's All Saints' Day, and Forefathers' Eve is coming up. So I'm walking along and all of a sudden what do I see but some grunt. That, I say to myself, looks just like a drunken piece of grunt walking by. So I head off after him, and presto, he disappears. You'll observe I'm talking in the present tense so write it down that way. I'm talking like this on purpose, so it feels like the reader was there. Anyway, half the streetlamps are burned out, so you can't see. But my eyes are used to the darkness, after all these years, so I can tell he's gone off to the ruins on the other side of the hill. I know all those ditches and nooks and crannies pretty well myself. I go over to have a look. I see him flash past before he vanishes again. Now I know he must have gone into that bomb crater, the one with all the bushes around it, you know, where we did Gigantophallus that one time, remember?'

'Oh, right! Right!' Lucretia knows exactly who she's talking about.

'Anyway, the grunt slips through the fence, the one with the sign on it about there being an excavation in progress. I pull up my slip and *voilà*! Of course I know where that loose board in the fence is. I keep walking, I'm already pinching my nipples under my camisole. I'm all mouth. I go down, down into the crater, and just like I thought, there's my grunt standing in that dark, bombed-out pit. Slowly he turns and...'

'What? And what?'

'I look at him, and... It's the *Countess*!'

'Her *ghost*?'

'The ghastly, ghostly slag herself. There's a white light glowing out of her eyes, her gums, her ears, as if she had a candle stuck up in her. She's wearing that jacket she got off the market, the greenish one, but it looks like it's covered in mud, in caked dirt, like the contents of her grave have been mixed with the rain and mud. I cross myself, and she says to me: "Here did I come for grunt, here did I come for the holy rod, through these ruts and underbrush, e'en after death! We observe this day Forefathers' Eve! Give me jism, give, and I to thee this moral lesson shall impart, that he who never..."

"'Why, that's blasphemy, you whore! To mock our nation's literature even from beyond the grave!"

'As a whore she always was exceptional! She continues her mocking, and says: "My name is Million! My name is Million!" she cries. "Because I've done a million grunts!"

'Heavens!'

'A thunderbolt strikes with a crash somewhere off in the distance, and suddenly she turns to me and out of the blue proclaims: "Macbeth! Thane of Cawdor!"

"'Begone!" I say to her. "Begone! Be no more, thou vile shade!" But she keeps at it, something about wanting neither victuals nor drink, just a drop of jism, jism of grunt, jism and more jism. Oh, and then she starts making fun of the Bible, too, getting all prophetic like some off-her-rocker Pythia, or Cassandra; she says, "There, Nellies, shall you stand before the zippered gate of the nads of grunt, and it shall not be opened to you." And then she holds her mangled hand out to me and says, "Come to me!"' (Here they look at each other and breathe out slowly.) 'Obviously I'm shit-scared because you can see her skull showing under her hair, but I know it's her because even outdoors she always smelt of that public toilet where she worked in the underpass; all her life she had that pine-scented whiff of urinal cake about her. Even in the dark I could always tell whether it was the Countess crouching down in the bushes, or some grunt. And I know it's her because she's talking exactly as she did when she was alive, the same country accent. I stand there like I've been hypnotised. All I know is that I need a drink, that if I don't have a drink, I'll lose it. Finally I dig a crumpled fag out of my pocket, and my hands are shaking, like this.'

Patricia's hands are skinny and covered with liver spots. She has long fingernails and wears a metal bracelet with the word LOVE etched on it in English, like the ones they sell on souvenir stalls at the seaside. She shows us how her hands shook. The bracelet rattles and clanks against a large, gold Russian watch.

'Somehow I manage to light it, probably stuck it in backwards with the filter lit, and I try to talk some sense into her gently (inside I'm still trembling like mad). So I say to her:

'"Get a hold of yourself, girl! We were best girlfriends when you were alive. All that sperm has gone to your head if you can't recognise a girlfriend after death, the same sister you shagged all that grunt with, and went visiting the Russians at the barracks with, and all that cum you milked out of them – if you poured it into a bath, all of it at once, it would've been enough to take a bath in, wouldn't it? And with a fat girl like you in there, it would've brimmed right over! *Kyrie Eleison!* Begone! Can't you see I'm not grunt at all? It's just me, old Patricia from the Centre." Her eyes were all cloudy; you could see she carried on knocking it back in the next world just as she had in life. It looked like she was starting to recognise me, then she mumbled her disappointment:

15

'"Pachisha?" (It wasn't "Patricia" she said, but something weird like "Pachisha" or "Chisha", as if her mouth were full of potatoes, but maybe that's what it's like when you're dead.) So I said, "Huh!" Then she muttered something, more garbled words, and went off to carry on cruising on the hill. Without so much as a goodbye, she took off, vanished without a trace, even though we hadn't seen each other for a good ten years and she probably had lots of stories to tell. Anyway, there was this old slapper there,' Patricia snorts with laughter, winking at Lucretia, 'You know the one: Owl. When she saw the Countess coming out of the ruins, she followed her right up the hill. Was she ever in for a surprise. And then there was something else I'd noticed earlier: a group of what looked like skinheads coming up from the river on the other side of the hill – they didn't look too friendly. I thought about warning her, but then I thought, what can they do to her if she's a ghost? It was all I could do to contain my own fear. For one thing, I had a ghost on my hands, and then there were the screams I heard coming from the top of the hill, as if someone were getting beaten to death. But I wasn't so frightened that I couldn't... I mean, that Zbigniew-with-the-moustache turned up right then. The one who's always on a bike.'

Lucretia knows. She stands up and smoothes the grey residue of her hair. She turns the record over. She tugs her cheap jumper with its naff pattern down over her protruding belly. She's ugly. Even though she's practically bald, she has dandruff. Now her lips curl up in a malicious smile, and she says smugly, through clenched teeth: 'Well, the Countess was highly strung even when she was alive, so I'm sure her own death must have come as an enormous shock to

16

her. Do you remember that time we went with her to visit the Russians at the barracks?'

The two old men become animated. Patricia goes over to the drinks cabinet ('high gloss finish') and reverently pulls something out of it. A second later, she sets down on the table a number of sealed plastic bags with brown things inside them. I start to open one, but they both lunge towards me.

'The fragrance! You'll let the fragrance out! For God's sake don't open it! We only open them on *anniversaries...*' They'd stashed their sorry relics in the bags for safekeeping: army belts, knives, foot wrappings, a few sepia or black-and-white photos torn from identity cards and stamped with the purple half-moons of large and long-invalid official seals – mugshots of twenty-something Russian musclemen with potato noses and mouths, faces wholesome, salt of the earth. Or else ugly and crooked, their fringes like triangles pasted over their foreheads. Dedications in Cyrillic on the reverse. Over the kitchen door, where you might expect to see a picture of the Holy Virgin, they have a tangle of rusty barbed wire hanging from a nail. They'd cut it down recently; it came away easily enough, all they had to do was twist it round a bit, right, left, done. They filled their pockets with the barbed wire, so they'd have some for Uterina and the others, for later on, when there was nothing left.

They show me pictures of the ruined barracks, the graffiti on the wall around the windows, carved, scratched, scrawled in hard-to-reach places. For example:

*Брянск 100*

I don't get it.

17

'The number 100,' Patricia explains matter-of-factly, 'means they had a hundred days left until their discharge.'

'Discharge!' sighs Lucretia.

'And Bransk, of course,' Patricia continues, 'is where they were returning after those hundred days. Why a hundred? Because they had to shave their heads down to zero every day for a hundred days before they left so they wouldn't take their lice with them. Then the party could begin. Their graffiti is still there on the walls today. Only today the walls are conspicuous, right on the street, while back then they were further away, back behind another wall, impossible to get to.'

'But not for us! Look,' Lucretia shows me another photo. 'Here's the private road (though it's not so private now), here's where the bushes were, and here's where Patricia would get down on all fours. Those barracks on Barracks Street, we used to call them "*head*quarters". I'd always say, "Come on Patricia, let's go to *head*quarters." There were other barracks in town, of course...'

Lucretia starts to bawl. Patricia's voice cracks. Lucretia recounts her initiation. A moving tale replete with the poetic motif of lost gloves:

The first cock I ever laid lips on belonged to a Russian soldier behind the railway station. That was a thing of beauty! It was just before Christmas, I rang up Patricia, deepest communism. It's hard for me to say now what year it was. It was before Christmas, and there wasn't any snow, but it was certainly cold. And I had a pair of new gloves. Really good ones too, which I left in his car, and had to go back later to collect. I had a porn movie, I had this one porno, you see, and I knocked on the window, my heart pounding wildly, because I'd seen how Guard Lady did it! How Guard Lady gave blowjobs. At first the cars all parked in front of the station, later on they'd be behind. And they would sit there in those military lorries, one in each – behind the wheel, often all day long, freezing outside. Later on, after the fall of the system, they'd be parked behind the station, so people wouldn't notice them. So I mustered up the courage and went with that porno, because I'd seen how courageously Guard Lady would approach them. And I went up to this soldier (a boy, eighteen), and the soldier says to me:

'*Chto ty hot'yel?*'*

And I say: 'Umm… *Pogovorit' s taboi…*'**

'*Ehh… Ya vizhu, chto ty po ruski govorish, no zahodi…*'*** I started talking politics, and he told me he was from Rostov-on-Don, how they have Kazakh traditions there. By now I was totally turned on, my cock hard, my heart banging, and I'm thinking 'I'm gonna explode!' So I say:

'*U menya yest taka pornucha, hotyel' ty uvidyet?*'**** And he says:

'*Nu davai, davai…*'† So he watches it, and then he says: '*A chornuyu ty uzhe yebal?*'†† 'No,' I say. '*Nyet, ya yeshcho nikogda babiy nye yebal…*'††† He's visibly pissed off:

'*Ty nye yebal babiy? Ty navyerno pyedik, da?*'†††† And I say:

---

* *Russian*: What do you want?
** *Russian*: To talk with you.
*** *Russian*: I see you speak Russian, come over here.
**** *Russian*: I have some porn. You want to watch it?
† *Russian*: OK, show me, show me.
†† *Russian*: You ever fucked a black [woman]?
††† *Russian*: No, I've never even fucked a woman…
†††† *Russian*: You've never fucked a woman? You really are a homo then, yes?

19

'*Da! Da!*' The Russians used the phrase *Pyedik Gamburskii* – Hamburg Homo. You know how Slavs usually associate anything pervy with Germany... And he says:

'*No, ya tym nye zanimayus...*'* And I reply:

'*A nravitsya tyebye, chui tyebya stayit? Nravitsya tyebye?*'** He says:

'*No nravitsya, no ya... u myenya dyenyeg nyet. Skolka hochesh?*'*** And I say:

'*Ya nichevo nye hochu, ya tyebye yeshcho dyengi dam, hochu vrot!*'**** And fuck if he didn't look around nervously to see if anyone was passing, then unbutton his fly. And right there, fuck, the palm tree loomed, and Lucretia didn't have even the slightest gag reflex! One two three, and the lad shot his load down my throat... I immediately spat it out into a tissue, and when it was over I asked him:

'Do you want to set a date for moving in?' And he says:

'Never! Bye.' Huh. I continue walking, and fuck if I haven't lost my gloves! So I walk back to him and tell him I left my gloves there, and he gives them back to me and everything, but with such a screwed-up look on his face, he wasn't at all happy, he probably wanted to chuck those gloves away. In my euphoria I rang up Patricia and said:

'Patricia, I had cock in my mouth!' He was a really clean-cut bloke, I have to admit. But I say, 'God, what am I going to do to stop

---

* *Russian*: Well, I don't understand that.
** *Russian*: But are you into me? Is your dick getting hard? Are you into me?
*** *Russian*: Yeah, I'm into you, it's just I... I don't have any money. How much you want?
**** *Russian*: I don't want anything. I'll even give you money, but I want something in return!

myself catching the clap in my mouth?' And Patricia says:

'Cretia, go to the late-night chemist and get a bottle of Sebidin, all you need is Sebidin, take it and gargle, that's the positive gamma, the negative gamma kills everything. And don't worry if you deepthroated that brute either, I'll set you up with some Doxycycline, I have some at home and all you have to do is take it. So now you've done it, now you see what I've been talking about. Now you've done it, just like you said, so now you see. Right? You'll have to reinvent yourself, you'll have to start making the rounds.' There was no going back.

\* \* \*

I can't bear it any more. I excuse myself, put my cigarette in the ashtray (a large glass brick meant to look like cut glass but obviously dislodged from a wall), and go to the toilet.

This is horrible. Horrible and fascinating both at once. There's no way I can publish this. How can I? What can I possibly do with it? An investigative piece for *Polityka*? A special segment on *Eyewitness*? Impossible. Highway prostitutes, thieves, murderers, smugglers, kidnappers, spies – anything but this. Even though there's nothing criminal going on at all. There just isn't a language for this. Unless it's *arse, cock, blowjob* or *grunt*. Unless I could repeat those words over and over for so long they neutralised the taint of the barracks. Like the word *vagina* in *The Vagina Monologues*. I'm not surprised reporters have shied away from this topic!

My thoughts meander along in this manner while I pee and have a look round their bathroom… First of all, right in front of my eyes, pinned to the wall above the toilet, is a photo, carefully cut out of some magazine, of a grunt being led away in handcuffs by two very grunty-looking policemen. It could be someone famous, but he's completely immobilised in any case, and the perverse thing about it is that you can't pee without looking at it. Then there's the washing machine – not an automatic one, but a grotty toploading thing – which is rattling like mad. The tap is dripping. The sink is full of pots of ferns and dreary houseplants like the ones you see on the windowsills at any public health clinic. I look at the pathetic products lining the rim of their yellowing and only partly tiled-in bathtub: an uncapped bottle of Three Herbs shampoo, a shaving brush thick with dust, bottles of generic aftershave and lotions, an extremely frayed and yellowing toothbrush. There's even a tube of self-tan – proof of their reckless struggle for beauty. But anyone who caught sight of Lucretia and Patricia in broad daylight would simply shrug his shoulders out of pity. All those cheap cosmetics, survivors of their own sell-by dates, collected by Lucretia, used on the sly by Patricia, those piddling anti-cellulite gels he thought would make his fat belly go away… All of it evidence that the room I'm in isn't a lavatory at all, but an armoury. Suddenly the gas water boiler behind me starts up with a roar – no doubt one of them is washing his hands in the kitchen. I look at the blue filaments of flame, the sallow bathtub. There's a saucepan filled with yellow water sitting at the bottom of it. The curtains on the window over the toilet are yellow, too. A flat for old ladies. And everywhere houseplants in flowerpots… Old ladies adore growing plants.

* * *

The tin, the tin can, the cottage, the tearoom: for fifty years it did for homos what today's shopping centres do for the middle classes. Located somewhere in a park of ill repute, coated with rust, built before the war, usually sporting remnants of the original trim. From a bird's eye view they looked like stars, each cropped point an entry-way, and the stars all went in! Inside, in the middle, was the shaft – a pole or thick column pissed on from all sides. Waste floated around its base, fetid as the foyers of old buildings.

They were part of the municipal infrastructure, along with street-lamps, benches, and those railings that stopped pedestrians from falling into rivers or lanes of traffic. Under communism they were the only public space of their kind without a toilet lady sulking in the corner. While the streetwalkers had their streetlamps to stand under, we had our tin: we'd stand in front of it – and it was more like stand-ing at the pillory than anything else, since any passerby could spit at you. Inside, the place stank invariably of disinfectant and piss. You'd go in, fish out your cock, splash the blotchy, rimey wall. Sometimes there'd be graffiti scratched with a fingernail into the palimpsest of rime, a peace sign or some completely incomprehensible joke. If you only came in for a piss, you'd walk right back out. On the other hand, you might circle the tin for hours waiting for someone else to go in. When this happened, you had to wait a few minutes, then walk in after him, stand off to one side and start masturbating, throwing sidelong glances at the man, who usually wasn't even pissing, just delicately, slowly stroking his foreskin. By then the ice was broken and you could stop pretending. Without even looking up at his face, which you may not even have seen at all since you'd been following him at a distance, you grabbed hold of his cock and let him grab yours, too. You didn't look up because you still felt some residue of shame, accompanied by the monotonous spatter of drops, the echoes and the cold, which was even more extreme than at the station. Since the tin had no doors, it was never completely dark inside. At some point every night, a mysterious Park Authority simply blocked the entryways with grilles.

But not always. When it rained, the entire park caught an incurable venereal disease called drizzle. Sometimes the Beaux Arts was open on nights like that. Standing in the narrow entry, there'd be this bloke we used to call the Rainy Lover. He'd be there with his trousers around his ankles and his sweater yanked up just under his beard. He'd be wet or masturbating, half-hidden in the depths of the entry. He never wanted anything from anyone, just the echo of rain beating against the tin walls, the amplified sound of ordinary, everyday raindrops. He probably didn't even feel the cold, nor the embarrassment, nor the wind. Who knows, maybe that was what he was into? How does it feel to have cold drops of rain slowly trickle down your naked body, and the water's not even clean, but leaking from the rusty roof of a latrine? Sometimes it's hard to remember what he looked like. What kind of face does a moustachioed thirtysomething make when he's got his unfashionable sweater all bunched up against his neck in one hand? What does he think about? Does he get excited by the slightest rustle in the nearby bushes? Is he disappointed when it turns out to be nothing more than a hedgehog? Maybe it excites him a little too much? One night I saw him during a summer storm. He was standing there smoking a cigarette while the tin was attracting a barrage of lightning. A mound of wet sheet metal. To die in the public conveniences. In Romantic drama it's always the villains who get struck dead by lightning. Like Balladyna, who died on the throne. The Rainy Lover looked pale, somewhat statuesque, the condensation slicking his hair back in an old-fashioned, pre-war do. Even his moustache looked a little like Hitler's. Any good mystery novel has the killer going after his quarry on a rainy night. At night the park promised everything, and there was no time left for it to deliver before the cold day dawned.

Anyway, it's interesting how most people see being struck dead by lightning while sitting on a throne as entirely different from when it happens in a cottage. Or, for that matter – to pick somewhere even closer in location and dramatis personae to the park lavatory – in that rococo folly in the English Garden, the Gazebo of Revery. It had other names – the Kiosk, the Wet Goods Shop – and without a doubt kindly, rococo matrons had read their share of romance novels in it. This sentimental outhouse had another name, too: Cupid's Grotto. Often it had plaster *putti* installed over its doors, their arrows aimed at whoever walked in. The romance novels that were read in the 'Kiosk' were just as likely to tempt the reader to sin, and I'm quite sure that this secluded spot was the rendezvous of various infidelities as well. Yet something tells me that there are very real differences between these two park conveniences – even if people do the same thing in both (and if they're not doing it then at least they are fantasising about it). And that's just fine.

Did they have cottages before the war? There's a photo of German Breslau that shows Plac Polski with an elegant privy made of carved wood in the place of today's rotunda. A number of top-hatted gentlemen with canes are strolling down the gravel-strewn boulevard among flowerbeds and fountains. Does the Rainy Lover's prewar countenance count as evidence? Maybe he was simply the ghost of some prewar German, murdered, say, by unidentified perpetrators? The history of homosexual life here has yet to be written, unless you count streams of urine on a tin wall as writing. Were there as many 'inverts' before the war? Where did they meet? Where did they have sex?

The only place I knew of was the 'Scorched Picket'.

Someone was always setting fire to it. It wasn't actually a cottage at all, but an elegant stone pavilion, solid German masonry, with little columns and statues, rendered in typical nineteenth-century lavatory classicism.

It was the 'alternative' cruising ground, for those who didn't want to take any chances, since it was always quiet – not many people even knew about it – and there were never any skinhead attacks. The Scorched Picket. A gloomy corner of the park overgrown with bushes, where hardly anyone ever walked, a long way from the boulevard. Left to grow wild, like an English garden. Long ago, before the war, this was where German homosexuals would meet. If you want proof, just go to the University Library or the Ossolineum and ask to see the crime reports on homicides and scandals. The really ancient divas will tell you how, in the fifties and sixties, the German queens who had stayed and, for whatever reason, had not been expelled, still frequented the Scorched Picket. Even though it had been torched hundreds of times! They went there again and again to celebrate their ritual of disbelief about what had happened.

The place had not caught on with the Poles yet, having been badly burned during the war. But that didn't bother the Germans. They would circuit round, say hello to everyone, and camp it up among themselves. They'd pretend their cruising ground hadn't been scorched at all, that nothing had changed. They'd shake hands, wish each other a pleasant evening.

Not until the eighties did the Poles start to go there, and then it was almost grudgingly. Sometimes there would only be one or two. Zdzicha Anaconda, some bloke passing through town who'd read about the place in an out-of-date guidebook… No one knows who kept setting fire to it. Did it have something to do with the war and the Germans? Was it some rite for purifying the place, a cleansing by fire? Or maybe the tin windcock on the roof really did attract lightning? A sturdy fence was recently erected around the Scorched Picket, and workmen were seen clearing the rubble, the fluorescent colours of their garb contrasting oddly with the age-blackened brick.

Sometimes grunt would show up in the tin at Cruising Central, looking like a hundred-zloty note – and a crisp, newly minted one at that. Some chanteuse would immediately duck in after him, he'd unbutton his fly, then pull out his badge and declare:

'Police. Give me your papers.'

The Communist Queens, the 'System Queens', the ones in with the Party and authorities, quickly wangled their way out, but others would be stuck in the nick for a long time. I didn't know a single Solidarity Queen, the ones involved in the resistance. Nor any Militant Queens. But it's interesting to consider what role they might have played in that men's game, when the women in the shipyards were slicing bread and helping out. They had no place in the theatre of the sexes. Somehow, too, that feminine submissiveness typical of both homos and older (pre-emancipated) women kept them from taking part in the resistance. They wanted the system to take them from behind; they enjoyed being passive, submissive, obedient… Or else they simply lived in their own imaginary universe, so reality meant nothing and nothing meant anything to them.

* * *

It's hard to say if anyone ever felt pity for them. They would have had to feel pitiable first! Jessica had a job as an orderly at the hospital. She was mean and stupid. Her life was dominated by television shows. First it was *Dallas*, then *Return to Eden*, then *North and South*, and at the end, before she died, *Dynasty*, which she watched in the emergency ward. Jessica would wash the dirty windows in the hospital corridors and see herself reflected in the glass as Alexis. Perhaps it was due to the distance, or the dim light, or something else entirely, but in the glass Jessica's grubby apron, plastered with ID tags and purple stamps, looked just like the white dress worn by Alexis in the last episode. Jessica's sweaty locks were transformed into a new perm. She was speechless with delight, bursting with pride. Slowly, keeping her eyes on the windowpane, she climbed down the ladder and set her bucket on the floor. On the other side of the window, in the courtyard, cats were yowling and screeching like monsters, tearing each other apart. They were all black and bad-tempered. Jessie knew full well what they were fighting over! Only members of staff knew about the corner of the courtyard, where, surrounded by a wire fence, there was a rubbish bin marked Biological Waste. Jessie once had to take an amputated leg there. It was surprisingly heavy. She was ordered to leave it at the courtyard for a special unit to collect the next day. For a long time afterwards, Jessie could not accept certain facts: how could she, as Alexis, have carted someone's leg around? How did this relate to her? But she learned to live with it, and that's when she started telling everyone what an extremely tough and noble job she had, how she was 'saving lives' and came into contact with death every day. Meanwhile, the unit usually waited for biological waste to accumulate before picking it up, and the fence and the red No Entry signs were no deterrents for the cats.

At least Jessica realised, to some degree, that it was all a fantasy, that those dirty gloves from the flea market weren't the lambskin finery she pretended they were, and that the vodka she drank at night down at the tram depot wasn't champagne. It was just a bit of make-believe, something to make it easier to knock back the goblet of her life, which tasted nothing like champagne. 'Fine. On closer inspection, it isn't entirely true,' she'd say to herself while cleaning a clogged urinal or emptying a bed pan. 'I'm still a far cry from Alexis, but maybe we can just pretend, like children do.' And she winked at the mirror as if she were lobbing a sardonic joke at Blake Carrington or, better yet, his wife Krystle. So just for today let's pretend I'm her. Jessica was filled with joy; she gushed; she was the very picture of a respectable lady! She put on airs and let the patients light her cigarettes and refused to thank them. She held her head high, put her hair in curling papers, smeared lip balm on her lips and pretended it was lipstick. Often she would go over to the other orderlies and cleaning ladies, take a seat in their cubicles, and fall into the role of the star.

'Zdzisio [Jessica had been given the unfortunate name Zdzisław] just sits there like an empress with his legs crossed, and refuses to eat bread and butter left over from lunch! He uses a glass cigarette holder to smoke his cigarettes! Oh, how he smokes!' The orderlies couldn't understand why Empress Zdzisio never harassed them. One of the nurses, an ignorant woman with cheap curls who went around singing chart hits from San Remo all day, once stumbled across Jessica in the boiler room in an obvious clinch with the boilerman. She was so shocked she dropped her syringe, which henceforth was useless as the needle had come into contact with the floor, which was filthy, covered with coal. 'Maria, Maria, Maria' — the nurse hummed her favourite song under her breath with malicious satisfaction and decided she'd shadow Jessica. Thereafter, whenever anyone said something nice about Jessica at the nurses' station, she would mutter under her breath: 'The *princess*... Princess *Diana*! But there's nobody to empty the bedpans...

As if in a dream, Jessica picked up shreds of the nurses' everyday conversations.

'Turn the telly on, the broadcast from San Remo's on tonight. Good job I'm on the night shift so I can watch it.'

'Stay down in Emergency, they've got colour TV down there. I always go down to Emergency when the figure skating's on. You can hardly watch the telly in TB for all the ghost images.'

'They say TB is haunted.'

'It's true, haunted by the health service.'

Jessica loved to tour the old hospital at night, and that nurse would follow her every step. It was an enormous edifice on which each era had left its alterations and annexes. Only the Church of the Infant Jesus in Warsaw is as architecturally bizarre. At every turn Jessica came across long-forgotten store rooms full of chairs, broken lamps, and operating tables. At night the deserted hallways, long and low-ceilinged like corridors in a bunker, were filled with pallid flourescent light. It was hard not to get lost in such a labyrinth. You could, of course, follow the white arrows on the green emergency exit signs, but then you'd get lost even more quickly, because the arrows were all mixed up and pointed the wrong way. Jessica would come across one pointing directly back the way she had come. The innumerable glass doors between the wards and the stairwells were locked shut with chains that rattled menacingly. On the ground floor the kiosk, when open, offered patients an array of stunningly dreary wares, telephone cards, fruit juice, and issues of *Detective* magazine, so that they wouldn't be bored and could curtail their own anticipation of death by reading about other people dying. Down another level was the cellar, and who knew if they stored corpses there? For – as Jessica was fully aware – an average of five patients died every day. But down there, with the generators humming, in the sad, cold light, she never ran into a single ghost. Modern death ruled this hospital: empty as a blown eggshell, clinical, it hummed with electricity and smelled of Lysol.

During her nocturnal sojourns, Jessie would lock herself in one of the spacious, empty, unheated lavatories. She would inhale the smell of disinfectant. Once she opened a window and peered into the well of the courtyard. Her face grew frosty, and something seemed to be moving about down below. On another of her night walks, she discovered a lavatory she'd never noticed before in Cardiology. The heavy doors creaked loudly, the echo repeating itself over and over through the sleeping ICU. The lavatory was freezing cold; it had clearly not been heated since the budget cuts were implemented. It was used now as a store room: IV-drip stands, wheelchairs for patients too weak to walk, ancient fire extinguishers, cracked and shattered vitrines – all piled up in the dust and petrified by the cold. She also came across a mirror marked with white streaks of evidence, dirty and unclear, but all the more beautifully deceitful for that. At such moments Jessie would pull her lipstick out of her pocket, along with her cheap, white plastic hairslides (nicked from a bedside table in the women's ward), and then, and only then, could she be Alexis! She opened the window and noticed that across the way a patient – a healthy patient who was clearly only being held for observation – was looking back at her and smoking a (strictly prohibited) cigarette. Jessica approached the situation, or the window at least, head-on. She lifted her smock and without a thought for the darkness or the cold began pinching her nipples. She couldn't tell whether the patient knew she was a man, or if he was taken in by her plastic hairslides, scarlet lips, and purple eyelids. But he stared and stared at her, all the while making a kind of monotonous motion with his hand. Or maybe that's just what it looked like to Jessica; darkness plays tricks on the imagination, after all. The next day she saw the man being wheeled into Surgery and figured she must have made a 'killer' impression on him.

Jessica unlocked the lavatory doors with keys hanging from an enormous ring, like the keys to the old chambers. The doors had been painted over at least a dozen times, and peeling off any one of the oily layers would take you back to a completely different era. Jessica would sit on the commode and imagine she was having her period. This turned her on immediately, especially since she always left the door ajar and at any moment one of the patients could walk in on her. It never crossed her mind that this patient would probably be a tubercular grandfather dragging a catheter around. She was happy simply to be living in a palace, an enormous, ancient palace – the hospital's foundations dated from the Middle Ages after all. She had vodka to drink, cigarettes to smoke, and an endless supply of cock to suck. She wouldn't have traded it for anything. Not even Alexis had it so good...

The other queens found Jessie, sweet-and-sour Jessie, unpleasant. Alexis had provided her with a long and effective apprenticeship in the tricky art of intrigue. She'd stand freezing at pay phones and waste her small change ringing up girlfriends, dishing out dirt, dialling wrong numbers, making crank calls, masking her voice with a handkerchief. In a word, she was a right bitch, and that's exactly what she wanted to be! Eventually the queens were all afraid to have anything to do with her, because it always ended in some elaborate plot, not to mention the rumours she would spread. Jessie was skinny and had a long, pock-marked face. Her sunken chest was wrapped in a snug, pink sweater, and around her neck she wore a scarf run through with silver threads. Knee-high white boots bearing the word *Relax*. 'Jessica Masoni is my name – sit up straight when you're talking to me, lad! Come here, puppy dog, I have something to tell you.' And after he gave his straight ear: 'Say "blow me", and queenie will give you a blowjob. Just look how fleshy my nipples are, some day the girls will show you what nipples are good for. But you'll have to wait till you're grown-up, pup!'

One day Jessie was riding the tram, without a ticket of course. The conductor approached her: 'Ticket, sir?'

Not even for an instant did Jessie lose her nerve: 'Don't you know who I am? You're speaking with none other than Jessica Masoni! You don't believe me? Why, call and ask them on your radio! I've even been written up in the Russian papers...'

In fact, Jessie only ever sororised with Angelica the social worker. They would turn up together in the park and at the sauna, known back in those ancient times as the State Bathing Works. At the picket line they would stand on either side of the road by the Racławicka Panorama and chat up motorists, so that afterwards they could make up unlikely stories about them. 'I shagged a German; he wants to take me to Germany.' 'I shagged a millionaire.' But the biggest sensation was always the one set off by the simple confession: 'I shagged a grunt.' No millionaire could inspire that kind of envy. Double-breasted suits and attaché cases with combination locks were nothing compared to broken teeth or a ruddy face, muscle-bound thighs or beery belches.

✿ ✿ ✿

A bottle of homemade liqueur lands on the table. It tastes of herbs; it's cloudy, strong, and a little too minty. We drink and smoke. They start to loosen up. They explain how life just isn't what it used to be. No soldiers, no park; and now the queens entertain themselves in modern, elegant bars that anyone can go to, bars crammed with journalists and wannabe movers-and-shakers. But they're not queens anymore, they're gays. Tanning salons, techno music, frou-frou. And no one has any sense of filth or wrongdoing – it's all about having fun.

But in the old days… In the old days they would stand in the street by the public toilets and no one could fail to see that something filthy was going on. During the whole of communism there was a little Orbis-run bar across from the opera house that everyone called the Little Fairy, or the Orbs, or the Nellie Bar, or – as those just passing through would call it – Fairy Bar. All of five metres square! In the café on the corner there's a concert every night. Two fat ladies stood behind the counter serving mostly coffee and cognac. You only had to walk by on the street to smell the coffee, the odour of sweet decay emanating, no doubt, from the jam tarts in the refrigerated case, the cheap perfume. Where did that smell come from? How could someone in a blindfold using only his nose straightaway detect that out of twenty café bars, this was the one infused with the stink of decay?

Patricia, Lucretia von Schretke, the Countess, Cora, Joanna the Priest's Girl, Giselle, Jessica, Madame d'Aubergine, and Golda, aka La Belle Hélène, spent all their free days there. Now and then a lonely traveller would wander in, take a seat on one of the high bar stools, and, immersing himself in the stench, watch the men walking by outside the window. Out of boredom he would ponder the word ORBIS painted across the glass, which from inside was inverted: SIBRO. *Sibro*, the most beautiful word in the world! More often than not it would be raining, more often than not he would light up a Carmen, and more often than not he would not leave alone. But before he left, all of them – Patricia, Lucretia, the Countess, Cora, Giselle, and Jessica, who was the first to get AIDS – would begin winking at him, buying him cognac, and glancing impatiently at the toilet door.

They were all hoping for a stroke, or more, of good fortune, for something that happened maybe once a year, at most: that the door would open and in through the heavy, plush, crimson curtain would come a soldier, or fireman, or teenage boy who was thinking of trying it for the first time. No one ended up there by accident, even though the place was utterly nondescript: no neon sign, no suggestive name. Whenever a newcomer finally did show up, he was usually nervous; his hands would tremble as he stirred the grounds of his Turkish coffee in its plain glass cup, and he would keep getting up from the stool, which was awkward to sit on. Those infamous bar stools, always either too high or too low… For the novices, the bi-curious, after chancing upon the place where the pederasts congregated, the bar stools were always the first hurdle.

A boy would sit there fidgeting. He'd drape his jacket over the stool and sit down on it. But then he'd remember he had a pack of cigarettes in the pocket, carefully hidden from his mother! He'd realise he'd have to retrieve them somehow, light one, his hands trembling, and make sure they all knew how grown-up he was. And above all, he'd have to try not to fall off the stool, not to flinch at the sudden roar of the espresso machine behind him, not to jump at his own reflection in the window with the inscription *SIBRO: Brandname Beverages, Cakes to Order, Coffee, Cognac,* and definitely not to collapse from excitement or embarrassment whenever the other men winked at him, fondled their crotches, and glanced at the toilet door. And they'd all be winking; they'd wink at each other and point at the boy.

I was that boy.

I, who back then confused art with smoking, who confused being an artist with drinking, who confused writing with being a whore, with autumn, with everything. It was 1988. The espresso machine howled like a fury, and a melancholy song was always running through my mind. Outside, autumn was underway, and it smelled of burning leaves. The first frost of winter is not a great time for a young man with an awakening lust for life. After a few cognacs I began to feel ill and puked into the urinal a brown mélange of sugary coffee and spirits. Someone walked in after me and squealed with exaggerated horror: 'Heavens, chicken here's about to be sick!' I must have been fifteen. The man, who had a moustache and a shoulder bag, was probably thirty. What was I thinking, engrossed in the spluttering sound of the espresso machine, on that wet, grey day when I bunked off school and spent my lunch money on coffee and cognac instead? He told me that if I was up for it, we could go to the toilets at the railway station, that the toilet lady rented out a special cubicle with an Out of Order sign, and that by slipping her a hundred thousand zlotys we could both sit in the cubicle for as long as we liked.

It was horribly cold at the railway station. I was shivering, and my legs were like jelly. My fingers smelled of cigarettes and stale, dried vomit, nervous sweat and cologne. My legs continued to shake as I stood in the cubicle, although it wasn't so cold anymore. Afterwards, when it was all over, I had the taste of genitalia in my mouth – salty, syrupy – along with that awful aftertaste of cigarettes: I wasn't used to smoking. I vomited a few more times that day. My jumper reeked of it, too. Love bites surfaced on my neck, reddening treacherously like the first symptoms of AIDS. I'd hide them under a polo-neck, under a scarf. My lips were sore, dirty, chapped. The guy took a liking to my watch and asked if he could have it. I was so out of it I gave it to him without a word. Later, of course, I remembered that I wasn't even a grown up yet and that my parents were still curious about what happened to my possessions.

That was how I first met them. Years later, returning from some literary event or other, I ran into Patricia at the railway station, and we arranged to do an interview.

The Little Fairy was managed by Mother Joan of the Homos, aka Pani Jola – the only real woman among that crowd. She must have been sixty. She was heavyset, crude, with piercing eyes that were always winking, always reflecting the moustached or smooth-shaven faces of her conversation partners perched along the bar, their glasses of cognac raised in a toast. She tended the bar but never served anyone. Instead, she drank with her patrons, denouncing them as slags and whores, and they loved her for it. Her eyes, always a little bleary and bloodshot, reflected not just people but entire histories. They were so shiny and glassy you could watch the front door opening and closing in them, and see the heavy crimson curtain that kept the heat from escaping; you could also see who was doing what to whom and for how much. Mother Joan of the Homos could have – no, she *should* have! – written a book of the Wrocław streets.

Every day she should have written the stories down on the bar tabs with her Orbis pen. Story A: Two cognacs, one coffee, one strawberry torte with jam; story B: coffee and a pack of Carmens; story C: four vodkas followed by four shots of the same, on the tab. Oh, what has become of those bar tabs of 1988? Where are those stories now, sticky from sugary cakes and grimy with cigarette ash? Where are Mother Joan's enormous bosoms now, their spacious luxury, which went unheeded, unneeded, by everyone? Bosoms that no doubt had a little amber heart dangling between them, an inebriated and good heart, filled with understanding for everybody's problems. With the obstinacy of a true maniac, Mother Joan of the Homos insisted they were all affairs of the heart. All of them. And that's exactly what she would say: 'Jessica's not about, she's in the toilet. Some affair of the heart has banished her there.'

But Mother could talk like that because she'd been endowed with two enormous hearts, not to mention that amber pendant rocking between them. Her puffy face, her emergency loans, her giving of booze on credit, her buying a stolen set of Finnish knives and all sorts of other hot merchandise, and her discreet anti-Semitism, shown for example when she hugged one of the queens:

'Sweetness, you know I have nothing against Jews, but for God's sake, *shaaaave!*' she would gurgle, nestling the unshaven face between her bosoms. But she sniffed out the Jew in all of us. I had only to go to the toilet for Mother Joan of the Homos to exclaim:

'Look at Snow White's profile... Wouldn't you girls say she's got something of the *Ahashrachabash* about her?'

As a woman of at least three hearts, she had more than enough maternal instinct to spare for the black-market moneychangers across the road, in the café of the Hotel Monopol. Out of all the queens in the world, the moneychangers tolerated only Golda, aka La Belle Hélène. I don't know much about her. She always wore an impeccable suit, and she went through life without ID papers, until they were procured for her at the old people's home. Before that, after she'd lost her money, she lived in the kitchen of her former maid. On her fiftieth birthday the moneychangers threw her a party at that awful Monopol, and Golda sat on a golden throne wearing a golden jacket. But none of the other queens went because they weren't allowed in.

In any case, although the moneychangers entered the haze of the Little Fairy with visible revulsion, certain interests kept luring them back. Mother would buy gold from them, and she operated as a kind of one-person pawnshop-cum-bureau de change. The money-changers would stand at the high bar, embarrassed by their satchels (known as fag-bags), shifting their weight from foot to foot. Their legs were invariably wrapped in bright nylon tracksuit bottoms, their waists girdled with bum-bags. Russian signet rings, watches, all sorts of tokens – Mother would test each item with her teeth, then deposit it in her bra, or some other cranny of her ample body, to keep it warm.

Goodness, how jealous Mother's regulars would become, how they hated the moneychangers! Was it because she referred to their petty, dirty business, all of which reeked of illicit hard currency, as affairs of the heart, too? Was it because of her generosity? Or was it ultimately because she satisfied the moneychangers' need for mater-nal love and kindness, as well? No, there was another reason for the queens' hostility: the moneychangers viewed her with completely different eyes, and she, for her part, played erotic games with them.

'Pani Jola's grumpy today, Pani Jola can't have got much sleep…' Without the moneychangers, Pani Jola was simply Mother Joan, but in their presence she became a Woman. When she talked to the queens, she would smile indulgently and show curiosity. She looked at us as if we were two-headed calves. And she never tired of hearing the simplest jokes: 'That's what *she* said!' Or: 'I'll pick up my skirt and leave *you* in the dirt!' Whenever any of us uttered one of those one-liners, Mother Joan of the Homos would burst into paroxyms of laughter, and with her chubby fist mop away the tears that smeared her makeup. She loved talking to us like we were women, but her own repertoire of witticisms was far skimpier than the ones that made her laugh.

Pani Jola was one of those people who disappeared completely after the fall of communism. The ground simply swallowed them up sometime in the mid-nineties. Even as late as 1991 she had a go at setting up a little sweet stall, but it didn't work out. If I ran into Pani Jola today, I'm sure she'd either be in the gutter or else stylishly slim, all done up like a spoilt European.

And instead of her book of the streets, she'd only be interested in her chequebook.

❋ ❋ ❋

Today I know what I need to ask them about. Will they talk?

'When did you first start going to the barracks?' Both of them, as if on command from their corporal, lower their eyelashes and start examining their faded fingernails. Lucretia stands up and in one move switches off the record player. This is serious.

'Oh my God, the things that used to go on! Like once when the police came, they were hauling off the drunks near the barracks and they shouted at us: "Off to see the Russians at the barracks again!?"

'And you, Trisha, started jabbering and swinging that empty vodka bottle in their faces:

'"What? We are friends with the Soviets, aren't we? All I want's to drink a vodka to my Soviet friends. *Na zdorovye!* I'm a member of the Polish-Soviet Friendship Society!'

'And then that one cop slipped his finger in and out of his mouth:

'"That's what you mean by friendship! Fucking homo!"

'And all the other cops sniggered in unison!

'Then Trisha shouted:

'"But I just want to go out for drinks with them!"

'And the cop says:

'"Right, get so plastered your arse won't hurt!" And they all started sniggering! Oh my Lord, when the Russians left, some queens hanged themselves!'

'Please, ladies, one thing at a time!' I say. They get serious.

'When I moved here from Bydgoszcz... Well, at first I was going to go to Legnica, because the other queens at the station in Bydgoszcz had told me how pansies from all over Poland go there. But the crowd there turned out to be too big, the soldiers couldn't stave them off. You know what, I told myself, they have armies in Wrocław, too. And the Russkies have no money for prostitutes because they're kept in their barracks without pay. And with them, of course, no one wants to be the bitch. So I put on my thinking cap and said to Patricia:

"'Girl, now's our chance." We talked about it all through the night. We took a number 17 bus and got off next to the bushes, then made our way over to the barracks. We went during the day, so we could see what the fences were like and everything. But there were no fences there, just a high wall plastered with harmless phrases that in four different languages warned you against coming within shooting distance. It was topped with coils of rusted barbed wire, and every dozen metres or so a watchtower and a guard. I said, "Patricia, what are we getting ourselves into?" But it all worked out, and twelve months later it was all a matter of course. One never appreciates what one has until it's gone. Later on, other queens claimed they'd been there first, but who believes that bunch of kangaroos? You're at the very fount of all knowledge here.'

'What was it like?'

'What was it like? What do you think it was like? Day in, day out is what it was like. Around one o'clock in the morning, we'd climb the wall, one of us giving the other a leg up. In no time a helmet would appear in one of those guard towers in the wall, and the soldier would ask in a whisper:

"'*Chto?*"*

'And we'd always answer:

"'*Eto my, dyevochki!*"**

'Snow was falling, the walls were bathed in moonlight... that's

* *Russian*: What?
** *Russian*: It's us, girls!

43

how you should be describing it for him – the gentleman is a novelist after all!'

'Oh, it didn't matter if it was snowing or pissing down with rain, we were there all the time, with our *Dyevochki prisli, vpustitye nas!*\* And the soldier would whisper either *tyepyer nye nado,*\*\* or that we should come back *za pyat' minut…*\*\*\* Once upon a time they had a huge pile of coal for heating their barracks on the other side of the wall, a whole slag heap high enough to jump on to. Supporting each other, Patricia and I would leap on to that pile of slag… More fuel for the fire! And there they were, five of them, waiting, steam shooting out of their drawers! We got ourselves all dirty because there was still barbed wire left on the wall and we had to jump several metres on to the heap.'

'Oh my God, *to se ne vrati!*\*\*\*\* Patricia downed a full shot glass.

'We used to take them porn magazines, Taiwanese ones; we'd take them coffee in thermoses, and booze. All those queens standing in queues at the butcher's weren't there on their own account; they went so they could make kielbasa sandwiches for them! Lordy, Lordy… They were always competing, who could piss the furthest, or spit the furthest, who farted the loudest. What a shame, Michał, that you weren't even born.'

'Oh please! Don't remind me!'

'So why didn't you go to Legnica?'

'We don't like crowds…'

* *Russian*: The girls are here, let us in!
** *Russian*: We can't now.
*** *Russian*: In five minutes.
*****Czech*: It will never come again!

'There was too much... What is it called? What's that word? What is it now?' Lucretia can't remember.

'Competition?'

'That too. But there was another word, too... What was it? When there's plenty of something? Oh, *supply!* Supply exceeded demand. At the barracks Mirejka said to us, "A person can only work it so much, you can only work it so much, right? Well, I couldn't do it. No sense carrying coals to Katowice! Patty, come and sit down beside me here in the grass. Come on, you whore, sit down, do that for me. We'll drink some vodka, I'll put a Validol under my tongue, feeling weak like I do... Oy, I've probably had eighteen of them... The one was ready to beat the crap out of the other, they were fighting cause they all wanted to... I mean, fuck if I'm taking every last cock down my throat!"

'But in Legnica, they couldn't process so many queens.'

'The Legnica queens...' – Patricia donned an army cap adorned with a red hammer and sickle and stood in front of the mirror, carefully arranging it like an old woman does her beret – '...the Legnica queens would stroll by the barracks all tarted up like women. At first they actually pretended they *were* women; they'd tell them they couldn't do it from the front because they were having their period... And if one of them was being especially cheeky, she'd say, "I'm still a virgin and I intend to stay that way!" Right! "But you can still do me from behind..." – Virgin! – "or I can give you a blowjob!" And for a while, there in the dark, those soldiers even bought it, I reckon. But you see there was the Legnica school, which was all tranny, and the Wrocław school, which we're the founders of, and the Wrocław school wasn't tranny at all. I mean, they were used to their punks anyway, so it didn't much matter whether it was their punks sucking them off or someone from outside the barracks. They'd even piss on you, if you asked them nicely...'

At that last remark, Lucretia froze at the table with the teapot in her hand. The blood went out of her face, and she said through clenched teeth: 'Tell me you're making that up.'

'I'm telling the truth. They pissed on me, three of them together, as I lay on the gravel, on the coal, the slag! It's just that you – ha! – you were laid up with syphilis in a hospital bed that night, eating cold milk soup! That's right, my love! And the steam shot right out of them...' Patricia took obvious pleasure in teasing Lucretia.

'If that's the truth, then I don't want to have anything to do with you any more. God, you could have at least told me they'd even agree to something like that, that there was even a possibility...' Lucretia slowly started to put on her jacket and beret. At eight o'clock every evening she went to mass.

'And there was one of them...' – here Patricia's face lit up with an ironic, jaded smile and twisted into a grimace – '...there was one I took a real fancy to. But he always kept himself to himself, off to the side, and didn't seem interested. So what do I do? I put on my proverbial thinking cap and say to myself, "Patricia, it looks like you'll need a bit of psychology with this chap." So I go up to him, this big blond – actually he wasn't, they all had mousey hair, just mousey brown. So I go up, and he says something like, "*Kak eto? Malchik s malchikyem?*"* And here I'm thinking: Aha! I've got you. There he was, Alyosha from *The Brothers Karamazov*. Fine, then I'll be Grushenka. So I say to him:

* *Russian*: What do you mean? A bloke with a bloke?

46

"'Look, I've been in *Gyermania* – three years – and there – *eto normalno* – lads with lads." And he just looks at me, dithering:

"'*No, ty nye zhenshchina.*"* And it was like a bolt of lightning hit me; I flew into a fit, squealing so loudly they started hissing at me to shut up:

"'What do you mean I'm not a woman?!" I said, "I have a mouth, don't I? And a vagina, too?" – and I showed him my bare arse – "I do, I do!" But my *Gyermania* is what did the trick. For them it was like paradise, unattainable, to travel to Germany! Those twentysomething young men, their whole lives in Russia, and other than Poland, other than their barracks, they never saw anything of the world!

"'*Kak eto, v Gyermanii tak eto dyelayut, eto normalno!*"** And hardly had he unbuttoned his flies than I was on it like a leech!

'But one time they came to us at night outside the wall. They were leaning against it when – whoosh! – one of their caps slid off, and a shaved head flashed in the darkness, and then another, and then a third. We burst into tears:

"'You're leaving! You're abandoning us!"

'We went down on them then, but we were mourning them, too. In a hundred days they would be gone! But then, oh, the things they told us... For instance, how they would never forget us, even when they were far away, when they'd started nailing pussy again. They told us we were their first loves...

"'*Ty znayesh,*\*\*\* for happiness we not need very much, any

---

\* *Russian*: But you're not a woman.
\*\* *Russian*: What do you know, that's how they do it in Germany, it's normal!
\*\*\* *Russian*: You know...

vodka, a little pussy. I'm simple man, I find woman there, and job in mines, but you here, you keep going after the cock and thigh."

'He was a Cossack. White face, moustache, a Cossack legionnaire (they smell so different, like the steppes, like Asia!). He told me he'd never done this before with anyone. He was surprised when Patricia took him in her mouth. At that she said:

'"But you eat pussy."

'Then he said not really, because "pussy – *vonyayet*".* And then Patricia gave him such a simple, austere answer, it was like she was born a Buddhist:

'"Then the pussy should be washed."

'It's true, they'll never forget us. They're lying there on the banks of the Don, married now, with children, old and fat in their deer-stalker caps, no longer the young men they once were. But they're there – they told us they would be – looking up at the sky, at the stars, thinking: "Somewhere, under these same stars, my Andriyusha (Patricia) is at the barracks now, far away in Poland."'

'I once fell in love with a certain Dmitri. I got myself all dolled up for him: new shoes, perfume, my good Wrangler jeans, and over at the barracks Radwanicka, pissed and all bent out of shape because her dentures were hurting her, shouted over at me:

'"You stupid slag, you dumb cunt! What do you think you're doing? Those are normal lads! Hmm, I really like that, I like the way you dress, you have good style, it's similar to mine. But so what? Under normal conditions you'd be reviled, he'd spit right in your face; but here you think you're fucking in love! In a normal country, where

* *Russian*: It smells.

a lad has a choice, he'd sooner eat out the oldest, most festering piece of snatch, and he'd beat the shit out of the pansy and spit in his face, no matter how young or tarted up! He'd kick your arse! What kind of life is this? Completely abnormal, and no place to hide!"

'Later, when they were leaving, everyone was schlepping around, complaining how nothing was happening, and Radwanicka says to me:

"'You fucking slag, don't you dare complain! No faggot ever had it as good as we did, and you've got memories to last you a hundred and eighty-five years! And now you won't, now we won't get jack. Tossing off something drunk on a bench once a year, that's what our new life will look like. That's the kind of life we'll be living now." And she burst into tears.'

*Tak prieroda zachaciela, paciemu—nie nasza diela.**

❋ ❋ ❋

As soon as Zdzicha Aidsova started getting really sick, everyone in the park began to shun her. They didn't want to sit on the bench drinking vodka from her bottle, they didn't want to sip the warm backwash. Once silky, her hair was ragged now; once sonorous, her voice a yelp; her eyes, once anthracite, were little pieces of coal. They stopped talking to her because her breath had gone sour. A fungus, some kind of fungus must have taken root in there. They'd say: Zdzicha, that banshee. Then, Zdzicha Aidsova's pretty but pimply and acne-scarred face began to take on a tinge of bitter irony. No

* *Russian*: That's how nature wanted it; why it is so—isn't our problem.

one could forgive her for continuing to trick with outsiders, for infecting them. All along the path in the park they'd throw empty vodka bottles at her. One of them landed with a thump on the ground. Some dog limped over, thinking they were playing fetch, that they'd tossed her a bone. Zdzicha took me with me to her coach, before I learned her nickname. What could a teenager like me know? Right, so she was walking to her coach. She'd discovered it behind the station once when she had nowhere to sleep for the night. A coach in the siding, windows boarded up, and wherever you looked, rows of points and crossings. Railway sleepers, withered shrubs, signalboxes, lights that shone only red, steel rails bearing impossible weights, poles with wires carrying thousands of voices, electronic signals, internet chats, laughter, tears. All together it sounded like distant racket from a school sports field under a viaduct, a sight in summer for passing travellers. Freight wagons loaded with long-forgotten timber, left standing for decades. Others were fitted out with roofs, even chimneys and windows, through which a signalman's kingdom would come into view: a time schedule bound in an old oilcloth, a pot-bellied stove, thick gloves. Grease coating everything opalescent, violet-grey. Grey ribwort overrunning the gaps between grey sleepers. Grey flowers emitting the scent of creosote-treated wood. Eau de Polish State Railway. Such were the tracks of Zdzicha's fate. The strangest thing about it was her looks; her face was pale and thin, and her practically white hair was falling into her eyes – but for all that, she'd let herself go, she was dirty, and there was the fungus, too. They said that Zdzicha had had a lover who lived in Paris and that's how she got sick. With nothing else to lose, Zdzicha started to drink seriously. She had a huge

German shepherd who would lead her, when she'd been drinking, back to that coach of hers, like a blind man.

Once, back when Zdzicha still had a job and a flat, they called her Jessie.

＊ ＊ ＊

They come to life at night. Their vision is better then, too – in the daytime they always wear dark glasses, ugly, gold-framed sunglasses from the market. At night, when they roam the parks and Polish Hill, when they find their way into the station waiting room, with its sleeping soldiers, drunks, and junkies, and poke their long noses, protracted from constantly sniffing out quarry, into the rotund, tin-walled cottages, then even the faintest silhouette of a distant passer-by will awaken a frisson of hope: that's him! Desire must have driven him here, too, into the night! They're not ones for beating around the bush – beating off in the bushes is more their style. And they're not especially fussy – old or young, sick or healthy, crippled – as long as it's not queen or cunt. The park at night is pitch black, and every now and then a patrol car passes by. It cruises slowly, majestically, cutting the darkness with its sharp headlights; it forces its way through the shrubbery, climbs the hill, circles the yard around the public toilets, then disappears. A phantom car. Some-one had inscribed something on a tree with its bark torn off; but it wasn't about us – even when people know about this place, they always act as if they'd never heard of it before.

After ten hours of 'picketing', their throats are parched from smoking, shoes caked with mud from walking in ditches and cruising the bridges and ruins. Their lips are chapped, their feet pinched and chafed, and their single handkerchiefs rolled up in soggy knots in their pockets. It's time, time to go home, but all of a sudden: they freeze at the sight of a figure in the distance, which, close up, turns out to be a tree or a stump. The imagination works wonders. What counts is the tingly excitement, the hope, because anything can happen. And no one would even think to go home now, though the birds have started to balls up the atmosphere of night, and it looks like the sun's coming up on the other side of the hill. But experience tells them that now is the time when miracles happen, when the nets of night start to teem with golden fish!

Before the walls are streaked with the day's first light.

Now is the time when their drunken Orpheuses might appear! A lush passed out on a bench, a tanked-up teenager on his way home from a party – whatever. They don't give up. The park is cold, pitch black; the park is evil. At night the park turns into a wild forest, bristling with stories of big bad wolves and Red Riding Hoods. The wolf might infect Red Riding Hood with some disease or other. The roots of the trees swell to fairy-tale dimensions, and in their hollows roost malevolent owls – decrepit, grey poofs hungry for one thing and one thing only. They sit there on their benches, gossiping – what else is there? They harass and annoy the passing grunts, but as soon as some yob comes to beat them up, they flutter away like owls. No surprise when a grunt wrecks the benches in a rage – they're always looking for something to bang. From their hiding place, the queens watch the grunt smash the benches up and think: Always banging something! In the evening, when the queens cross the threshold of the park, they feel a rush of excitement, like the junkie about to shoot the syringe into the vein, like the gambler sitting himself down at the scarlet, felt-covered table. Anything can happen; something always happens. Who knows who the beneficent God of the homos will send my way tonight. Queens do believe in God, after all, like all the other old ladies in their tasselled berets. And they really don't think of what they are doing as sinful – after all, they're hurting no one!

At five in the morning, panic sets in. It will soon be daylight, and all the imagined lads will have changed back into trees, No Entry signs, boulders, and monuments. No deceptions remain, the emperor has no clothes. Something had been stirring in the bushes all night, and now it's clear what it was. Not some grunt standing there in front of the hole in the fence – just an old, abandoned vacuum cleaner, its long hose wrapped around it, looking like a tracksuit with a thick neck and close-cropped head poking out! In a moment, the park will fill up with people. Unfortunately, it won't be drunken, horny grunts, but ordinary people taking their shortcuts to work, nannies with children – they'll look at us from the other side of an invisible wall. Fragrant with shoe polish and toothpaste, fresh newspapers tucked in their shoulder bags. Hideous and sober, freshness unfurls along with the breaking day and spangles it with birdsong. Brrr. It's better to run away from this scene of desecration. To run away from people, to avoid their faces. To go home, to sleep.

❋ ❋ ❋

Lucretia is crying. She stows the souvenirs in their plastic bags into the drinks cabinet and carefully closes the door. But not before we each had a sniff. I, too, inhaled. At first I smelled nothing. But then I detected the faintest *soupçon* of prison funk, sweat, and Lysol. Maybe I'd got a whiff of some musty footcloth! Now, on the table, all that was left were pictures. They stared up at me, most of them teenagers, not even in uniform yet. The pictures had been taken somewhere beyond the Volga, some far-off Soviet photographer's studio. Patricia picks up one of them, wipes it on her sleeve, and examines it as if for the first time.

'This one must be back in the Caucasus now. My beloved Sasha. And here's Vanya. Sometimes at night, when I can't sleep, I pick up a map and look at it. Where is my Sasha now, where's my Vanya, my Dmitri? They didn't leave us a thing. Even the camp has been donated to the university. Nothing, no park, no barracks, no nothing. Everyone was all in favour of the changes, the new order, but not Lucretia and me; we prayed it wouldn't happen to us. Everything's going downhill. Under communism, plucking a recruit off the train was a piece of cake… All those Stasyas and Romeks came straight off the farm, and there were no girls in the army back then, no leave either… As soon as I heard they were making the army more "humane" I knew it meant bad times for the queers. Now every recruit can get as much as snatch as he wants.' Lucretia weeps. Suddenly Patricia straightens up and asks in a hopeful voice:

'But maybe we'll be invaded again, Lucretia. What do you think? Maybe we could get occupied by the Germans?' Patricia quite evidently has never heard of NATO.

Lucretia looks anxiously at her watch. Church won't wait, and she wants to go and say her prayers for her Vanya, her Dmitri, and her Sashenka. Or maybe that's just what she says, and in truth she's off to her usual haunts. Dressed in black, of course. But before she leaves, she calls back from the hallway:

'Eh, they'll never invade us again. *To se ne vrati.*' Suddenly she brightens up. 'Unless we could... You! Unless we could get ourselves sent to prison! Oh! They'd make a prison pansy out of me, all those criminals. I'd be their bitch, I'd put out for each and every one of them...'

'Don't you start! We've got company! Goodness, there she goes again... You'd better get to church and say your prayers. Look at her, going to church and praying to those saints of hers, but she's still got the Devil inside her!'

'... every last one of them, I'd do each and every one. I'd be their whore, their widow... And there'd be one who looked like a murderer, who'd say, Wash the floor with your face, bitch! He'd cough and spit on the stone floor and piss on it. Lick it up, bitch! And I would – I'd lick it up!' Lucretia's nostrils flutter like a film star's, and she runs her fingers up and down her chest, her stomach, further down; hunger has dragged her down into the depths of abjection. Something is itching away at her, something is sucking at her insides. Who knows what it is, but wherever it takes her, it definitely won't be good...

'Shut your face already! Fine, so you'll be his whore, we already knew that. Now shut up!' Patricia can't cope with this image. Suddenly she's reminded of something, but it's clear she's waiting for Lucretia to leave. Lucretia turns and tries on some old caps; finally she chooses one that makes her look like a fat, old grandad going fishing. A brown leather one. She sticks her tongue out at us, then curtsies politely and walks out the door. Patricia gives a sigh of relief, and is gearing up to tell me something when the door opens, Lucretia walks back in, grabs a pack of cigarettes and lighter from the table, waves goodbye to us, and then leaves. Patricia gets up and from an enormous kettle adds more hot water to my coffee grounds. She gives me a glug of peppermint vodka, too. Suddenly she's a completely different person. She gets serious, stops talking in the feminine. An old and tired life. Compulsively she starts to tidy what's left of her hair. And at that – arghh! – Lucretia walks in again.

'Remember that time we went to Oleśnica, to the prison? While we're on the topic of prison pansies… I really have to tell the story again, for posterity's sake, because I'll be coming home late and Reporter Man here will have gone. Remember, Patty? It was late autumn. All day they'd been sitting in their windows, gripping the bars, staring at the street. All rough-and-tumble, dingy-grey, chiselled, their heads shaven and hard to make out. You can see both wings of the prison from the street, not like the one by us on Kleczkowska. Sometimes families would stand under the windows, using hand signals to exchange information with them, but that evening no one was around. And we went up and just stood there. They sensed us immediately.'

'No, first one of them asked us, "What are you gawping at?" We practically shat ourselves. A great hunk of a criminal like that, talking to us! And locked up too, so it was like he was in the army! Say what you like, but to my taste, a real lad is an incarcerated lad. If he's out of jail it means he's behaved himself, just a brown-noser. A real lad's got to be all piss and vinegar and full of himself! No education, just a normal lad, you know, in prison, in the army, a young offender perhaps. Even a fireman…'

'And they were there braying, and we said nothing.'

'Nothing at all, we just stood there, craning our necks, stopped in our tracks. Nothing. Then by some fluke they figured out what was going on, because they started shouting at us, and people walking by stopped to point and stare.

'"Hey you! Whores, queers! Hey, you queers: I'll fuck you up yer arsehole!" Those people had a week's worth of gossip. And we stood there rooted to the spot, we were so turned on; it was like gulping a whole box of sweets down all at once. Oh my God, were we hot for them! And we were turning them on, too! They could feel the punk in us, they already knew what they would do to us, they'd dream of it at night while they were wanking themselves off. They'd ask each other, "Which one you wanna do? The one with the cap or the tall one? I'll take the tall one, the one with the cigarette. Already know what I'm gonna do to him." That's how those straighter-than-straight macho men would talk about us in their bunks. In their bunks, bunking in their bunks!

'And that's when I whispered in your ear, "Patricia, wiggle your arse!" Her face and lips were motionless, it was like she'd turned to stone. "Be dramatic, girl! Camp it up! They want to see us as women, so let them. They'll fantasise about us later! They'll get hard thinking about us! They'll cook chai off a razor blade, off a lightbulb. Give them a little sophistication, girl, be provocative! Something refined, delicate, smooth! Oh Patty, dear old Patty, just camp it up a little..." Then you lit your cigarette, and that was enough. They shouted bravas at us and stamped their feet. They roared until the guard appeared in the corner tower; they were shouting at us from all the windows. We couldn't take it any longer and ran off...

'So we made a little tour around Oleśnica's main square, and what do you know, we ran into Oleśnicka there. But all she could do was roll her eyes when we told her what we were up to. She'd discovered that game twenty years before, and had long grown bored of it. Everyone knows about it, if you're from Oleśnica... So we ditched her and moved on. Then I said:

'"Look, you nutter, it'll be dark soon. Let's get the train home. Because if we miss it, we'll have to hitchhike, and you're the one who's going to have to lift your skirt up for the drivers." Then I said:

'"We've been found out, the guard saw us." And the prisoners had kicked up such a fuss, starting fights, smacking each other in the toilets and the showers, that the guard in the tower had to order them to pipe down on the megaphone! We didn't hear it exactly, just rumbling from the horn and the even louder din of their response. Our womanly passivity had driven them wild, along with their being incapacitated while some poofter, some queer, some loser was standing there free as a bird, smoking a fag and watching them; they were locked up and couldn't fuck us up or anything, not even light up... Some bloke with a steel pole was walking down the street, and they shouted at him:

'"Beat the shit out of them with your stick, mate! Beat the shit out of 'em!"

'The bloke just started walking faster. But we went back, even though we'd already been found out. What? We're not allowed to stand on the street? And right next door there was a hair salon, so it was as if we were waiting outside for some other queen to come out. Well, she just went in for a tanning session and that's why it's taking so long, and then she was going to get her highlights redone, and her nails done, ooh! And the minute they saw us they started shouting for the whole world to hear:

'"Bitches are back!" They saw through us immediately. There are people I've known for years, people who've had years to figure it out, and they still say to me things like, "One day when you get married and have kids..." But one of those convicts – only later did we find out that the prison in Oleśnica was for the mentally ill – one of those psychiatric prisoners starts right off talking our talk, like he was a big whore just like us, whore to whore... the same fucking language...

'That's when you squeezed my hand even harder. "Pansies" is what they were shouting at us. One of them stood in the window, taking up the whole window, behind the bars, rubbing his crotch like he was going to fuck the bars... We just stood there. Like we were made of stone, something out of the Bible. Volcanoes seething inside. Over to the main square again, back round again. We'd already given up on the train. It being night and all, we figured we should see what we could make of it; those lads no doubt had but one thing on their minds. There was only that one in the window, but after he saw us he disappeared for a moment, then reappeared with a few others, then they all started beating themselves off on the sill and grunting. Soon they were in all the windows, lighting up the place like a Christmas tree. And we were up there, in there, with them! Above them, someone began signalling something to us with hand gestures; I instantly regretted never having learned their sign language. Then they shouted at us:

'"Heh! Whore! Answer him!" But it was hard to make out their words; after each barrage of shouts we convened a meeting of two,

59

a convocation, combining all our resources to figure out exactly what they were saying. "Heh! Whore! Answer him!" is what we came up with.

'Anyway, as I didn't understand their sign language, to reply I just stuck my finger in my mouth and slid it back out, addressing him in the universal prison jargon of sex. But it was all too much; I could no longer contain myself, so I went and hid myself around the corner and had a wank. But you stayed put – why don't you tell me and the gentleman here what happened next?'

'Well, umm, you'd pissed off, and before me there commenced the great Balcony Scene of my life… One of them started whistling at me, and it was like the whistling of a skylark, that herald of the dawn… It was like the most beautiful concert ever played, the most wonderful music imaginable. As if he was whistling to the faithful bitch at his heels. And all in tune. *Towhee-towhee-towhee.* And I approached his window – not right up to the wall, but a couple of metres away, as I wanted to be able to see him – and it was as if I was hypnotised, like a cat following a call, like a performer on the stage of instinct, lit solely by the latticed scum of light. And I went to those brutes with my heart aflame. And then he raised his hand, shook it, and drew it across his neck as if he were threatening to kill me, as if he were vowing revenge. That I'd be found with a knife in my back on some dark street – Book of the Street indeed! – like Mańka from the song… Shivers went up and down my spine. But I was still on my feet. And then he started quietly whistling to me again, and so softly, as if he were silently stroking my heart:

"'Come here, little one, come over here… Come here, come here…" and he whistled: "*Towhee – towhee – towhee…*" Like he was a young boy again, calling to newborn kittens before roasting them alive in a dustbin... Gently, gently they would call the baby kittens – because they *were* gentle. They'd say, "Here, little one," and the next minute they'd be tossing the carcass into the bin. And in the ferment of that heterosexual prison all their heterosexual traits were fortified, exacerbated. A rage of tenderness and hatred, they wanted to rape us and kill us at the same time. They hated us and they desired us. And we just stood there as if we'd taken root in the ice. Our passivity, their explosive mayhem: like a bumblebee caught in a bottle. Young lads, all of them. Until finally we couldn't help but break out in song: "And the walls will fall, fall, fall!"

'Dawn was upon us, the last train had already departed, and we just stood there like we were waiting for Judgement Day... We were already thinking Judgement Day had to be on its way, and God would come down and say: "Lordy, Lordy! What are you girls standing there for? Why on earth are fruitcakes like you standing *there?*'

'Later we went over to the young offenders' home. But that can be really dangerous, because there they can go in and out. We called up this one queen from Gdynia, and she said:

'"Ooh, the clink... I'd keep my distance from the clink, girls! The queens here used to wait in front of the clink until they released a prisoner. Then they'd cook for him, give him a place to stay, do his laundry – and not one of them remains alive today. Ooh, girls, I'm not carting my arse over there to sing 'Asleep in Jesus' for you, not even if you pay me..."

'Go on, Lucretia, move along now and say your prayers. I'll stay here and chit-chat with our guest..."

Once upon a time, and this was long before there was ever any talk of barracks, I was still living in Bydgoszcz. I even had a boyfriend there, you know. Matthew-Mary they called him. What a nutter that boy was. She worked as an orderly in the hospital – did her national service there, then stayed on to empty the bedpans. We never went out together because we both had the same taste: masculine lads, straight if possible. And the railway station was going through a dry patch then, and it's not like we could go without. Just like a junkie needs his fix. The one time, though, we picked up a soldier together. We got him drunk on vodka, and he did a striptease for us; but he wouldn't take off his boots, because they never take off their boots; their feet get so manky in them, and they're ashamed of it. And it was so funny, him dancing with his trousers down, but with his boots and footcloths still on. He couldn't take those trousers off completely… Another time we did a young lad, another straight boy, heavens above… And once I got beaten up. It happened really quickly. I was walking through the park one night, see, not afraid at all, and I noticed this group on their way back home. Twelve o'clock at night. By the time I saw them they must have been about ten metres away, so I just looked away, acted normal. But they appeared from behind a building, from around the corner. So I started walking faster, acting like I was coming back from somewhere, like I was in a hurry. And I'm listening and already thinking that it must've worked – and then there they were, coming up about five metres behind me, saying something. Not a second later, one of them rushes up, kicks me, pushes me to the ground. With my face stuck in the tarmac like that, I couldn't get up. Another one pinned my neck with his boot, probably one of those heavy ones that skinheads wear, but when I pulled myself free, he just stepped on my neck again like it was nothing! Until something cracked. The others took my belt off me, and started to whip me with it. My mouth was all gritty with sand and blood. But I didn't feel the pain; I didn't feel it even though they were whipping me. And I heard them say: You gonna die, poofter. And I said, please, stop it, please, and that's all the words I could cough up. They ripped me off, too. I took my watch off myself, and started to give them everything I had, because I thought that with each thing I gave them they might ease the pressure on my neck. The fact that I'm still alive today I owe entirely to a passing car; it passed by on the street, and I heard them say: let's get out of here! And though I wasn't in any pain at all while it was happening, because I was so upset, the minute they left I started vomiting blood. They later told me in hospital that I had internal haemorrhaging. Matthew-Mary came running to me. We flagged down a car and took off for the hospital. And that's where I found out I had that haemorrhaging, and a deep cut to my head, and a concussion, and a broken hand, too. I didn't have any papers – they took everything; they left me there with nothing but my underwear on. Pepper spray? Who ever heard of pepper spray back then? I'm telling you, nobody would've dared to use it in such a situation, because if those lads had got any angrier they would've killed me; it would have been enough for them just to step a little harder on my neck. And them standing there on my neck was the worst thing ever! I was shaking so badly, I could've taken an oath never to go to the park ever again. So later on we usually just went to the barracks, though that was in Wrocław. And the barracks were a godsend, a real luxury, not just because they were all straight there, but it was pretty safe, too. And it was like they even kinda liked us. But those skinheads – brrr. Though we finally got our revenge on those straights for that!

✱ ✱ ✱

The elderly concierge smiled when he gave me the keys. Keys and towels at the sauna, handed out by none other than Wrocław's most famous queen – Lucia La Douche! Lucia was famous for her stormy dalliance with a criminal who got her drunk and robbed her. After that, she announced, 'I'm never touching vodka again if it's the last thing I do, not even if it's made of solid gold!' At the reception desk at the State Bathing Works, she watched me out of the corner of her eye, the hair around her bald spot dyed and permed so tightly it looked like sheep's wool. Her face ruddy and robust, her bloodshot eyes glowering. You could see she came from the country; you could tell, even if it was just her typical country penchant for talking about metaphoric gold that gave it away. And it wasn't just that she'd sworn off drinking 'solid gold vodka', but all her friends had 'hearts of gold', too, and everyone she met she nicknamed 'Goldie'. Like the madam in a house of ill repute, Lucia retrieved an enormous key from a narrow drawer; but it was only the key to a locker. She handed you a folded sheet that would, by night's end, be transformed into a Roman toga, sheathing a body damp with sweat; she handed you a towel. She took a sip of her coffee. She was utterly relaxed, she never hurried; other people could do the hurrying. Nothing had changed for her in over a decade. So Lucia would draw out her vowels, speak slowly, slovenly, lost in thought:

'Ooh, Goldie Girl, go on, hurry now... A real hunk just walked in there. A golden hunk of a man! I gave him the key with that little heart-shaped charm on it, a little gold fish. Let me tell you something, just between you and me, love: get a move on, shake a leg, he's waiting for you in there... I gave him number sixty-two...'

If Lucia were around today, I'd ask her to decipher the stains and blotches on all those sheets that were tossed into the dirty linen basket, to reconstruct their history, to write her own book of the streets – a book of solid gold. She'd pick them out under the dim fluorescent lights – it's always night at the sauna. She'd squint and gripe under her breath about the trouble she was having with her eyes.

Half the people who frequented the sauna back in the eighties are no longer alive. Those old queens would warm their bones up in pairs, ambling majestically, cloaked in sheets; they would come for the whole day, bringing their lunches with them in canisters, and eat in the locker room. The beautiful, marble hall of the State Baths was much too grand for them. They weren't worthy of those Greek columns. Clouds of steam would float low over the giant tiles. Back in those days buggery was still a sin. Everyone was naked, or had towels wrapped around them like togas, one arm uncovered, gowns made of sheets. Gaunt clavicles, sunken chests, freckles and liver spots. Sitting in the marble pool filled with lukewarm water, I would look at those old queens: Comely Cecily, Catherine the Purse-Seller, Jehanneton de Millières, Catherine la Bouchière, and any number of Villon's other women. They came around the corner, baring their corrupted flesh, licking themselves lasciviously, pinching each other's nipples as they walked past the pool. They went off to the steam room in hopes that I'd join them. The decay of time had magnified the decay of AIDS unfurling within them. Special offer! All ten Egyptian plagues for the price of one! It started with the red spots that appeared on their bodies. That's when they realised that something was about to end, that the time for farewells had come... So they forgot their inhibitions and rushed headlong after the fugitive remnant of life... The less time they had, the more wild they grew. They had no shame; they were like unnaturally libidinous lepers. They reckoned that because everyone was sick already there was no reason to worry about safety. They pissed on each other, tore out what was left of their hair, and gave every perversion, even death, a whirl. The Roman baths began to look like a scene from the Marquis de Sade, from a film by Pasolini. With what tenacity those deteriorating, paunchy, fifty-year-old bodies would cling to one another! There was no secretion that couldn't be licked, no motion that couldn't be interpreted as an invitation to... sex? Was that still sex? It was more like a dance of death. It defied words, but maybe whimpers and wheezes would do. Rats started showing up, or maybe that's just how it seemed to them. After the first deaths, the municipality ordered that the steam room, the pool next to it, and the locker room all be disinfected. Clouds of smoke wafted between the majestic columns in the Roman hall; Lucia La Douche was burning the towels and sheets, setting the dried sperm ablaze. The smoke refused to rise to heaven, but coiled downward, underground.

I'll never forget the stench!

* * *

Thoughout the communist era, Lucia La Douche had lived above the butcher's on the high street, where the Green Cockerel tavern is now. She used to bring grunts from the picket line back home with her. One time, they robbed her – never mind; another time they beat her up – no matter. Once, out cottaging, she met three guys and brought them back up to her place above the butcher's for a drink. They tied her up, beat her, and started rummaging through her high-gloss wall unit and the drinks cabinet, where she kept all her valuables. But she didn't care, because what she valued was something else. They found her old Party identity card:

'Eat it!'

Nothing, just 'eat it'. Lucia refused; she hadn't, after all, brought them home so she could eat her own ID card, in its hard protective wallet no less – I can't remember now if it was plastic, but it was certainly hard, and certainly not edible. Lucia always did her hair up in a woolly perm with a curling iron, and they took that Russian curling iron, and they heated it up, and they branded her with it. Until she ate the whole thing, until she was no longer a member of the Party. Then they finally fucked her. With the red-hot curling iron. And that was the final straw. She died in hospital, and may she rest in peace. And now in her stead, Oleśnicka, who used to be her assistant, is the most famous queen in Poland.

Under communism, Lucia La Douche used to sell vodka under the counter at the bathhouse. And she kind of had a thing going with Zdzicha Anaconda. Zdzicha was called that because she worked in the snake house at the zoo. She used to feed them; she'd walk in there in her dirty overalls, without an ounce of fear. Oh Zdzicha, Zdzicha! The serpent lady! Our serpenty, snaky Zdzisława

Anaconda! Her hair was blonde and she had blue eyes and wore a denim jacket... And she looked so pretty in her rubber apron, walking from the monkey house over to the sea turtles, which were as big as small cars, and then from the turtles over to the snakes. She smelled like jungle, like apples and fish food.

Once, back on the Scorched Picket, the queens said to her:

'Zdzicha, you could make a fortune off smuggling those snakes into West Germany.'

'Just a couple of those snakes, Zdzicha. You'd make a mint!'

'Hide them in your drawers, act stupid, and fuck off over there! You can say they died...'

'Oh, Zdzicha, Zdzicha... don't be stupid, smuggle them into the Reich!'

'What are you waiting for? It won't be the first time you've had a pair of snakes in your drawers! Ha, ha, ha!'

So one Friday Zdzicha Anaconda stayed late at work. She chatted with the lady in the ticket office for a while, then with the nightwatchman, and at last she announced that she had two sick snakes on her hands and she had to go and take care of them, because snakes like that need looking after, you know, they're not cheap... Her hands trembled and her legs shook as she walked through the pitch-black monkey house, and in the silence the keys to the cages rattled in her pocket, and those monsters howled inhumanly. She turned on her torch and saw some behemoth hulking behind the glass. Planet of the apes, planet of the dogs, a preserve for wild beasts. Somehow she made her way to the snake house, but she wasn't really sure which ones to take. The little snakes wouldn't fetch enough, but boa constrictors? In the end she compromised; she stole two little ones that would grow into big ones in the future: one that the veterinarian had recently treated because it had swallowed an egg that broke inside it, and another, pretty, opalescent one. And thus Zdzicha became a smuggler. She put the snakes in a burlap bag and threw it over the fence, on to the Odra embankment. Bawling her head off, she went to the porter:

'They've died! And they were so cute, such lively little fuckers, and now they've gone and died just as I've put them back in their cases...!' Then she sauntered out and circled back around the zoo, down by the fence to retrieve the writhing bag printed with the slogan *Chemistry. Feeds us. Heals us. Clothes us. Houses us.*

But Zdzicha failed in smuggling the snakes out of the country; she was caught at the East German border. She lost her job, and after that she really went to the dogs. That's when she started robbing people! She stole all the time, did Zdzicha, and sometimes they paid Lucia La Douche a visit and complained: 'Your Zdzicha robbed me again.' And Lucia would clench her teeth proudly and say:

'Excuse me, mister, but leave me out of it. I'm a grown woman and I really don't care to waste my time with frivolous matters. I have problems of my own!'

❋ ❋ ❋

So how did you get your revenge on the straights?

'Well, it was like this. The two of us were having a terrible case of fellatio withdrawal, and everywhere we went the cure was unavailable. The park was empty; it was cold; the railway station was nothing but beggars. And we were like a pair of beggars ourselves, begging for the blessed nob, the holy balls, the sacred arse. We'd made a kind of religion of it, after all. And then it was like... Oh, I don't know... I'd prefer it if you wouldn't record this...' – I oblige and turn off the tape recorder – 'So, there used to be this one discotheque, see, that was popular with grunts from all over Bydgoszcz. Primavera was its name. It's not around anymore, like everything from back then. So... there we were, and we'd been trying all night to score some drunken grunt. The dark, the cold: it was a nightmare. They were playing this music, too: disco polo. And we were starving, literally on our last legs. And behind that disco there was this river. Bydgoszcz, as I'm sure you know, has water all over the place. And the river had embankments on both sides, and again and again a grunt would go back there in the dark by himself, or there'd be a whole row of them all taking a slash. And they were tempting us, like this, see?' – Lucretia demonstrates – 'They'd stand there with their legs spread like this, feet wide apart. And then, oh... How can I explain? We got ourselves a knife, see, and we waited, in hiding.' Here, Lucretia's voice cracks again. 'Because they didn't... they didn't want to do it as a matter of choice. So we had to choose for them. There they were, pissing with their legs spread apart like that, all cocky and provocative... They were getting us all hot and bothered, and then they would walk away, and a lad like that, you know, not over his dead body... So, anyway, there we were watching, and this hunk comes by in these jeans. Jeans, you know... Back in those days, that really meant something. And they were so tight, and he had this bubble butt, and his crotch was bulging out, a real symbol of everything that's masculine. And he was totally bald too. And then he started going down one of those dark paths, and there was no one around, and we… How should I know if he's still alive? But we got him with that knife, in his legs, so he blacked out… He must have survived; really, I think he just blacked out… Because, well, it was like this: the minute we went after him with that knife, he screamed and started thrashing something awful. But we weren't scared at all, we were so determined! He just shrieked and thrashed about and kicked. Did he ever! But then I remembered that what you needed to do was poke him in the eyes, poke his eyeball into its socket with your thumb so that he would go unconscious from the pain. And while Matthew-Mary was twisting his arm back, I used my thumb to poke that eyeball in as hard as I could. And he blacked out. And then I unbuttoned his fly and pulled out a glorious cock, glistening all over like it was coated with saliva. Then, right there in the bushes, we undressed him like he was some kind of mannekin… Well, that's why I had to get out of Bydgoszcz. I was afraid he might've survived and that he'd recognise me. There was so much blood, but I think he only blacked out, because in the end he got a hard-on, and corpses don't get hard-ons, right? But you know, as soon as we were able to have our way with him, we lost all interest; groping him just felt like going through the motions. If only that stupid slapper hadn't thrown him into the river. In fact she just left him there near the bank, but his head was in the water. And that kinda worries me.'

＊ ＊ ＊

These stories certainly have some fire in them. Candles have been lit on the graves of Jessica, Angelica, and Lucia. But in fact, they're constantly going out, because it's cold, practically winter, and it keeps on raining and snowing, and the wind never stops howling. But we have little lanterns in our bags, too. All we have to do is stick matches inside them and make sure we don't burn ourselves as we do so. The embers of cigarettes glow in the darkness. Throats burn. That's how people usually start to die. All of a sudden, even in the early phases, the colours start to fade, to turn grey, no, not grey – it's just that everything starts looking completely different. The oranges Jessica brings to the hospital and places on the white table with its chipped enamel. She looks at them, surprised they're still there, because she no longer is, and existence has become something utterly foreign to her. This is what they call looking back from the other side. On the other side the pain is constant, as if Jessica's body were trying to debase itself for her, so she won't regret having to leave it behind. Jessica is afraid of her own body because she knows that in a couple of months it's going to stink. She looks at her nails and can already see the livid crescents beneath them. Her old job told her of the charms of decay only too well. Oh, how she'd love to send that body of hers to the scrapheap! But it's not possible. She doesn't want her body any more, which is destroying itself, which suddenly turns out to be as durable as a soap bubble, as a drop of egg white. Especially when seen from overhead – and as a matter of fact, she sees everything as if she were on the moon looking down at it. Only now does she fully realise that never, not for a single moment, did she believe in the possibility of her own death.

Nightly talks with the telephone hotline are in fact rather comforting.

It took Jessica forever to die. It started with the throat infections,

72

which were quickly remedied. A few days later, strep throat; like-wise cured. Then the flu again. The doctor's question:

'During the past three months, might you have had...?' Hysteria. Jessica vomits into the toilet. Blood tests, but not for that yet, just for antibodies, which, it turns out, she doesn't have. The norm is 18, she has 22. She was practically donating blood, sent a total of five samples to the lab, getting the verdict a week later. During that time Jessica almost died, her pneumonia undiagnosed. For the first time she wasn't winning against her own body. The medicine relieved her sore throat, but only for a few hours at a time, and then it came back like a fire that can't be put out. The next time the nurses took her blood (cheerful, clueless, cracking jokes), the radio was playing Budka Suflera's latest release, and Jessica regarded it as a breach of tact. In the toilet, while peeing, she noticed a sticker advertising some PVC window manufacturer; she seethed at the insensitivity. All around her the bustle of life was continuing, utterly unaware of how ephemeral it really was!

'Please, sir, calm down, please calm down, sir, please stop shak-ing, sir!' says the doctor, but he answers straightforward questions with an appalling earnestness, and on top of that he's suspiciously friendly. Fuck this! He's constantly asking if he can be of help with anything – that's what worst about it! He acts as if he's my friend or something! This toxic atmosphere, where everyone's so nice and understanding, it's revolting! Someone offers to go with her to get her results, because 'you oughtn't be alone at a time like this'. Some-one else offers her a lift, because it's practically winter, after all, and 'you mustn't be out in the cold with your immunity compromised like that! Besides, somebody might cough on you on the tram!' All at once, everything turns into a mass of sticky pap; the pap envelops Jessica and penetrates to her lungs. Discreetly, so as not to cause panic, the doctor palpates her lymph nodes – neck, armpits. He washes his hands; but the armpits continue to reek: why bother showering when you have pneumonia?

Her entire organism was out of tune like an old piano, and not only that but some secret enemy had battered the keyboard with an axe. And the dryness – a fire blazed in her throat, and whatever she drank was instantly soaked up like water in sand. Not even antibiotics were helping! There was no denying it. And Jessica, who always had so much verve – lift up your kisser when you're talking to me, kitty cat, and that's what *she* said, et cetera – was too embarrassed now even to mumble those two words: *risk group*. She sat there on the examining table, staring at the pharmaceuticals behind the padlocked glass doors of the medicine cabinet, tugging at her hair, muttering incomprehensibly, her lips drained of color. Her voice began to break, 'cause maybe, maybe... maybe I have... When at last she landed in the hospital, it was as if she were going through life half-asleep. The strangest thing for her was when she began to feel strangely consoled... But what kind of consolation could that have been? Whole processions of long-dead people filed past before her eyes. They were dead, so what? Consider it another way – it wouldn't be long, a few thousand years from now, and even if it's a million years, so what? At some point in the future there won't be any humans at all left on this planet. Not even the earth is immortal. Even the universe isn't immortal, let alone humans. Then, right after that, came memories from childhood, from a time as-yet unaware of the sad inevitability. Her mother's head in a then-fashionable wig of big, russet curls. Her face still young, like in those old, black-and-white photographs that have lacy, jagged edges. Then came a tremendous gap in Jessica's memory, although she did experience the sixties. She was in their new flat, in their newly built block, sitting in the kitchen, and her grandmother was holding her in her arms. She gestured with her 'little piggy' at the windowframe, which had some kind of lever at the bottom for opening the double panes, and asked, 'What that?' 'Ohhh, that's where the baker man bakes his bread,' is what she heard. One of the never-explained enigmas of Jessica's childhood, since from the window – and she looked for it many times – there was no bakery to be seen. And ever after, in that little knobby metal box sloppily daubed with white paint and fastened to the old-fashioned window, the baker man patiently baked his bread, and he must still be there baking away, because the only person capable of breaking that spell passed on long ago. Then the nurse came in and put her on the drip, but Jessie wanted to go as quickly as possible. At a certain moment, just as they were deciding to insert the tube in her throat to help her breathe, her deceptive calmness shattered and she flew into an hysterical rage. She screamed at the entire ward. When she had first got there, she would wake up at night and cry silently so as not to wake up anyone else. Now she stopped caring and ran out into the corridor, running and running until she collapsed by the radiator next to Surgery. She pulled her hair out, scratched up her face. She saw red spots in front of her eyes. She rubbed them and saw a crowd of people coming at her, yelling:

'Pull down your pants, Jessica! Moon us, Jessica!'

'But watch out, your hole's been fucked so hard the shit's pouring out! Everyone's too disgusted to screw you, they don't want to get your AIDS-infected diarrhoea spilling all over them!' It seemed to her that someone was probing her anus with a cold, aluminium torch.

'Moon us! Show us your arse! Everyone's looking at your cunt! Oh look, you have a cock too – ooh, so soft!'

'Noooooo!' Jessica bellowed at the entire ward, at the entire, vast hospital. 'Noooooo!' she bellowed so the scream would kill her, so she'd finally expire. 'Noooooo!' She broke free, jerked back, hacked, spat; then someone caught her and held her tight. Jessica gnashed her teeth and bit that someone, drew blood, and got punched in the face, and already that someone was sticking her in the arm, all over her body. A tingling heat spread out from her arms and through her veins, burning, then a foaming cloud of mugginess spilled into her brain. Suddenly Jessica saw herself lying bare-arsed and arse-up on a cold examining table, covered in blood and discharge, and all around her patients in gowns were crowding in, nurses and order-lies too, until the consultant ordered them all to get out. One older fellow whispered to a nurse, 'That AIDS really is awful – they say it attacks the brain and nervous system, people go off the deep end.' Jessica fell asleep, feeling as if she were being carried somewhere in someone's arms, probably to the common room, or maybe to isola-tion, or what if she was being taken somewhere else altogether, somewhere where nothing existed at all?

# PART II
# THE LEWD
# BEACH

# Hey

Not sure if this will work (I don't believe in ads anymore), but who knows, maybe I'll find a good-looking gay guy on here, someone I can build a long-term relationship with, one that's about more than just sex and stuff. I live in Wrocław. I'm straight-acting, good-looking (told so anyway), and a student. 5'7", 70 kg, 5" ;-), blue eyes. I enjoy cycling, I'm polite, drama-free, friendly. No pic, no answer. Well, I'll stop now, guess I'm out of charact ...

# The Old Dears of Lubiewo

*Jeeeesus!* I've got a case of Georgette, camping it up in my speech and my gestures, I'm flaming so hard you could grill a steak on me!

I'm dripping with sweat; a tricklet slowly seeps out from under my hair and comes to a halt on my brow. I struggle to roll from my stomach on to my side, smear on some suntan oil. From my hollow in the dunes I gaze upon a blond between two tufts of beach grass. I write. Grains of sand on the card. Now the tricklet slithers on to my nose. Once it drips off the end, a new one starts. And another is already forcing its way through my hair, tickling my scalp under my visor cap. Little twigs, cigarette filters, grains of sand. All of it yellow, independent, translucent, part of a whole.

Long live Wolin Island! Long live the beach at Lubiewo!

The name 'Lubiewo' is a cognate of *libido* – the insatiable libido that saturates this place. And we swim in it, foundering in the warm, gooey muck.

From Międzyzdroje, you have to walk west along the coast towards Świnoujście for an eon or two. Long enough to get sun-burned by the time you get there. About forty-five minutes. One way, your back gets it; the other way, your face. I prefer walking on the bluff, through the woods, along the dunes. Amid the feverish buzzing of dragonflies and bumblebees, with green pine cones getting into my sandals, with a view of the ruined army bunkers behind the barbed wire fence. Ghosts of SS men in the cellars, the standing water, the swarms of mosquitoes... Yes!

If you're walking down there and you look beyond the green, wooden steps, you'll see the nudist beach, and there, some way (an appropriate distance) further along, is where we hold court – with our suntan lotion, flasks of coffee, and bodice-rippers! With our noses – and only our noses! – covered with maple leaves. Wearing coloured sunglasses studded with fake diamonds. With tanning oil, and keys to our rented single rooms in Międzyzdroje. Because it's nothing but lonely single men here. The older regulars, the ones no one wants to go with, rent in Lubiewo, right where the green steps end at the top of the bluff, and all that is up there is a single shopping centre (which has – irony of ironies – a huge rainbow as its logo), the woods, and an unguarded pay parking lot. As the other visitors, the young ones, frolic in the dunes like kittens with soap bubbles, I carefully rearrange my blanket, take out my lotions and cigarettes, and beckon some old chanteuse to come over and keep me company, but not for the reason she thinks. I entice them for their stories... I want them to become my storytellers, like the ones in Pasolini's *Salò*. And every day they'll tell an even more perverted tale for the State, standing at the piano, in front of the burning doors. It's a faggot *Decameron* I'm trying to turn out here.

The only problem is that there's no such thing as sin any more.

It's vanished, soaked up by the sand like a couple of drops they'd flicked off themselves after coming out of the sea. Where did it vanish? When?

Today the waves tossed a red flag right on to the middle of the beach. Right where our section starts. This red flag marks the boundary of our People's Republic, a concept these lady pensioners understand full well. One of them was just arriving at a nearby spot on the beach, so I took advantage of the fact that a bumblebee had started to attack me there on those sweltering dunes, lured no doubt by the fragrance of tanning products, and the old dear screamed 'Begone!' at that bumblebee, swatting the air with her book, and immediately set about getting acquainted with me.

'That bee certainly had it in for you...'

'Well, it *was* persistent...'

'They're awful when they get angry! Here, see? They're... they've built a nest here in this heat. Can you rub some cream on my back?'

She sets down on the sand the book she'd been waving about, swatting the bee, which was no less persistent than she was – oh, but that's lovely! I'm dripping with sweat, the bumblebee comes back. I glance over: whatever was she reading? *The Beach*. Gold lettering and the face of Leonardo DiCaprio against an illuminated sky. They made a film of that?

'Yes, he was divine in it! Just right for a beach read. Shall I go a little lower?'

'Thanks, but no thanks. Uh-huh, I just did it there myself.'

'Do you fancy some coffee?' She's brought her entire world with her. She'd put together a little 'bag of essentials', something for her to think about during the long winter evenings, and including everything that could possibly come in handy. A first-aid kit, some multifunctional pocketknife she'd bought off the TV...

'But of course.' I watch as she pulls two cups out of her bag of essentials, each printed with her likeness. There she was, all dolled up! Wearing glasses, a gold plastic necklace, dressed in her Sunday best, as if she was off to church!

'I've been coming here every year since the mid-nineteen sixties, when they were still holding those Miss Nature contests... And every year since 1989 I've had my picture put on a cup on the promenade. I always have it done on my last day; there's a bloke there who charges five zlotys. That sort of thing was unimaginable before. And on every cup, I'm a year older.'

'You'd never guess...'

'Oh, get away with you!' She looks at me coyly. Now we're approached by another elderly queer whom everyone calls the Pensioneress. She's running with a newspaper in her hand, some crappy, glossy tabloid, and even before she's joined us: 'A UFO! A UFO! Girls, get on your knees! A UFO is landing!'

'Here in Lubiewo? Why, that can't be possible!' we respond sceptically.

'They said so in *Fakt*. They even have an interview with a Martian!' She won't let it drop.

'Is it an official interview?' I joke. But they don't get it, both of them being model tabloid readers. They just soak them up! They probably don't really understand what I'm talking about either.

'What? Huh? Of course. But here, listen: "Yesterday Usedom, today Wolin. Those weren't meteorites. The balls of light that Genowefa and Zenon Kozów saw flying over their barn were flying saucers. Our reporter succeeded in speaking with the pilot of one such vehicle. Asked why they had decided to visit Earth, the extra-terrestrial replied: 'We've come to Earth to try out our antennas,'" – here my queens sighed in unison: 'Oh! Their *antennas!*' – "'Although the extraterrestrial did not specify how the antennas were to be used, he did announce they would land today on one of the beaches on Wolin Island.'"

I shout at them, but they're lost to the world, at least this one, this earthly dimension. They're engrossed in the newspaper, can't get enough of it, sighing, talking about how handsome he is. For a Martian.

Finally I can't take it any more. I explode:

'Do you tarts know what I do with crap like this? I use it for wiping my arse! See?' I rub my bottom with the newspaper and crush it. 'Martians! What the fuck!'

The ladies seem a little disconcerted, feel a bit stupid. They look around and burst out laughing. To make amends, my bumblebee queen proposes more coffee.

'You're making such a fuss! Care for another cup of coffee? Perhaps with some *cream*…?' And would a queen dream of uttering that word *cream* without some smutty allusion in her eyes? Never!

Then the newcomer, the one who joined us, notices the cups, the ones adorned with her aging self.

'Oh how lovely! And the photo, is it glued on?'

'It's a *transfer*,' my old dear says through clenched teeth. 'A permanent transfer. I get one done every year.'

'And where does a girl get a thing like that?' She primps her hair, poses for the camera.

'Right over there, behind the fish and chips stand, and the shooting range, and the rubber balls. Right in front of drinks and ice creams. Up by Pizzeria Florida.'

'You mean by the old Workers' Holiday Fund that got converted into a beauty farm?'

'Exactly, just a little to the left, on the way to Lightning Lodge 11.'

'Care to reveal what you paid for the pleasure?' the older one asks.

'Five zlotys,' my old dear drawls, already a little bored.

'Ooh, that's a lot...'

'Well, it ain't cheap,' she says, proud as a peacock.

'I used to come here on caravan holidays in the fifties. You know, here and Niecko. But it's much better here. No comparison really.' She laughs effusively.

They both agree. We pour coffee into those mugs of hers (mine has a picture of her circa age forty), and light up. They smoke Mars; I'm smoking R1. I make myself comfortable, lie down. The sky overhead is amazing, eggshell blue with fluffy white clouds. The skin on my face tautens in the hot sun. It's not long before they start pressing themselves against me and groping me down below. I let them because I know that otherwise they'll get mad and there'll be no story. They may as well have a bit of fun. And get off, too, why not. On that dickery-dock of mine. I close my eyes and puff away. It's nice. It's slick. Warm. It's entirely possible I'll be staying here late today, and when everyone, and really everyone (except that blond), has left, then I'll reign in perfect solitude; I'll go skinny-dipping, I'll romp around in the sand and take a pee wherever I like! And I'll stroll about in the dunes, where the day's flotsam will still be looking to get some... That's the sort of holiday I'll be having, too, until I get back to my rented room at the Deaf Hag, where I'll pull out my scholarly texts, papers, and pens, and dash off a page or two of cultural criticism. But here... I've got *Cicadas in the Cyclades* running through my head... And while one of them is sucking me off and unable to talk because her mouth is busy, the other one starts thinking aloud:

'They said we're going to have beautiful weather tomorrow.'

'Oh-uh,' the first one affirms with her mouth full.

'On RMF FM...'

'Uhh.'

'A good station, that one.'

'Nnnn...'

'And a UFO...'

That was a ruse for getting my pecker, because the minute I hear the word 'UFO' I grumble angrily, turn on to my other side, and there's a change of scenery at the well: the first one loses her place and the other one moves in on me. Then the tension grows: the empty-mouthed queen is quiet, until out of the blue she's reminded of some snippet in the tabloid and says, 'Janda's oven exploded in her face.'

To which the other queen, the gorged one, mumbles something that sounds like, 'Already read about it.'

Then I explode too. The two old gazelles slowly wind up their work; they got what they wanted. With younger queens, cruising someone can take weeks: first a movie, coffee, chatting about the weather and the birds. An old queen will tell you: 'But what if it's pointless? What if there's not much in his trousers?' The older queens learned Villon's bitter wisdom long ago: Take only boys, while there's still time. Their time was up long ago, and yet they keep taking it, they take belatedly, even if what they get isn't quite as photogenic. They stand there like late arrivals at a party that's just coming to an end, where all that's left are the crumbs.

I turn over lazily on to my tummy and ask them to rub Eris tanning lotion on my back. It's suddenly all so Polish. While only a few miles away, on the other side of Świnoujście, latex is all the rage in Ahlbeck. Everyone's buff there, clean-shaven, tattooed, nipples pierced, barbells dangling from their penises, metal bands around their cocks. Did you see all those Western gays, eyes bloodshot like pigs, on the nudist beaches outside Amsterdam, Berlin, Utrecht, Zurich, Stockholm? Phalluses like the teats of female savages – stretched out, saggy, worn out. Gorged. Wrinkled. Shaven. Lubed. The sweltering heat, the mosquitoes, 'The Night Chicago Died' playing on the radio. They're nothing if not physical in that Western sun, every last spot, every last pustule on a neck or in an armpit, every last bruise or reddish blotch. The farther off in the woods you find them, the more pustules they have; they can't be got rid of all at once, can't be frozen off in the portable cooler, where bottles of Corona chill among the ice cubes. Waiting to be drunk with a slice of lime stuffed down the neck. Only a few short kilometres away these and other Western customs prevail. Butch men. Bald men. Shaven men. Skinheads. Hunks. Reeking of poppers. A headrush of latex.

Thank God it's only queens and jolly old ladies here. The radio warbles Maryla and Budka. We have our Mars cigarettes, our Eris sunblock, our memories of caravan holidays, when you'd spend a whole night on the train just getting there, honey, and a crowded train at that, standing in the corridor the whole journey, but happy just to be going to the beach.

'It's not the same now at all… All you have to do now is board the coach or express train, sit your fancy arse down, and off you go…'

'Our employment enterprise used to have railway cars that they'd converted into dormitories, regular camp beds with clean, starched sheets stamped with the enterprise logo. And artificial flowers on the side table, and loos out in the forest, because the cars were in the forest.'

'In the forest, in the forest… Pine cones would be dropping to the ground. When we made a bonfire, everyone would sing, "We're on holiday, in this forest on the coast"… or wherever you were. You could put that forest wherever you wanted. In the mountains people would sing the original version "In this forest in the Tatras", and at the lakes they sang "In this forest in Masuria", which sort of changed the meaning. And the chorus would end up with a split personality, some singing "in Masuria", others "on the coast", and a few older girls still stuck in the Tatras. And a bottle of vodka making the rounds. Back then we always took our holidays in such out-of-the-way places. Say there was a little river flowing peacefully somewhere, before you knew it a holiday camp would pop up there, with folks singing "In this forest on the Vistula". Except that under communism, as soon as you discovered some really scenic spot, they'd hang up those gigantic rasping megaphones in the trees and destroy the peace and quiet. From morning to night you had to listen to things like "Karolina's Gone to Gogolin", and have your bath in the lake. You're not used to that sort of thing I suppose; you wouldn't have managed.

'Back then it all just felt a lot more like Poland. We had Polish products, Polish music was played on the radio, and you could really only travel in Poland, what with it being so hard to get a passport. There we were with our Ludwik washing-up liquid, listening to Maryla Rodowicz, and dreaming of holidays on Lake Wigry. Today you feel like an *Ausländer** in your own country. The way it was in West Germany: everything so expensive, you can't afford a thing, colourful in its way, garish, alien, but not a Polish product in sight...'

'But we still come here,' chimes in the second old dear, 'while the other queens are all off in Ibiza or Cap d'Agde. They have conventions there for porn stars in those gay movies; they all go in aeroplanes. They say the sex is non-stop. All those Latinos show up, and it's off into the bushes. I like it here much better. I take the slow train, which drags along but is cheap, and I sleep in a tent at the Gromada campground. It still reminds me of when I was a child, the smell of the sea. No southern sea smells so deliciously of pine trees and salt and chips from the snack bar...'

'Yes, but under communism...'

They recall how under communism you had to come here in secret, because everyone knew each other, and all the employees were housed in the same railway cars.

At that, Old Dear No. 2 says:

* *German*: Foreigner

89

'Forgive me for being so forward, but perhaps we should introduce ourselves.'

'I'm Michał.'

'Zdzisław...'

'Wiesław...' Smooch. Smooch.

'Michał.' Smooch. 'Zdzisiu.' Smooch. 'Pleased to meet you, Zdzisiu.' Smooch. 'Wiesio.' Smooch.

'You can call me Wieśka...'

'Zdzisia! Zdzisława Sośnicka...' Smooch, smooch.

'Michalina...' Smooch.

'Oh! Michalina Wisłocka!'

'So, Michał, there was one time that I was walking here, and I'd already taken off my drawers and I was checking out the lads on the dunes, each one hotter than the last. And all of a sudden, who do I see? It was that witch, the secretary at my enterprise, I don't remember if I was at "Fortune", "Rainbow", or "Daybreak" back then. She'd ventured all the way up from Międzyzdroje, only she was near the green steps, at the nudist beach, the straight one. She was looking around to see if anyone noticed her.'

Yes, it's all elderly ladies here, spreading their pensiony warmth all round; the kind of ladies who bring soup in flasks and chit-chat about their ailments.

'So anyway, that witch found herself a place to make her camp, and I made it as far as here, walking along the bluff, so she wouldn't see me, since back then you had to walk even further, further down; that beach gets closer every year. Oh yes, back then you had to walk a really long way.'

'You had to walk a long way back then,' repeats the other. 'What year was that? '69? That beach practically reached the Levee.'

'Except that under communism it was a little different here. Different atmosphere. Basically it was a cruising ground on the dunes. And people didn't smile like they do now; they all looked like they were up to no good, as if just being here made you a criminal. It used to be you had to be so covert here...'

'And now everybody's utterly overt here...'

## Berging Queens

'How do we get by? Well, it's hard. First, you're lonely your whole life. Second, you're poor, you're on the outside, retired, beyond the pale of reality. Even the young ones, they're on the outside, too. Doubly marginal: first, you're poor; second, you're a poofter. So you have to create your own world. It's true. The first part of your life you're bent on finding someone to spend the rest of it with. But it's not exactly easy, especially in times like these. And then there's wanting to be somebody important, to be someone... Later on you get used to being alone, to being a no one. And that's when the fun begins. Oh, you can spend the whole year (in secret, at work, under the table, under the covers) looking forward to coming here, just waiting to spend your whole summer getting laid, lubing yourself up in the sun and heat, cruising... The tanning lotion from last year squirrelled away somewhere like buried treasure... and sometimes, when you're really sad, you take it out, open it, sniff, and remember the feeling of getting off... the train... the hot sun on your face again, and the sand dunes! But you can't go sniffing it all the time, or else the memory will gust away... You escape into your own private world, where it's as cosy as the hollows between the dunes... And everyone thinks this is the bottom. But they don't have breezes like this at the bottom...'

'Or those chanteuses who actually think they're women. They're not even transvestites, they just feel like women inside...'

And with that the other Old Dear gave me a little nosegay of blue flowers that she'd been gathering all day long on the dunes. So tiny – perhaps they were forget-me-nots. She knew exactly what she was doing! She wrapped a towel around me, a makeshift dress, and stuck the nosegay down the front...

'That's how these queens have fun with each other! They just make a few compromises: they dress up so no one can say they're in drag, but they'll have on things that you might find a real woman wearing, too. Under their jackets they'll have on a deep v-neck vest with a medallion dangling in the cleavage – *voilà!* instant décolletage! And they'll slip on a bracelet or two, and if anyone asks why, well: boys wear bracelets, too, these days! And lipstick, or lip balm actually, which you can get at any chemist's... And if they accidentally gave you the tinted lip balm, whose fault is that? And now the fun can begin. In secret, when no one's around, you make yourself up in the toilets, put on your face... Your fingernails might be a bit on the long side, too, but still acceptable...'

'So it's Berg! A faggy Berg!'

'What?' I can see they're laughing. Even if they've never read Gombrowicz's *Cosmos*, they know a thing or two. In their bones.

# St Rolka of the University

'It's all right for you, you're in a doctoral programme... You really don't have it so bad... Uh-huh!'

Rolka sits in the reading room studying the catechism. Has been for years now. She wants to get into the Papal College on Ostrów Tumski. The first time I ever saw her was in the local nellie bar, back in her disco days. Long hair, but a receding hairline, rolling eyes, fanatical, inspired, but in the depths of those eyes there also lurked a kind of affectation. Then the news broke: Rolka's gone crazy! She went mad and was locked up in Kraszewski Street, in Zegadłowicz Street. In that enormous red brick cloister, behind sky-high walls.

Five years later, Rolka was standing in front of the mirror in the toilet at Scene. She had some kind of rag draped over her head and was prattling to herself:

'You're pretty, I love you. You're pretty, I love you. Mwa, mwa!' A moment later, in the main room:

'Everything's fine now. I just have to get my stuff from the mental health centre, all those plushy things of mine.'

Rolka inhaled nervously. Nervously! A drag on her cigarette, a sip of beer. And she raised her eyes in her eternal perturbation, a little too untethered, all that endless relocating, and now she had to get her plushy things out of isolation, too. All her teddy bears and threadbare stuffed toys, so they won't throw them out, but they hadn't given her permission to take any of them. So she rolled her eyeballs, a little too evidently terrified (somewhere at the bottom of her eyes), smoke, beer. Finally she lowered her eyelashes, looked at her fingernails. I never go anywhere, not out in public, I'm *persona non grata…* Uh-huh!

'You have it good, I come here to read.' Two years later, and I see Rolka every day in the reading room. She doesn't budge during the breaks, when they ventilate the hall. She's wholly absorbed in her studies, but still she rolls her eyeballs (all that bother she's had with the administration), and her hair keeps getting longer, too, and it's grey now. Grey. Streaked. But gathered up in a pointy tassel on top of her head, like a little girl. If they take her at that college, they'll canonise her, no doubt about that! And she was always the first on the picket line! And at the sauna. Only today she asked me:

'Have you been to that sauna over in Zelwerowicz?' She giggled, wanted all the juicy details. But suddenly got serious, spooked:

'I have to get back to my catechism now, to my prayer books, my little pictures of saints and sheep. I have to get back to the reading room. *Bye-bye.*' I have no doubt they'll canonise her at that college; and there she'll be, a figure in a fresco, St Rolka of the Cruising Ground with a teddy bear in the crook of her arm, her eyes rolling upwards, the patron saint of perturbation, crisis, and transiency.

## SMS from Paula

Dear Vicômte! Carriage has gone ahead. Your Marquise is in the summer palace, coming by coach to take the waters this pm. How are things with la intrigue, don't forget the hat

# The Painted Swede

At the gym a lady we call 'Miss Cat' comes over to me. A svelte blonde in a tight-fitting black jumpsuit that makes her look like a figure skater. All she needs is a tail. She crouches nimbly, feline, lying in wait for me to begin my workout in the little room with its scales, mirrors, and mats; she leans against the wall and steers the conversation to the topic of makeup. How I was sweating so much, how I was even glowing...

'Don't you use any powder? Really, Mr Witkowski, between you and me... You're such a worldly man, always off to Berlin, Zurich, Budapest... You really should know more about such things: in the West lads wear makeup. Nothing too obvious, just something to create an effect. But you can't actually prove it. Listen, I'm renting a room from this Swedish guy who's working for a company here, he's the boss.'

'And he's letting a room...?' I look at myself in the mirror over the sink. I really am glistening with sweat, like a dog's balls in springtime...

'Maybe there's a reason, maybe he's not rich enough yet, or maybe he just doesn't care, or else they can't get set up here? He's so… quiet. It's as if he's not even there. One day I was in the bathroom and came across a little bag from Sephora and there, inside, he'd got himself some foundation, mascara, eye creme from Christian Dior, and what else? Eye creme, mascara… Oh, and he got himself a blush brush made of… it was written right on it… Chinese goat hair or something like that. Nothing special. But the receipt was in there, too: four thousand zlotys!'

'Please, they must make something like fifteen thousand euros a month working in those Swedish firms. Michael Jackson said in some interview that he spends four thousand a month on makeup alone – in dollars!'

'Well, it doesn't do him any good. Anyway, I went and hid in the kitchen and waited to see how that Swede would look when he came in to boil his eggs for breakfast. It was just as I thought: his face was smooth, golden, but you couldn't tell he was wearing makeup. He just made himself look really nice, so you'd think, Just look at that nice-looking man. Tanned, sharp features. You know? It was enough to make me jealous…'

'And he didn't have a boyfriend?'

'Yes, of course. That goes without saying!' She burst out laughing.

## Invasion

They'd fallen asleep on my blanket. I was reading their tabloids, and to tell the truth I was utterly revolted. Krystyna Janda's oven had blown up in her face: that's what they had on the front page as the day's top story, along with a photo of the actress with an appropriately alarmed look on her face (heavy makeup, her eyes popping out of her skull). 'Krystyna Janda escaped death by a whisker yesterday. When she went to open her oven...' Suddenly there was a swooshing sound, and a droning, as if a gigantic oven were exploding on the beach, but in fact it was some gang riding up (even though it was banned) on motorcycles, in leather jackets, music blaring! The Old Dears blanched with fright and hid under their blankets, hoping somehow or other to survive the invasion from outer space; they must have remembered from health and safety training what you're supposed to do in such situations. They were pressing masks made of underwear to their mouths and noses, and jumped under the blanket, into the hollow. Later on they started digging a bunker in the sand. That got a lot of laughs because they took branches from the woods above the dunes to cover their 'bunker', i.e., the hole they'd dug out in the sand all the way down to the water, so now they had a trap for all the most handsome Martians flying over the beach, and one after the other they set their lures in order to catch something. But those weren't Martians at all, just that team from Poznań that was here yesterday. Weird, Americanised, beefed up. They had faces straight out of an American movie, square-jawed, upper lips raised like Rambo or Rocky or something. They went about in boxers even though it was a nudist beach (America is prudish). And they were a 'team' because in the United States the individual doesn't count for anything, only the group, brainstorming, teamwork. They all act in unison, as if they were playing football, a team sport! Clones. When they want to swim, they jump up suddenly from their blankets and rush into the water at full force, diving right in. And as soon as they run out, they start rolling around in the sand, all of them at once, as if it were choreographed. They were all cut from the same cloth, even if they didn't know each other, and they would all do exactly the same things, behave identically, even on a completely different day. No doubt they thought they were being masculine, boyish even. Because the lady pensioners and the other queens, once they'd mustered up the courage to go in the water, would take half a day just to stick their pinky fingers in, then they'd recoil with a squeal, roll their eyes, and swoon at how cold it was, how they wouldn't step foot in there for all the tea in China!

## Dune Patrol

'This one time I looked up, and all the chanteuses were fleeing the dunes, running helter-skelter down the hill to the beach, their drawers in their hands, running in pairs, until they disappeared in the water. That whole colony of Poznanites camped out at the end of the beach, beer-drinking youths – they were running away, too. As if someone had let dogs loose in all those bushes. As if the sweltering heat had set the evergreen forest at the edge of the dunes on fire. But it was patrolmen – border guards. In full gear. Our first thought was: swim to Sweden! We're already part of the EU, after all…

'Then came the shouting: "Can't you see the signs? Everything's prohibited!" And more signs, warnings: Tick Alert. And still more: Don't Litter! Don't Spoil the Environment! And how every weed on these dunes had been planted there by a human hand? And more and more and more signs, how this is a military zone and might have mines in it! And then the fines. We were just over there… Under that tree… until we bolted. But not far away this old thing had been watching us, peeping at us from behind the bushes. She was so engrossed she didn't even see them coming and she fell right

into their clutches. Her comeuppance for watching us like that…
And they said:

'"Your ID, your passport."

'And she replied:

'"Can't you gentlemen see I'm standing here as nature made me?"'

# The Nonchalant Blond

I sent one of the Old Dears into Międzyzdroje for cigarettes, newspapers, and mineral water. The other went off of her own accord to
Lubiewo for lunch, to the Społem cafeteria (they still run one just for
her in the woods). And I went off to my blond! He'd been standing
there in the bushes, trying to attract my attention, as naked as Adam.
They're all Adams here anyway, and none of them, no matter how
much they've sinned, even cares: they're still not ashamed; they don't
feel their nakedness. What's nakedness after all when everyone is
equally, legally nude? Everything here is out in the open, in broad
daylight. No prohibitions, no sin. He was standing there. And he
kept on standing there. Even though I ostentatiously made room for
him on my blanket, tidying away the cigarettes and sunblock. I even
patted the blanket a few times, so he'd know... Finally he came over,
stood a couple of yards away from me, and... talked. He talked and
talked, all the while stroking himself. But nonchalantly, as if he were
pushing away a lock of hair or petting a dog. He was young and
handsome, and had a yellow mane of hair, but it seemed as if he was
covered in dust. And though he was young, it was like he was old,
and though he was good-looking, it was like he was used, chipped

(bruises on his legs, an appendectomy scar). And after a minute I realised: he's poor.

He's poor. That's how his story starts. What his name is, he doesn't say, but he has a daughter(!), Olivia (pretty name). They've taken away his benefits for some reason or other, I don't really understand. Any day they'll cut off his gas. The anonymous 'they' are always taking something away, cutting something off, lurking everywhere. He lives somewhere near Szczecin, and today or yesterday a friend in Międzyzdroje told him on the phone that he'd give him a hundred zlotys, but that he had to come get it. So he hitchhiked here. Olivia went to the neighbours. The route, which by train takes two hours, took him from five in the morning until twelve noon, from one village to the next, then two more hours waiting in the dust and heat. And all for nothing – his friend had lied. And the blond spent his last grosz on the trip. Now 'they' were cutting off his gas, and his landlady was going to kick him out (kickin' me out, she is), and he'd be living on the street again with his little one, and it wouldn't be the first time. He even went from house to house in Międzyzdroje today, asking everyone for a zloty, but of course no one gave him a thing, because they've got beggars there in droves, what with all the buskers, street artists, and mimes... Hasn't he tried to have Olivia taken into care? He wanted to, but decided against it; he'll raise her himself. And what about the mother? She doesn't want anything to do with the child. The whole time he was talking he was playing with himself, but it was like he was doing it without realising! Completely nonchalantly, absentmindedly. So I said:

'You could always sell your body!'

'No, that's something I can only do for love...'

Unfortunately, if that's what love looks like for him, playing with his willy like that, nonchalantly, just going through the motions, then I, for one, am incapable of reciprocating, Marquise! Eventually he thanked me for listening to him and asked me for some money. But I couldn't give him anything, because – following the old cruising-ground custom – I never take money with me to the beach, so that I won't get robbed when I'm in the dunes (I keep my key on a chain around my neck), and what if there's no one to watch my blanket when I go in the sea? I always give to the Great Christmas Orchestra Charity, but I really didn't have anything on me today! He thanked me again anyway for listening to him and went off into the dunes. A moment later I saw him there, standing on top of a dune among the brush, stroking himself, just like before, nonchalantly, as if he were petting a dog! At the same time he was looking about to see if 'they' were anywhere in sight.

## Mistake No. 18

Throwing caution to the wind, I amble down the beach, crossing over towards Międzyzdroje. Maybe there'll be some action over there, because honestly, Vicômte, I don't think that blond would've been of any use to you... But, why... there he is. He's here! Here! Oh, wonderful! Wonderful! And I'll be fucked, he's in sports kit, too. Mmmh, very nice! You better get out your best bag of tricks, Marquise, he just looked your way... The first rule in situations like this: under no condition let the totty know you're interested! Slow down a bit, but keep walking. Don't turn around, and whatever you do, *don't stare*! Let him come after you. Because if you throw yourself at him he'll think you're just some old trollop who'd go off with the first thing that comes her way, without even bothering to suss it out first. So with my chin held high I slow down, and without looking back at him, I walk straight ahead. I try not to swivel my hips, I straighten my posture as much as I can and turn my left profile (the better one) a tad towards him. Sucking in my stomach, I reach down and pick something up from the sand and hurl it, and with a manly kick I send a can flying. He catches up with me, overtakes me, glances at me. He's thirty, I can tell out of the corner of my eye...

Athletic. So I slip my slim pack of cigarettes out of my bathing suit – I only ever strip off in the hollows between the dunes – and ostentatiously I sit down on top of a dune. And now, according to all the rules of the game as I know it, he should sit down, too, a few yards further on, and we should begin exchanging glances, back and forth. Only the real pervs start jerking off right away. I smoke, and my hands are atremble with the thought of what an easy catch this was, what tonic for the heart...

But then, Totty commits Mistake No. 18. He can go to hell for all I care! He does sit down, but it's much too far away, and all the way down in a hollow, so he's invisible, and there's no way for us to look at each other! Basically, I know he's right there, but what now? He's probably kicking himself, too, for pulling an 18, but it would be awkward for him to stand up now without a good pretext. And he was *so* hot! And he had his jeans balled up in his hand, and now he's probably laid them out on the sand under his naked, hairy, ruddy little tush. He's probably got his hand down his pants, too, not that it matters, it's so completely out of view! And it's not like I can stand up either, cruising being cruising after all; we'd both end up acting totally embarrassed, as if we didn't know what was happening, that it was all purely coincidental, that was the thrill. So it's not like I'm going to get up off my arse to walk over and start chatting him up. I can see smoke rising from his hollow. Maybe he's sending me smoke signals? Oh, if only I could write words of love in smoke in the air, but I've already extinguished my cigarette (and stuffed the butt-end back in the pack – I'm no litterbug). Well, after fifteen minutes I simply don't care any more whether or not it's appropriate: I get up and walk over along the top of the dunes and look and – no one's there! He's gone! Just a dent in the sand where he'd been sitting. But how? If he'd got up and walked away along the beach I'd have seen him! He must've gone over the top of the dune. I comb the area for a good half hour, but nothing. Vanished into thin air. A *fata morgana*…

## Gypsy

Suddenly I look up – there's a deckchair there. But what, or rather who, is in the deckchair? It's Gypsy. Her legs are crossed and she's reading the paper.

Paula already told me about her, about her uncanny way with straights. Well, I'd love to see her try it with my bit of totty!

'She's an absolute troll, that one, traveling all over Poland selling rugs. Her hairline starts way down her forehead… Her hair is bushy and bleached… But the peroxide can't get through all the dye, so instead of blonde, it's totally orange. "Bottle blonde" is what they call it. Hideous. And it's not like she's really interested in a shag; she just comes up to you on the street, on the picket line, all serious, and says:

'"Hello. Pardon me. My name is such-and-such. Very pleased to meet you, sir. I am a homosexual and I have an offer for you. You won't regret it, I assure you. You will be completely satisfied. Please, allow me to explain." Then she sits with you on a bench and the words keep coming (the grunt probably expects her to pull something out of her bag and try to sell it to him).

'"If you do not mind, sir, I should like to masturbate you. I promise, you will be 100 per cent satisfied. I'll do anything you like, for free, here, right now – behind that wall. Please, consider my offer, I mean it seriously..." And she doesn't even crack a smile! She's completely with it, like she's trying to sell you some new retirement package or insurance policy. And they fall for it.'

Ah well. That was some time ago, and here I am running into Gypsy in Lubiewo, in a beach chair. She tosses the newspaper away and engages me effusively, telling me all about her recent adventure in Ostrowiec – grammatically, she speaks as a man. She's utterly earnest, as ever, her brow furrowed:

'I was travelling. On business to Ostrowiec. To buy some used Taiwanese rugs. In Ostrowiec, I hopped into a taxi, a very handsome driver (complaining about his wife, children). So after we've driven a little bit, I say this to him.' Here Gypsy gets even more serious, clasping her hands as if she's going to pray, bowing slightly. She continues:

'I have something to ask you, sir, a proposal, if you will. I will pay you double your rate, twice the amount on your metre and a bit more on top, if only you will agree to my request. Please, sir, allow me to give you a blowjob. You will not regret it. Here, we can stop in these woods for a moment, I'll suck you off in mere seconds, suck you dry, right down to the very last drop, and I'll swallow as well. However you like it, your wife won't give you better service. You can do it to spite her, sir (Gypsy remembered that he'd been complaining about his wife...). You need only to unfasten your belt, sit back, and presto. Really. You will be satisfied.' The fellow stopped the cab, wham bam bam, Gypsy did what she had to, paid him double, and said:

'I am very pleased that everything went so masterfully, but I have another proposal for you, sir. As I am here often on business, why not meet again? In a month's time I'll be back for rugs from China; I'll simply get into your taxi, once again I'll pay you double, and once again I'll suck you off.' The bloke agreed.

At this point Gypsy vigorously expels smoke through her nostrils and mouth.

'So you see,' she continues, 'I found myself there a year or half a year later, in Ostrowiec. I went to the taxi stand and looked. The cabbies were all standing in front of their cars, in a group, talking, and I started walking towards my cabby, then he whispered something to them, and they all fell about laughing! And stared at me. What do you think he could have said about me? That I did everything he wanted me to do and paid him, fair and square? Is that what he was blabbing to them about? And what was so funny? I ask you. What's so funny about me…?'

And she's still asking… Gypsy sits there in that beach chair, fanning herself with the newspaper, sweat streaming down her face, fending off the mosquitoes, and so serious in her distress, so utterly preoccupied, and hideous, frowning…

# The Actress and Apparel

By way of reciprocating, and to clear her mind of that unfortunate incident, as well as my own of my unpleasant loss of Totty, I quickly tell her a story about a certain Actress, and offer her a cigarette.

So there was this one famous Actress by the name of Iga. And all through communism she learned her lines on the picket line in the park. On a bench. In an interview in a local newspaper, the Actress was once asked where she most enjoyed learning her lines, and she replied, 'In Hanka Sawicka Park. Go ahead and laugh!' Fans would approach her there and ask for her autograph, and she always gave it. The queens would ask her what role she was learning, and then they'd learn it, too, and later they'd go and camp it up on top of the hill. Back then they had one of those communist bandstands up there, just the thing where queens could put on their burlesques. Like all good things, it's gone now; somebody objected to something or other, desperate people chopped up the stage for fuel. They would stand in that bandstand and read their lines by heart, but that soon got boring, so our chanteuses would sing – arias, recitatives: What do I see, who is that woman whose hat resembles all the flowers of

Araby? Has she come to avenge her unhappy brother?! O, forsooth, I knooooooow her! They'd find a stick and an empty bottle, and presto: a microphone. Sometimes the Actress even joined them. One winter, after a snowstorm, I was taking a stroll there at night, and there they were, the queens together with the Actress, sledging helter-skelter down the hill. All I could hear was their squealing:

'Luuucreeeeetia! Ack! A tree! A tree! Help!!!'

So the Actress would stand there out on the street together with this ballet dancer, in front of the State Department Store, which was right next to Cruising Central, of course; they'd stand there at that traffic light for hours, chit-chatting.

'Look, what I bought today,' says the one, pulling a blouse out of her bag into the light, unfolding it and showing it to the other… Cars would honk their horns, but they were no match for two queens examining newly purchased garments. Though they were whispering to each other, they were theatrical, stage whispers; you could probably hear their conversation as far as the Rynek.

When the Actress got into a fight with her opera-singer boyfriend, she took all his clothes from their flat and hung them up at the moat (the cruising ground extended along the moat back then), on the fences that separated the park from the water. All day long she hung out his things, as if she were hanging them up to dry – underwear, socks:

'Take your mink coat and sod off! Go back where you came from, where you belong…!'

Golda, aka La Belle Hélène, turned up and saw the moat flooded in clothes – the Actress's boyfriend was evidently something of a clotheshorse. She took one look then trotted off to the

Monopol, and even before she walked in the door, she told the moneychangers:

'Gypsies are pitching camp on the picket!' Then off she went to tell the toilet lady, and the cloakroom girl, and the lift girl...

In the good old days, that is, in the seventies, the Actress frequented a cruising ground known as Sądówka. These days even a three-legged dog wouldn't be seen there, but back then the place was in full bloom! Normal straights, men, *paters familias* from the nearby flats and council blocks, would come down in their houseshoes and shorts, in a hurry, because the wife had dozed off in front of the telly, and before you knew it they'd been serviced. I was told this by Kitty of the Stinky Breath, who was young enough then for Iga to snatch her up and take her, like it was the most natural thing in the world, back to the theatre, clear across the stage, through all those nooks and crannies, and right into her dressing room. Actresses were going onstage, there were people shouting and bells going off, you know the way it is in the theatre, and no one gave a thought to Iga walking through with Kitty in tow. They made love there among the props and Iga's dust-covered costumes, since that was before Kitty's breath started to stink.

The Actress had a doppelgänger who, in addition to looking like her, had altogether failed to distinguish herself in life. She was a boring, old queen who'd worked her whole life at the post office; the only nice thing about her was her pretty sobriquet: Rachel. Young actors and students were always sucking up to her, and as a result she'd been able to bed her fair share of young men, or else they would follow her on the street, smiling at her. And more than once that envelope pusher found herself telling them the secrets of the actor's craft, expressing her views, really speaking her mind, and they'd listen with rapt looks on their faces, dressed all in black. But that Rachel lied to them; she invented all sorts of adventures from her 'early years in the theatre' – though it's unclear whether she'd ever actually been to a play even once in her life – how this or that famous lover had courted her, and all the men who'd sent her flowers in huge, overflowing baskets. Her image of the world of the theatre was more Hollywood than Wrocław. In the end, one particularly intelligent poof got mad at that stamp licker for cashing in the actress's ration coupons, which she got only because she looked identical and which she obviously didn't deserve. So she sent her an anonymous letter with the Jew's words about Rachel from Wyspiański's *Wedding*:

> *They say that music fascinates her,*
> *But a man has yet to captivate her;*
> *Maybe I'll find her a job at the post office...*

# UFO!!!

They come back. First one, from lunch. But seeing that I'm alone on my blanket, she doesn't dare approach me (the one condition of her sitting down here is that the other one, her accomplice in age, be there too). She walks on a bit further, spreads herself out on a towel, places a leaf on her nose, slips off her vest, and starts tanning, looking over again and again to see if I'm watching her. Finding that she is, unfortunately, being watched, the least she can do is to place a leaf on each of her nipples, too.

I look up and see the other one returning with a lot of shopping; it's clear she's planning to sit here until late in the evening. I pounce on her: I've run out of cigarettes, and sitting in the dunes always makes me want to smoke, especially if there's a beer to go with it.

She treats me to some of her bad cigarettes, but she also got me a pack of R1s. She also treats me to the news that she believes she may have seen, in the Międzyzdroje spa park, with her evil hound at her side, Oleśnicka – evidently they let her out. Which may be true since Oleśnicka is like the chairwoman of the Polish National Committee on Faggotry. Anyway, I look over and notice that my Old Dear No. 1 has emptied her bag of various books of the bodice-ripping kind, as well as – people get more childlike in their old age – one of those yellow inflatable arm bands for swimming! In a flash she inflated it (pulling such faces from the strain!), picked it up in her skinny hands, and, after asking politely if we'd keep an eye on her things, which were all packed into one of those flower-patterned cloth bags that old ladies use for their shopping, she went off to bathe. She must have houseplants at home. Violets and geraniums and ancient, sprawling aloes.

'That's right, I saw Oleśnicka on my way back from lunch...' says Old Dear No. 2. At which Wiesław steps back and sneers and says quietly:

'And on my... on *my* way back from lunch... I saw *it... It!*' She makes as if to flee.

'What? What did you see?'

She looks back and cries:

'The UFO!'

Then I start chasing after her, infuriated, and she squeals and runs away. She stops mid-run, turns on her heels, and shouts:

'A giant ball, a great ball of fire, a light, glowing over the dunes, a giant ball, a ball, a ball!'

Finally I catch hold of her, tackle her to the ground, and drizzle sand in her eyes, in her face. 'Don't do that to me, what are you doing? Oh God, what is this bitch doing to me?' The whole scene is interrupted by Zdzisia yelling:

'Here it comes!'

'Oh no, that too!'

'What are you talking about?' I ask seriously, the two of them having gone completely off their rockers. On the horizon, though,

I notice someone, not a UFO at any rate, but some poof or other. Zdzisia exclaims:

'Hare Lip's coming, girls! Duck!'

'Who on earth is that?'

'Everyone knows Hare Lip because of that affair she had. Look at her, how meticulously dressed she is.' And it's true; in spite of the heat the figure's wearing a black, long-sleeved blouse, long pants, a hat, gloves...

'She must have an aversion to showing any skin... Ha!' says Zdzisława, and begins to tell me the story of Hare Lip...

# Hare Lip

The metropolis of Wrocław, on a summer night, just before daybreak. It's about four in the morning. The tarmac lit by streetlamps,
the streets empty. And all of a sudden, there between those mori-
bund buildings and shuttered shops and offices, a bald bloke of
about forty rides by on a bicycle. Quickly, looking uncertainly from
side to side. Hardly cause for surprise, except that one thing stands
out here – the man is naked, stark bollock naked. No underwear,
no eyeglasses, no watch, no shoes, no bag: just a naked body on a
bike! How he managed to get back into his flat, nobody knows, but
then nobody was around to start with.

Hare Lip owed her sobriquet to the impressive cantilever of her
upper lip and the funny way it made her speak. She was a doctoral
student at the University, though maybe it was the Polytechnic. She
would spend all Sunday correcting student papers until evening
drove her to the picket line. But 'nothing's happening', 'no one's
around', 'slim pickings', were the usual prognoses in the park, and
had been for years. It was a kind of key phrase. Nothing is happening, nothing is happening... What's happening? Nothing's
happening... There was something Buddhist about it, a kind of

wisdom informed by the concept of nirvana... There's nothing, nothing's happening... Causes, effects, nothing... Suffering... The utter nonexistence of time, of space, of people. Nothing, nada, nix. Waiting for Godot and nada. And even when there's something – that's nothing, too... It was no different that evening. And it wasn't until three in the morning, utterly knackered from constant strolling, smoking, cruising, that she spotted some grunt. Oh. My. God. He was super! Totally straight-acting. They went down to 'city hall'. Into the shadows of looming columns, into the bottomless gloom of their crevasses, into shadows cast by statues. The lights were on a timer and quickly, obligingly, went out. Suddenly the grunt spoke up:

'It really turns me on when a lad takes off all his clothes.' Hare Lip responded in a breathy lisp:

'Turnth you on, huh? Hmmm...' she dithered. 'Well... thuper!' Then she wholeheartedly began ripping off her clothes, throwing them off into the distance, her backpack, shoes, keys, watch, briefs... The grunt ordered her to turn and face the wall, lucky girl; her striptease had excited him so much, he was going to take her from behind now... But instead the grunt carefully aimed a hearty kick to Lip's buttocks so that she fell, lacerating her face. He took her things and ran off; he left her bicycle (he had his own, and there was no way he could haul away a second one). He must have been straight, but that thought somehow ceased to give Lip any consolation. Because now, without her keys, without her money, without her underwear, she had to ride home on her bike... The narrow racing saddle wedged itself awkwardly up the crack of her almost forty-year-old arse, and between bouts of panic Hare Lip was struck by a deeper realisation. The clock on the cathedral tower struck three, or maybe it was four, but for Lip it was striking the hour of realisation. Fortunately the city was empty for now, but who knows when, out of an alley, there'd come a band of youths drunk on cheap beer, including, who knows, some of Hare Lip's students?! So it was better to take the side streets, although that would mean extending her route indefinitely – she lived on the outskirts of town after all! And she needed to make it home before it was completely light, before the birds woke up and the streets started filling with people. Before any of that took place, the dreamy, surrealistic hallucination that was naked Hare Lip riding her bike through the very centre of the city would have to disappear once and for all, melt away or dissipate in the morning fog. The distant ringing of the night tram – Lip's bottom felt wet; she stopped and looked: it was her own blood. Mosquitoes were stinging her mercilessly, and every inch of her skin was bare. She picked up speed on her bike and in a moment felt as if she were about to fly over the city, so free, so naked, so liberated, she'd bolt up the hill and soar over the awakening city like Margarita on her broom over slumbering Russia.

But then she remembered where she was; a cold sweat broke out on her forehead. Bells were ringing – Lip was thirsty. Her throat was parched; the last time she'd had anything to drink was at eight that evening, before leaving the house, and that was vodka. If it was four now, then she hadn't had a drop to drink for eight hours, and vodka makes you thirsty! In the course of that inauspicious night, she'd smoked a whole pack of Marlboro Lights (all that without a drop of water); who wouldn't be thirsty! The monotonous hum of some nocturnal electricity – Lip was hungry. The traffic lights tediously

blinking over the crossing, out of operation at this time of night –
Lip was paralysed by the realisation that getting home would bring
her no consolation, that she wouldn't be able to tuck herself away
in it like a pair of cosy, comfortable pyjamas, she wouldn't be able to
put on anything she had in her wardrobe because she wouldn't even
be able to get in without her key. A black cat crossed the road – Lip
circled back in a wide arc and decided to ride over to see a queen she
knew in Kozanów. She'd bang on her door at four in the morning.
On the outskirts. She'd ride as fast as she could on her bike and
maybe she'd even take wing above the city. Covered in blood,
naked. Elated.

## Kino Studio

'And you know what, Michał, they say that one time the very same Hare Lip walked into the first class of the school year and… there he was in the lecture hall! Her student! The bit of grunt who'd nicked her clothes! They say she got her revenge on him, all sorts of stories were reported. But only the good Lord knows what happened there…'

The first thing I did was read her bodice-ripper… There she was, sitting on the terrace at the end of the season, gazing at the autumn leaves, but of course right off she meets a doctor (because the book is in the 'Medic Series'), and they immediately start screwing (because the book is in the 'Spicy Series' too), and then it all ends happily ever after since he's a dog breeder and is loaded to boot, etc. A well-thumbed copy carrying the stamp of the Cheerfulness 4 Library of the Workers' Holiday Fund. The pages are coated with various blotches, dashes, and spots, like liver spots, like the hands of the old ladies who turn them.

I stood up from my blanket, stretched and looked out over the dunes. A lone fatty was standing there, scouring the beach through a pair of binoculars. I could hear the team from Poznań, from Scorpio, singing in the distance. Old Dear No. 2 was off picking forget-me-nots in the dunes, or else just pretending to as a cover for stalking someone. Meanwhile, Old Dear No. 1 had come back from the water, sputtering and squealing. The water's warm, bottom all sandy, I really should go 'for a dip', she'll watch my things. The sea's still as a lake. When I demurred, she asked me what my earliest (gay) memories were of. I answered: of the eighties and Studio Cinema…

Studio Cinema… where once a week the local chapter of Lambda would meet. Queens in jumpers and neck scarves would smoke cigarettes and sit in the cinema bar, which had a TV and plants in the windows. They'd drink tea from glass cups, bitch at each other, gossip, or listen to the president's speeches and try to be 'political', part of the 'struggle'. Sometimes they showed movies, like *My Beautiful Laundrette*. Once a month they held a disco, but this was back when the streets really ran with blood! The cinema was in Popowice, the most skinhead-ridden part of town, and the skins would wait outside the theatre like dogs; they'd throw rocks through the windows and hit their targets. Whenever anyone wanted to leave, he had to be escorted by a police bodyguard, because folks were always getting knifed or stoned and as often as not taken to hospital in critical condition. Blood, I remember that; blood on the faces of people who'd simply come to have a good time. I remember those bloody skinheads, too, who would keep trying to break free of the police, kicking their legs in the air.

But here my story is interrupted, for we both look over: someone is walking towards us. The Old Dears immediately begin whispering to each other: how it's a certain Apothecaress from Bydgoszcz, a really wealthy queen who's obsessed with her health. She always carries a bottle of water with her so she can rinse off her darling's cock before they get down to work. She always has condoms handy, and a lubricant gel that she prepares herself in the back of the shop; she mixes it in a mortar, since the chemist's where she works sells both ready-made and made-to-order pharmaceuticals. So she concocts all kinds of lube, mixing in anaesthetics, sometimes even psychotropics. She gave me one once in a white pillbox – it blasted me and my arsehole to outer space! She eats vitamins and definitely minerals. She's been spoiled rotten by her money like the lewd bitch she is.

## You'll Never Be Sated...

'No licking...'

'No licking?' We couldn't believe it.

'No licking.' The Apothecaress shows us a brochure, and there it is, black and white, you're not supposed to, because when it leaks...

'That's the pre-ejaculatory fluid...'

'That has AIDS in it too.'

'You mean HIV.'

'That's what I said.'

We sit down on the blanket and study the brochure. The Apothecaress pulls a bottle of Vichy sunscreen from her bag and dabs each of her moles individually. Then she smears her birthmarks with the Vichy 60.

'And girls: no facials!'

'And no rubbing cocks against your face if you've shaved less than four hours before – micro-abrasions, you know...'

'And don't lube your arse with Nivea, because it causes micro-incisions in the condom...'

'And no brushing your teeth before giving a blowjob! That causes micro-incisions, too...'

'No giving blowjobs at all: you'll come into contact with AIDS through your teeth, and through the cuts on your chin from shaving; you'll come into contact with all those fluids, and ruination!' At that the Apothecaress pulls a bottle of Vichy water from her bag and mists her pale skin with it. She says:

'I'm cooling myself. Furthermore, the micro-elements soothe the sun's irritating effects, which can cause adverse changes in my skin.'

'Look here girls, they say even fisting is bad.'

'*Fisting*?' We all sit up at the same time and tear the brochure out of the Apothecaress's hands.

'No kissing. You'll get herpes... That's because of the, umm... mucus membrane. You can't touch the mucus membrane, so no contact between your lips and anything, anything good at least... Because all those places where you'd be likely to lick him, that's all mucus.'

'You can't do anything. This is giving me a sore throat.'

'That's right, you can't do anything!' the Apothecaress declares triumphantly. 'From now on, don't touch any living thing. And for those of you who've already been touching penises with your tongue today, there's Doxycycline and Difflam. Exterminate all those chlamydias once and for all, and don't give any new ones a chance! Keep yourself clean down below with a personal hygiene gel; thoroughly disinfect yourselves; put on a pair of fresh white undies, and padlock them! And maybe then you'll manage not to catch anything. From now on, no more touching! Nothing at all! Nothing is allowed!'

'And here I was wanting to do everything...' Old Dear No. 2 starts up very quietly. 'Sticking my tongue down a bloke's throat, right into the lymph nodes, siphoning them up...'

'And licking arses and drinking cum!'

'Licking everything! Licking everything imaginable! Licking ourselves crazy! Lick-lick-licking ourselves to death!' Old Dear No. 1 pipes up, cheerful again. 'And pulling hair and spitting and stuffing our faces with bollocks!'

'But you've never seen a penis, a foreskin, under a microscope, have you? Do you have any idea how many bacteria there are on there? Not to mention in an anus? Haven't you ever heard of liver-infecting viruses like...' But everyone's tuned out the Apothecaress.

They've already sterilised her, she's aseptic, medicalised. All those doctors and apothecaresses have no taboos anymore, just petting; she's been washed completely clean of taboos.

I've had it with these doctors!! Spending all their time in hospitals, in clinics – that's why their sex lives are so bad. The things I've shown them! Whenever the doctor lady asks me if I've engaged in any 'at-risk behaviours', I say, uh-huh, then she says, when did the last behaviour occur, and I say, the last behaviour occurred sometime yesterday... Seems to me that 'at-risk behaviours' must be a term borrowed from English... And with all those samples, the blood, all those glass slides stuck up... Ugh! But washed entirely clean of taboos, starched and ironed, too...

So we said to her:

'Foreskins and anuses may look one way under the microscope, but cock and arse! Cock and arse is the thing!'

'And anyway, look what it says here: rubbing sperm all over your body is called a "Russian massage". Did you know that?'

'And fucking a woman's cleavage is called doing it "Spanish style".'

Everyone laughs. Oh those Spaniards!

'Well, no one's going to tell me it's not OK to rub two cocks up against each other.'

'But you can't let the holes come into contact because your mucus membrane is exposed there.'

'Well, I've been exposing all of myself all day!' Another round of laughter.

'But what if there's not much in his trousers? Maybe it's OK…' the Old Dears console themselves.

'You're idiots. What difference does the size of his cock make?'

'Oh, it can make a *huge* difference!' They giggle.

'You know, I don't really understand this. If a lad is clean and good-looking, how can he possibly have AIDS?' My Old Dears were beyond on this score. How often had I heard them say: 'Why, the boy's well groomed, and they're going on about AIDS…!"

'Well, just imagine this: AIDS is invisible!'

A moment of silence. They continue reading the brochure, giggling over the pictures.

'And here was I hoping to finally gorge myself on that lad.'

'You'll never be sated by him, my dear,' the Apothecaress replies philosophically. 'There's no quenching it. It's not like you can devour him anyway.' (We: 'Well, it *has* happened before…') 'You'll simply touch him with your tongue and wander along on the surface. You'll glide along it without penetrating. As if you were licking a computer screen.'

They agree. General robustness and hermeneutics of the body. Like a landscape, you can't penetrate it, it won't sate you. It's an illusion. A surface, a flat network, Deleuze and Guattari.

'An optical illusion,' adds Old Dear No. 2, playing dumb.

The Apothecaress pulls a copy of *Forum* out of her bag, along with pills that accelerate tanning, which she swallows down with Kudowa Springs mineral water.

'Did you read this article in *Forum*, about how in the United States 40 per cent of new infections are intentional? And in Western Europe... How the queens there are so degenerate that they even ask to get infected? They put adverts on the internet saying things like "Help me seroconvert", or how they've already got such and such a strain of HIV, but want a new one...'

We can't believe it. She shows us. The article. It's true.

'But why would they do that?'

'Well, why did that German guy eat the other German? As if it were a perfectly normal thing to do; when the police entered that house in Heidelberg, he still had remains in the freezer. What's really interesting is that he had a video of the other bloke agreeing to it. He actually consented to be eaten!'

The Old Dears stamp their feet:

'No! That's completely abnormal! I refuse to accept it! I'm an old woman, I want to stay healthy and live a long life, and I eat... the jams I make for winter, not Germans!'

We stand there in silence. Tra la la la... Suddenly one of them says:

'Listen, maybe that German was just really, really hungry?!'

'Huh?'

'Well, what you were saying, about how a lad can't satisfy you because there's no quenching it, because it's all surface and skin...

Well, maybe he just wanted to feel really connected to him?'

The others agree. But that's not the way to do it. Killing someone, cutting him up and eating him. Like a schnitzel. Like in a restaurant.

The Apothecaress scowls:

'You're all monsters.'

She was, in spite of everything, a girl from a good family, sterile and pure. She even had on sunscreen under her UV-protective sunglasses, because of eye cancer. Pale, skinny, red-haired. A wet, English chicken. I adored her.

My Apothecary Amazon didn't really have a sex life, no matter how much she tried; she'd read too many of those brochures. Instead she'd become addicted to chatting on the internet. She urged me to buy a camera, because the cyberqueens are all doing the nasty now, in full view and in colour, virtually infecting each other with virtual viruses. I thanked her very much for the suggestion and closed my eyes. Dozed off...

...

'I don't know about you, but I'm not laying my lips on a cock again for as long as I live...'

'Right. Let's see what happens tonight.'

...

'She was looking all over for a flat, first this one, then that. So I said to her: what the hell do you want, as long as the roof's not leaking...?'

...

'Look at that seagull... big, big enough to feed a whole family...'

...

'So I rang up that tart. And the line was *busy!*'

# Di

had scars on her wrists and came from Bratislava:

'Only an hour away from La Vienne!'

Her name was Milan. A drop-dead gorgeous, sixteen-year-old blonde with blue eyes, long eyelashes – like the boy next door in a comic book for well-behaved little children. But on the inside, inside that boy next door, a dirty old whore was lurking. A bit of a sloth, too. She worked in the metro, at the Karlplatz-Oper station. There was a pub in a glassed-in area, which we called the Aquarium as it had a view of the public toilets. Tons of teenage Poles, Czechs, Romanians, and Russians would make the rounds – and geriatric Austrians, too, of course. Some of them were beautiful; others, hideously ugly. There was no middle-of-the-road in there...

Di couldn't forget the pervasive stench of citrus-scented disinfectant, which mingled with the smell of shit from the toilets. She hated standing in front of the urinals, waiting for clients, so she would usually sit drinking beer in that glassed-in, subterranean pub, and watch, glassy-eyed, as the old men circled the conveniences. I said to her:

'Back to work, Diana! *Arbeiten!** Even if it's just for fifty schillings.' And she said:

'*Ja sem žena leniva…'***

Whenever she finally got her arse in gear, all she'd do was sit and drink beer with the bloke. Then she'd say to me, out loud since he didn't understand anyway:

'*Konečne som nasiel toho pravého chlapa…'****

Di wasn't really suited for this kind of work. Once, exhausted by a client, she rang for a cab. She had a hard time finding the stairwell, and the steps were steep, and through the open entryway she could see the car waiting for her. So she hurried down, started running down the stairs, carefree and happy that she was done and had a decent wad of cash in her pocket. Then suddenly, just as she got to the last step, the world disappeared and there was a great thud! Di blacked out. Coming from Slovakia she wasn't used to such clean, clear windows. She wasn't used to many things. And later it pained her no end that the cab driver had seen her fall, had seen her careening head slam against the windows at full force, and she was embarrassed about that.

Things went downhill from there. She had less and less money. She'd even started living on the streets, which made her look like shit. It was a vicious circle: she had no money, so she looked awful, but in order to make any money, she would need to get some rest, a bath, and put on clean clothes.

She was on her own, in the metro, and her shoes chafed her feet

---

\* *German*: Work!
\*\* *Slovak*: I'm a lazy woman.
\*\*\* *Slovak*: I've already found my stud…

so she couldn't go roaming round Vienna. She hobbled over to Alfie's, a bar for boys like herself (rent boys, in other words), sat down in the corner, and without drinking, without smoking, without eating, simply watched the goings-on, quietly humming Slovak rock songs to herself.

It was like a game of roulette: one day you might earn fifty schillings, but to do that you first had to invest something, because most of the time you'd sit there for hours before picking up a client. During that time you'd end up drinking five coffees, five Fantas, five beers, five whatever, because the waiters made sure that the rent boys ordered at least one drink an hour. So what you made in one day, you'd spend over the course of five just sitting and waiting. Di watched with envy as the successful ones at the bar stuffed themselves on enormous schnitzels with chips and salad, or chops and fried eggs. With beautiful halves of lemon to squeeze on the meat, on those chips, on all that wonderful grub! She swallowed her own spit and smoked a fag she'd bummed off someone, which tasted awful on an empty stomach. She wondered how long before they threw her out, since she wasn't putting money in the till. Even if she did dig up a few schillings, she knew what would happen: she'd trick once, then have nothing five nights in a row; she could lose everything. Even the Romanians – they've been dry for two weeks! Oh, and what Romanians they were! My God! Through their oversized, baggy, white trousers they showed Didi their gorgeous, fat cocks. Stretching the stained fabric around them. In their broken German mixed with Russian, they asked her to see for herself, starved as they were – two weeks. They wanted schillings, cigarettes, but what could she give them? They were handsome and masculine, had none of that unfeeling look in their eyes, like the Austrians, Swiss, and Germans had; they were straight. Eighteen years old, swarthy, with bushy, black eyebrows!

An elderly trick named Dieter, a copy of Günter Grass's *The Rat* wrapped in brown paper under his arm, makes the rounds of the bar like a professor. Wears a threadbare sports coat, has a little pipe. But he doesn't know what he wants. He once called Di over to his table, bought her drinks, and said:

'*Heute bin ich müde, lass mich in Ruhe...*'* Then they made a date for Wednesday, though Di wasn't even sure he'd live that long.

Vincent is behind the bar today, a tall, likeable Austrian; Di and her ilk are good for business. Old torch songs waft out of the stereo speakers, even Edith Piaf. In the other room the rent boys play the slot machines. There's a hideous, filthy African who smells badly; Di knows she's homeless, that she got sucked into the vicious circle, and that she'll end up the same way, too, if a miracle doesn't happen tonight. Then that sweetheart Vincent gives a nod to the security man to escort the African discreetly off the premises. Suddenly a jolly band of local playboys bursts in: middle-aged, colourful scarves on their heads, chains around their necks, rings on their fingers. Noisy and jolly, straight from a land called Miami, a land of movie stars, cocktails, and red convertibles pumping music at full blast. A land of moonscape wallpaper and faded dreams that's only as far away as the imagination of the next playboy. They order whiskies and smoke Marlboro Reds – they couldn't care less if smoking kills. Bald and monstrously obese,

---

* *German*: I'm tired today, leave me alone.

in the way that only the wealthy can be, because wealth always exaggerates a person's distinguishing features – thinks Milan, the philosopher of the Bratislava council estates. Because if someone likes to eat and he's poor, all that will happen is he'll get fat; but if he's rich (and for Di all Austrians were rich), then he'll end up looking like one of those behemoths. And if you have a really campy queen who happens to be loaded, she'll probably be wearing an entire jewellery shop, a coat of gold, furs – enough to trump any opera diva. The playboys' bellowing fills the bar; they're completely out of control, but of no use to Di as long as they're entertaining each other. She's been around long enough to know that only the shamefaced, solitary daddies stuck in the corner are worth eyeing. The bald men unleash another volley of rowdy guffaws. Meanwhile the real 'rowdy ones' – the beautiful young Russians – sit quietly in the corners, fumbling in the pockets of their grubby jeans, counting out their last coins. There was yet another kind of trick who got deformed by wealth: the middle-aged queens with their faces, their grimaces, each reminiscent of a different animal species: weasel, parrot, owl… dripping with bracelets and topped with hair transplants. A moment later those poseurs are joined by beautiful, two-metre-tall lads from the land of glittering lights and cheap entertainment, who come to take their coats, move their ashtrays closer, light their cigarettes, who exchange their place at the door for a chance to be chosen. They even pull out their chairs for them, sit them down at their tables.

But even as those lads hurry to serve them, the queens bat their eyelashes and slap them clumsily, tenderly, or make indignant faces: 'You look like a turd. I'm taking someone else home tonight! Pooh!'

Even though they were old and ugly, they didn't show the least sign of balding (transplants) or greying (dye), they had no wrinkles, they were tall, well fed; it was only the jaded expressions on their faces that gave away their ages. They'd already had everything replaced. But they put on airs like those Czech actresses, those old girls with frizzy perms... Old gazelles with their bracelets and rings and cigarette cases and lighters, and everything smothered in diamonds, rubies, a hoard years in the making. Right beside them: a table of strapping bears with huge bald pates – a gang of taxi drivers. They're knocking back beers, smoking those little brown cigars, cracking up for the whole pub to hear. Tin rings with skulls on them. And if they weren't bald, then they invariably had their hair cut in a mullet, sometimes down to their arse in back, a crew-cut up front, with highlights. Now one of them swaggers like an old sailor to the jukebox and picks out a whole variety show of bad German dance songs about love. The ones with the choruses. A woman's warm voice oozes out of the jukebox. All they need now are beer and schnitzel, thinks Di, chewing her nails.

The macho moneymakers are playing billiards in the other room. On and on and on, for six hours already. As if they didn't need to work at all. Oh, they're ordering sandwiches! The expensive ones... Garnished and served right at the billiards table, service on top... The sandwiches that have sausage and pickle and tomato... Sometimes they leave the door to Alfie's open and a breeze blows in. Some of the boys are always getting calls on their mobile phones – they're the real call boys... They place adverts with their phone numbers and photos in the gay papers. They take their calls and walk slowly past the bar towards the door, chatting away. Hi, this is Eros; hi, this is Hyacinth... Their names are always confected. Later, from pay-phones, they ring their girlfriends in Prague and Moscow, their fiancées:

'Hey baby, I've got a job in a restaurant. I can hardly wait till I've made the money for our wedding... Yeah baby, I got the socks and clean underwear you sent, thanks a million...'

Every now and then a skinny, nervous, bald queen walks in, sits at the bar, orders a beer, and spends the whole evening flicking her lighter on and off. When you ask her for a light, she looks at you for a moment with a completely vacant stare. Later a group of Polish grunt walks in. Straights. Their eyes brim with banality, hostility. They're here to make money; they suppress their disgust. They wear tracksuits with POLSKA in enormous red letters emblazoned across the back. Right off they say:

'Fucking hell, I'll fucking annihilate that piece of shit.'

Di is deliriously afraid of them. But there's one agreeable Pole among them. She hears him telling someone else how he's just returned from France, from Cannes, how he didn't make a penny, and in fact was cleaned out, and if his friend hadn't got lucky on a slot machine they'd have had no way to get back, would've got stuck in the old vicious circle there. Then he stops; there's no need to explain to anyone in that pub what the vicious circle is.

Now Di gets up and walks out of the bar, out of its heavy air thick with the smell of cigarettes, schnitzel, beer, and cologne... She walks to the little park next door, where others are stamping their feet on the ground to keep the cold at bay. They're like her – so broke they can't even afford to sit in a pub. Out on the street, it all looks just like it must have in the past. People standing; old, fat, and bald, the tricks walk between the parked cars along the street; sometimes someone beats someone else senseless, or else the filth comes round and everyone vanishes into thin air.

And that's when the lawyer turned up, who for the next three months would make her his domestic whore. In exchange for cleaning and sex, he tended to Di's legs, which were chafed to the bone, and all of the illnesses she'd contracted during those five days of being homeless. When she'd had to sleep... no, in fact, she hadn't slept anywhere. Because they shut the metro, pulling those grilles down from the ceiling, like they did in castles in the olden days. Everything was shut; drawbridges were raised; it was red lights everywhere for Di from Bratislava! The first night seemed as if it would never end. Milan stood in the freezing cold from midnight until daybreak. And nothing happened. Snowflakes fell against a backdrop of lit streetlamps. Was that all? Was that all that was going to happen? Sometimes an elegant, streamlined Mercedes would drive by; but Di no longer wanted a Mercedes – all she wanted was her own room, in her flat, in her tower block, in Bratislava; for her mother to make her tea; to be doing her homework. It's just that her passport... Well, basically, she had no passport. So why did Milan leave? Because the soup was too salty. Di came here a year ago because she was having trouble in school, and she couldn't stand the food at home, the smell of burned food in the kitchen... Things like that. Because they made her go to vocational school, and she was doing badly in it, that kind of thing. Because life was something that happened somewhere else; life meant dancing with millionaires and drinking champagne, not the smell of something burning all the time. The idea came to her suddenly. She started stealing this and that and selling it on, and as soon as she had enough she took off. Later, once she'd arrived in Vienna, she swore she'd arrived in paradise, that she'd never go back, and she chucked her passport down a manhole.

Around five in the morning she started eating snow. From the lawns, because she thought it had to be cleaner than the snow in the street. She hobbled down one of the main roads, studied the shop windows, and had a taste of that unique and inimitable flavour that the West acquires when you don't have a single penny to your name. She tried to sneak into an underground carpark, thinking that even the cars must have it better than she did, but she tripped the alarm and had to leg it. And so for five days and five nights she shambled all over that fucked-up city. When she went down the less frequented streets she would take off that awful shoe of hers, in the winter, in the snow. She wanted to freeze. She'd station herself on bridges and watch the Danube with its enormous, slow-moving ice floes. She inspected the kerbs, filled with a beggar's certainty that she was bound to discover money there at any moment, that it was statistically impossible for her not to find anything. In the metro station there was a vending machine, and in that machine, behind the glass, chocolate bars and hot chicken wings. Everything. She just needed to find some money, and she spent every night searching for it. Every single bottle top looked like a coin, and every stone embedded in the tarmac was begging to be picked up. When she had only a few coins left… That was awful. Three days earlier she was just about to call home, her mum and dad, and ask them to bring their car and come and fetch her, to arrange for a provisional passport at the embassy, but the phone ate her money. She pounded it with her fist, but nothing came out. There was a sign with a toll-free number to call and report such incidents, but of course it didn't work; all she got was an automatic message with some twat rattling off whatever. To get her revenge on those Austrian cunts, Di stuffed the payphone with sticks and matches (matches that would've come in handy about now).

She came to despise all the people getting into their cars, driving off to their opera, reading the newspaper in their little Eduscho cafés, carrying their parcels, running through their snow, kissing under their statues, and giving each other gifts of chocolates embellished with the heads of their Great Composers. Di glared at the huge boxes of chocolate like a starving bitch. Whole window displays of chocolate, each one individually wrapped in gold paper, painted with the profile of some musical fuckwit in an enormous, grey wig. Open round boxes of chocolate the size of carriage wheels shimmered in the empty street's nocturnal light. Di had crossed a boundary in her hunger and was feeling it less and less now. But she looked at those boxes of sweets and couldn't tear her eyes away, so highly improbable and fascinating had the luxuries of that world become. A poor man dreams of work and enough money to get by; a beggar dreams of nothing less than millions! Bells were ringing in the distance; crimson garlands lit up, then went out; and Di had the feeling that at any moment a carriage drawn by a legion of reindeer would come for her, here in front of the shop, and whisk her off into some fairy tale or other. She wasn't quite sure which one best suited her: the one about the little match girl, who froze in the snow? She'd stuffed her last matches into the payphone, and anyway, smoking was awful! It did nothing at all to make the hunger go away. Or maybe the story of Kai and Gerda was better? That must have been one of those Scandinavian fairy tales, because Milan remembered only that it was full of ice, whiteness, blue skies, and lucre. Just like Sweden. And just when it seemed things couldn't get any kitschier... Hmm, how to explain? There were these lights set up everywhere, and Di reckoned, to her surprise, that they were rigged with photosensors, because whenever she went near them they would start playing this one especially inane American Christmas carol. And in that empty, bitterly cold night, little bells really were ringing, but instead of reindeer came a combination street cleaner and rubbish lorry, which in Austria all look like things from a science fiction war game. Di was feeling like rubbish herself, and couldn't help thinking they must be coming on her account.

Di eventually stopped walking, because every time she took a step her shoe would cut into her foot, practically to the bone. At least that's how it felt. Those beautiful loafers – detested now – were a reminder of the life of prosperity (Ralf! Alex!) she'd had not long before, when instead of saving her money for times like now, she spent it all on heaps of new clothes. (*Geld sparen, Geld sparen, Di! Du musst Geld sparen!*\*) But later, when she lost the flat she had rented from a Brazilian queen (Sierra Ferreira da Silva), she stashed them all in a locker at the train station, threw in a coin and... and they were still there, but in order to get them out she'd have to deposit fifty schillings or something, because the meter was still ticking! The blinking display kindly informed her that if she didn't remove her things within twenty-four hours, she wouldn't be able to

---

\* *German*: Save your money, save your money, Didi! You need to save money!

get them out at all. Or something like that – she didn't entirely understand what those Austrian pigs had written there.

Di was no longer able to walk or stand up, nor could she put up with the sadness emanating from all the Christmas trees and lights and jingling, carolling bells everywhere. She was so done with that whole green-and-red festival of kitsch.

But then: a miracle! Di, filthy and hungry though she was, found a trick in the metro. A fat, sweaty, unshaven Arab. Who smiled lasciviously at her nineteen years and fawn-coloured hair. Milan thought she might kiss the Arab for joy, right there in the subway! She was already counting how many chops, chips, and sandwiches he'd be good for… How much could she get out of a bloke like that? Not much. But there was a shower at the Bahnhof; you just tossed in some coins and the doors parted. Only a few inches though, so that two people couldn't make it through at once. You had a half hour entirely to yourself. Washing was wonderful, but being entirely by yourself for a whole half hour – that was pure bliss! To be off the street finally; finally, to be alone! She'd go and have a wash, and put on a pair of fresh socks, which she would buy. It would be a holiday.

The Arab didn't have a place. She asked him, 'Have you got a place?' As if to spite her, the Arab didn't even have a place to go. But Di wanted to get the whole thing over and done with as soon as possible, so was about to drag him off to the bushes in the park or the toilet in the metro, when the Arab (Ahmed) insisted that he knew the perfect spot. He took Milan to an underground carpark that had some public toilets. They zigzagged between the variously coloured cars. It was dimly lit; the only bright thing was a green sign with the word 'EXIT'. They shut the door, and Ahmed sat down on the toilet. It was enough to make you puke: he had breasts like a woman's, except they were covered in hair, and he reeked of sour sweat. Every few minutes he would break into idiotic laughter and order Di to lick his corrupted body from head to toe. Or else he would fart and laugh as if it were the funniest joke he'd ever heard! Di did lick him, but all the while she fantasised about the cigarettes and chops, which allowed her to forget what she was doing. Suddenly someone started pounding on the door of the stall – it was the attendant! The carpark attendant! The guardian of all those underground carparks, one floor on top of the other, deeper and deeper, leading all the way down into hell! One of those attendants in fluorescent vests, yellow, maybe orange. He banged on the door and bellowed. Di didn't understand a thing because he was yelling in German, and for her to understand he would have had to be yelling in Slovak, which he wasn't. Instead he yelled in German, but Milan had no problem imagining what he meant. In a word, they needed to get the fuck out, because the *Polizei* was on its way.

'*Verdammte Schwule! Verdammte Schwule!*\* Open up!'

Well, the Arab managed to make a dash for it (without paying!), but Di was seized by the even fatter and more repulsive-looking guard. Without so much as a how-do-you-do, he lands his fist in her face and blood begins to flow. She falls on the floor, on the tiles. The guard grabs her by the collar, screams something about the police, then throws her a bucket, a mop, a rag. Di tries to escape, but the fucker grabs her by the ear and holds her with all his might. He keeps holding her by her ear, like she was a schoolboy. She was afraid she'd

---

\* *German*: Bloody queers! Bloody queers!

never escape, our Diana – she'd end up as cheap labour washing the floors. The guard cries alternately '*Polizei!*' and 'Washrag!' It's her choice. Eizer you gonna putzen zis whole carpark for me zright now, or I call ze police! Fucking queer! Di chose the rag. Bawling to high heaven, hungry and filthy as she was, she had to clean the entire multi-storey carpark, and then she had to clean the toilet where she'd been caught, the cause of everything. Finally she simply walked out into the night, with nothing, knackered. That's what they call it. She lifted her head and noticed an enormous luxury hotel in front of her. Hilton or Carlton. Snow was falling. Only one room showed a light. She'd seen her share of such hotels with clients, their laptop computers loading on their king-size beds, Chanel perfume in the bathroom, and room service bringing up champagne on silver trolleys. The light went out, and Di thought to herself in Slovak how unjust it was that so many rooms should go to waste, empty all night, while she was freezing and had nowhere to sleep.

How many times had I told her:

'Di, Dianka, calm down. This job is for people with the steel nerves. Who learn Deutsch, collect the geld, and fuck men from the Mercedes cars and the underground parkings! But not here – you must to go to München, to Zürich! No bleiben here! Nischt gut, here *kein Geschäft,*\* Diana. You will be surprised if I say you the many clients I have! Because I know how it is done! I even make little CD mit photos of me! *Ponimaesh?*\*\* You understand, little tart, Milan, *ptishku?*\*\*\*

\* *German*: No business.
\*\* *Russian*: You understand?
\*\*\* *Russian*: Little bird.

Now, at five in the morning, in front of the shop with the choco-late composers, my words must have been drifting through her head like snowflakes. That night Di realised that the West in its entirety was like an electric amusement park wired on high-voltage. The lit-tle lights kept on blinking whether or not you were having a wonderful time or dying in the metro, dear Milan, you lovely, you beautiful angel. Perfectly indifferent. Forever jolly. As long as the plug stays in its socket. And Di was a hair's breadth from turning into a socialist that night.

But the lawyer took pity on Milan. He locked him in at home for the whole day and went to work. Di had to do the kitchen, and all the other work, the computers... Bored, vacuuming, digging through wardrobes stuffed with boring suits on hangers wrapped in plastic. Eventually she started to regret that she'd ever run away from home and come to Vienna, where she thought she'd be quaffing champagne every night, where the streets were supposed to be full of hot lads and fast cars. In the meantime, there was Jürgen, that old, balding lawyer, who got upset over the slightest thing, shouting and everything – how normal is it for someone to wipe his arse with chamomile-scented cotton pads? Di looked suspiciously at all the unfamiliar contraptions. What, for instance, was that enor-mous toothbrush plugged into the socket for? It looked like it was for cleaning bottles, but it had some kind of setup on the handle, buttons, *nerozumiem tomu*.* What a laugh that 'toothbrush' caused when she turned it on! It was a vibrator, for heaven's sake!

Or once she washed her hair with some shampoo she found in

* *Slovak*: I don't understand it.

the bathroom, and Jürgen threw a shit fit because it was a special shampoo for grey hair – his – and it was very, very expensive, and she must to stay avay from it. And once he beat her to a pulp, for no reason at all! That too! He'd told her countless times not to use the metal spatula when scrambling eggs in the Calphalon pan, she must to use a vooden spoon! So what, big deal... Because vherever ze coating gets scratched, ze pan vill burn! Di really got it in the neck for that scratched pan. That's when she realised that the first commandment of the urban professional middle class was: 'Thou shalt not use metal utensils on Calphalon, only wood!' And these commandments had been revealed to the urban professional middle class by their yuppie god, scratched into the surface of two Calphalon frying pans...

Well, eventually Di rebelled. She began doing things wrong on purpose just to spite him: she used his shampoo, put his underwear in the wrong drawers, and – although he'd expressly forbidden it – she rang up Edwin, her friend from the good old days, her American... And she told him that she was going to slip out and visit him that evening, told him to wait. And Edwin once again gave her directions on the U-Bahn, because Di didn't really understand how it worked. She waited until evening. That's when she had her daily stroll, when she was allowed to go out for an hour on her own. But if she didn't come back at the agreed time, there'd be hell to pay. Edwin was a playboy of the first degree. Tall and slender, hair dyed blond, cowboy boots, jeans, chewing gum, and poppers, which were already illegal by then and you could only find in porn shops labeled as 'CD washing fluid'. He waited for her near Hammergasse and took her back to his place; then, an hour later, he sent her on her way.

Still dazed from the poppers, Di bounded down the stairs and bashed her head against a completely clear pane of glass. When she came to, she was in the vestibule. The glass doors to the stairs had snapped shut behind her automatically; in front of her was the exterior door, which turned out to be locked. She tried to open the glass doors, but needed to use an entryphone. What the hell was Edwin's last name, what floor was he on? She hadn't paid attention when they came in – how could she have known she might need to remember this later on? So there she was, trapped in a space just a few feet square, time ticking by. Jürgen was no doubt already home, cursing her in absentia. And probably no one would come through the lobby before morning, because all the Austrian yuppies had gone to bed hours ago. She rang one of the buzzers for the first floor; a woman answered. But Di's German wasn't the best... She tried to explain her situation in the same language she spoke with me, a mix of Slovak, German, Russian, and Papiamentu, but the voice started shouting something about the police, so Di stopped. She made herself at home on the stone bench and thought about how everyone in Vienna, quite everyone in that rotten city, lived in old buildings...

When she got home, Jürgen refused to let her in. He'd thrown all her clothes out the front door. In the end, though, Di whinged so much that he gave in and let her sleep that night; he was afraid of what the neighbours might think, and Milan kept sobbing louder and louder. But he wouldn't let her sleep in his bed; he told her to sleep on the floor. That night Di slipped into the bathroom, took the blade out of his safety razor, and... that's how she got those cuts on her wrists.

## The Team from Poznań

They think of themselves in the masculine. They march for equal rights. They take pics of each other with their mobile phones, upload them via USB and Bluetooth to their laptops. They send each other SMS's and MMS's – from Wroc, from Waw… Sup? L8erz!

They're from the 'emancipation phase' (unlike us, hence the boundary running straight across the beach, up by the defunct radar and red flag). They agitate for their right to marry, to adopt. They're constantly agitating, and agitated. They talk in the language of *Polityka* and *Wprost*. They came over, enthusiastic, with a volleyball and that sing-song Poznań accent of theirs. One butch lad with sideburns and designer stubble piped up:

'Wouldn't you like to come and play with us?' He introduced himself with a firm, manly handshake:

'My name's Błażej,' he said, bald and with an impressive package.

The two Old Dears were immediately overcome by their masculinity; they felt exposed and quickly slipped on shorts under their towels in order to hide themselves. Then they ran off to go berging, abandoning me: 'You stay and play the man with them. We're off to pick posies on the dunes. Pocketfuls of posies to adorn our bodies with! Ooh!'

Traitoresses! Leaving me behind like that! I pushed my sunglasses up on to my forehead and lay there, observing the pair of powerful thighs looming like columns over me. I parted my lips ever so slightly and was just about to start something, when the thighs began shifting restlessly, something about adoption, equal rights, the right to marry, the Green Party, civil partners, monogamy, safe (monogamous) sex, and condoms. We're civilised people, you know. We want to do this right, with a sense of morality, with the sanction of society, wearing white gloves (so as not to soil ourselves by association with you). Then he began telling me how it's people like me who give gays such a bad name; and that while we (i.e., me, the Old Dears, the Blond, and other frequenters of the dunes) were going at it like dogs in the bushes, they'd come here with their volleyballs, athletics, and fitness regimens to drag us out of our pre-emancipatory, post-picketatory gutter – in short, they wanted to give us something useful to do. No fats, no fems. No more opening my jaw the moment a bloke drops his drawers. It's love, mutual understanding, reciprocal respect that's needed now. Sometimes other things are more important. Like what? Friendship, intimacy.

I rubbed my eyes and thought, Lucreeetia! Help! Hmmm, I could see those turncoats out of the corner of my eye, having it off in the dunes, totally oblivious to the fate they'd abandoned me to. So I continued lending my ear to that beefed up, body-waxed, plastic boy toy until I lost all interest in doing him – with all that friendship and intimacy erupting between us it started to feel like I was talking with my therapist. Too intimate, too emotional – like talking with family, except with *my* family I wouldn't talk about it anyway... It's not as if I even *want* friendship and intimacy. Makes me think of my mum. What I want is a completely anonymous hookup, someone who'll thrash me like a bitch getting what she deserves, who'll rough me up, rush in like a tornado, and leave me too weak to stand up and shut the door behind him, a damp spot on the bed, drawn and quartered... And if he were a hammersmith, raging with his hammer, hammering away in his factory, what would you say? Would you make him go? Oh I'd shake! I'd shake and shudder, I'd shake, and shake and shudder! My hair a mess, he'd leave me there like the whore I am, spit on me, toss a paper towel at me, and go without shutting the door. He'll leave the door wide open. And with my face buried in the sopping pillow, I'll fall asleep – I'll sleep, without any friendship, free of intimacy!

He says, Us gays. Us. Us gays should do this, us gays should do that, together. A bird flies past, a seagull; the sun disappears behind a cloud. Not just sex, but sports, too, and protecting the environment, an alternative perspective on European culture, and whether I wouldn't like to subscribe to his discussion board, some website or something. What? An old codger like me and the internet? With my reverence for the past, for all those state-subsidised caravan holidays, it's as if I were moving back in time! And not one of them smokes; all they do is toss that ball that's got NIVEA written on it back and forth, and lie there in pairs, snuggling. I drag my arse up off my blanket and walk over to them. Aha! Those monogamous couples there, all cuddly in each other's arms – I've been doing at least one of each of them every day in the dunes... Now they all act as if they've never seen me before. There's monogamy for you! That peroxided chicken there lying in his daddy's arms in the setting sun on a Marlboro beach towel – I had him just this morning, right after I got here... And how many times have I been stalked by that lopsided nag over there! Now here she is, the picture of monogamy.

New troubles arise meanwhile. The rest of them, not having heard my conversation with Thighs, and seeing what a muscular young lass I am and what fashionable sunglasses I'm wearing, come up to me as if I were one of them, and start talking like I was just another emancipated queen. So what's going on down in Wrocław? What's it like at Scene these days? What about H2O? They're off to Berlin for the Love Parade – am I going, too? Is that why I've coloured and gelled my hair like that? I'm forced to speak in the masculine, but I mumble quietly:

'So how did all you ladie— lads first get together?'

They reply, Oh, through the ads. On gay dot pee el. Hi, I'm looking for a life partner, no pnp, d/d free. Hi, I'm a cute, laid-back twentysomething. I have a dog named Filip. Or else it's: I'm a student, just want to meet a hotty for a pint and get freaky! I'm at email this on AIM, number that on Gadu-Gadu, text me later at blah blah blah blah. They play games where one of them lies down on the sand at the water's edge and the other one buries him, moulding him into a mummy, adding an enormous cock out of moist sand with a pebble on top instead of a hole. An eruption of jism shaped like a sandcastle collapsing into the sea. Click, a digital pic, smiles for the camera, and a flourish: their postcard from sunny Lubiewo, addressed to: The Old Brewery, Kulczyk Street, Poznań, wish you were here.

## Write About Us!

I know those ads, I know them well. I've met loads of men through them in my time. The team ask if I'm going to play volleyball with them; they've stretched a net along a row of sticks all the way from the water to the dunes. One of them has peroxide dreds, another a tattoo, all of them are jumping, leaping up and down; they couldn't be more butch. It's all too much for me. I say:

What, me? Playing ball? Perhaps I could just take a seat on your blanket there, and, if you like, regale you with a story? Because that's what I do. You a writer? Why yes, I am an authoress of the highest calibre. Michalina La Belletriste they call me; formerly I was known as Snowflake. Wow, you should write pro-gay rights articles for glossy, high-distribution magazines! Are you active in the rights movement, have you appeared in the gay media? Hmm, why yes I have, I once wrote something for *Aktivist*. Jarek L. called in the middle of the night to ask me, because Violet V. failed to deliver her article. What about *Nowy Men*? No, I've no interest in publishing in *Nowy Men*, nor in *Inaczej* either. But I *am* writing a book about *you*. Is it political?

Not in the least. Oh, please do write a book about us, says bald, bespectacled Błażej.

Write a novel about us. Us Gays... It should be a narrative about two middle-class, educated gay men, doctoral students in management and finance, who wear glasses and woolly jumpers... Mornings they lounge around in the same bed watching the same telly together, and for breakfast they eat toast with sliced tomatoes off the same plate... They've established a stable, long-term relationship, and now they want to adopt a child. But they've run into some trouble, see. Society, you see, doesn't accept them, even though they're well bred and well behaved, as the reader can tell. You can make the contradiction even more apparent by giving them neighbours who have a wretched marriage, who drink all the time and beat their children, but whom the state would never dream of keeping from adopting. But our couple, who were hoping to adopt a little boy (a boy!) and couldn't have been more perfect homemakers – their application is rejected. Readers should be able to figure out on their own what an injustice it all is... In the end the couple decide to adopt a cat... I mean, really! Like, OK, you can't have a kid, so just adopt a cat! And they decide to give him the same name they'd planned on giving their child...

Oh, what a wonderful idea for a book! The perfect gift for Valentine's Day! All the gay couples can go buy it for each other at the galeria. I'll just pop along and write it. I'd better clear off now. I might even make some money!

Then they invite me to some gender-something queer-something conference at the university in Poznań, where all the gender-gays will be. German Ritz will be there – he's the keynote speaker – and there'll be a feminist talk about the body by Professor Borkowska... all of it informed by Judith Butler 'n' stuff...

## The Date

I had the following mishap on the internet:

This fellow answered my advert. Luckily he wasn't 'nice' and
didn't 'like to chat and have fun,' so he got five bonus points right
away. He wasn't into kayaking either, and he didn't go to the gym
five times a week, and he hadn't given up drinking, which was truly
odd. In any case, my ads were always written in such a way that only
people like that ever answered them. But this one was a scientist and
quite serious. To cut a long story short, I fell in love with him after
about five emails. I know, I know what you're thinking, Vicômte,
and you're right… But it was as if we were made for each other. Only
he never told me what he looked like, and I never asked. Eventually
he wrote that 'looks weren't important' for him. I wrote right back
and said the same, said they weren't important for me either, because
we agreed on everything. I printed out his emails, kissed them,
framed them. Sometimes there were ten mails a day and expensive
mobile phone calls, too, since we used competing services (he: Idea,
me: Era). Still, we'd sometimes spend practically an hour on the
phone; his voice was so young, so beautiful. He was… a scientist,
solar something or other, world-renowned, an astrophysicist. And

since the only physicist I'd ever known was a skinny boy with long hair who had a pretty voice like his, too, I simply pasted that image on to him in my imagination. Love can't survive on words alone after all. It just doesn't work. Abstraction is unbearable. After a few months of emailing I couldn't stand it any longer. Let's meet today, at the zoo, I said, now, right now. No, we should chat some more first. I don't care what you look like, I said. You could be in a wheelchair for all I care, you could be HIV-positive, I just want to be with you... And he was so smart, emailing in all those languages about that sun of his. That's why he never used Polish characters in his messages. Because, he said, he was used to writing in ten different languages, even some really uncommon ones. Finally he agreed to meet. After a whole day in the bathroom there I was, standing outside the zoo... and he didn't show up. A quarter past five already. Just some old guy in a wheelchair. A beggar, I figured, because half his face was mangled. It looked as if he was born that way, like he had that Elephant Man disease. So there I was, standing, waiting, checking my watch. And slowly it dawned on me: that homeless man's waiting for someone too... Elephantitis, bald, shabby clothes... He smiled at me and wheeled up in his wheelchair. Me: my face was a wall. The wind. Oh why, on this of all afternoons, did nature have to provide such a perfect backdrop for the protagonists' emotions? A sudden gust blew hair into my eyes. There was a storm in my head, too: what to do, how to hold back the tears? I was hardly going to run away! But the tears kept welling up inside me. Right before my eyes the boy of my imagination was disintegrating. That slender, long-haired, happy youth, who had spoken to me so cheerfully, so joyfully, and for so many hours over the internet, was dying.

The way he talked suggested he was younger, too; he'd say things like 'People'll get pissed off' or 'What're your digits?' My boy was dying, his dimples ebbing like foam, his freckles dissipating like sand... But – he had never been! No matter that I'd been snogging him in my thoughts for months! I'd been kissing a corpse all along!

I'd been kissing the man now sitting before me in a wheelchair. The wind was blowing, and he turned his eyes to me, azure, naïve... He had to be naïve if he believed what I'd said about looks not being important. I even believed it myself for a moment. Oh what does it matter, I thought. Love him now, love this man before you. I broke the silence:

'Waiting for someone?' My throat was so thick I couldn't make out my own words.

His eyes lit up. 'Michał?'

I croaked something through my clenched windpipe, something like Uh-huh, pleased to meet you. But I wasn't able to fake it well enough for him not to notice the plummeting of my heart. Shall we go for a stroll, I mean, a roll, I said, through Szczytnicki Park? He started trundling his wheelchair towards the pedestrian entrance. We continued in silence. And only a few hours before...! When he got home, an email would be waiting for him. Judging from the conversation, he hadn't got it by the time he left. How completely idiotic that email was now, in the context of our silent, funereal procession – my boy's funeral. I had written to him that the moment we opened our lips we would never again be able to close them, how we would rush back at once to my place and embrace for hours, and lick and kiss and make love for hours and hours until the end of our life together. Fat chance now, I thought. At that very moment he gave me such a look... I could see he found me attractive, and that this was fueling a hope in him. Maybe he even sensed that something wasn't right, but merely chalked it up to the wind, the bad weather... Suddenly he said:

'You have such beautiful eyes.'

Beautiful eyes! Fucking hell! I started to cry. I couldn't hold it in any longer. I said: Don't say things like that to me! Can't you see what's happening? Can't you see the tears flowing from these beautiful eyes on to my possibly more beautiful cheeks? Don't say another word. I'm attending a funeral here, this is a funeral procession I'm trudging in! One sepulchral step after the other in real, physical space! You're the physicist: you of all people should understand that!

I thought to myself: just talk to him, ask him things about the sun. At least you won't have to deal with the silence. At least you should be able to communicate on an intellectual level. But whatever it was in his voice that in the emails (from the boy) had sounded so brilliant, that intelligence of his was dull now. I started up a conversation anyway about university funding, research grants... It was as if I were talking with one of my countless academic uncles. In the end, an operatic element, which I had been hoping to avoid, came into play. He stopped suddenly, brought the wheelchair to a halt, and said 'I love you' right there in the park, under some sort of mannerist sculpture, a faun on a fountain, some rococo genitalia. I was forced to resort to a convention – I don't know if it was from *The Csardas Princess* or *The Hunchback of Notre Dame* – and said: 'Umm, I really hope we can be friends.'

Friends! Vicômte! The carriage pulled up and love's thunderbolt failed to set this heart ablaze, but perhaps we could remain 'good friends', just as those lads from Poznań wanted to be, bosom buddies... Our relationship would be about other, more lasting values. Which is to say: Keep your arse out of my bed and shut up already about the beautiful eyes!

When I got home I looked at the wall where I'd hung the printouts of my emails from my 'bespectacled boy', and I reread them. For a moment the boy in the emails returned to life, gasped one last breath before twitching a little, jerking his leg, then expiring for all eternity. And there I was on the sofa, my face buried in the pillow, braying like a horse. I was sick, feverish, like someone in a novel. Nature, the body – everything colluded to ensure my survival. And there was my poor mother saying, 'So your date didn't go too well, then...'

## The Leather Lad from Poznań

Right, I think, I'm getting the fuck out of here, and run away. I run back to my blanket, to the sixties, the seventies, to the flask, the tinned tomato soup that Old Dear No. 2 brought back from the Społem cafeteria. I escape with them. With us – a flock of queeny trollops from the picket line, occupying the margins of post-1989 Polish society like a chancre on its arse. I run off to write. But hardly have I left when I'm accosted (that's all I need) by that lad with the all-over tattoos and piercings and body shave, the bald one with the barbell dangling from his cock and the studded leather strap around his bicep. A bloke like that could have pinned me down and defiled me any day! Until he came up and started speaking to me like this:

I understand that you're a Polish writer… one who's spent some time in the West. Oh, ha ha, didn't we meet each other on… michal witkowski free art dot pee el, right? You don't fool us. (You have your photos taken wearing black leather and you go to Berlin regularly… But that's exactly what I was getting at: Berlin for him meant whoring around.) We're a tight little batch of lads who enjoy practising safe sex in a certain clearly articulated style. If you're interested… We're straight-acting, we're all pretty good pals, we've known each other for a while now, and we respect each other, too(!). If you like, drop by and see us in Poznań, at the 'Lech' Housing Complex, and do keep in mind that we have all the right gear. We have gynecological forceps, black latex gloves, lube, poppers, leather and rubber masks, and gasmasks, too. Whips, collars, cockrings, harnesses, flails, and – the Leather Lad whispers seductively – Bunsen burners… We're not perverts or anything like that; we have barristers, and artists – you'd fit in perfectly…

And so it went, on and on, for exactly forty-five minutes. Not one cigarette, not a single beer, and the best part of the sun came and went. Finally I just nodded and said, Sure, I'd love to stop by some day, but right now I really need to get back to my blanket, because I've got two… two gentlemen there looking after my gubbins. Maybe I'll stop by and see you lads sometime…

## Michał, I presume?

'I for one am an old, intolerant, out of shape, bad-tempered, camp queen, and the minute the lot of you start talking, I can't help but shut down like a communist-era butcher at six in the evening!' I mutter to myself, to the bushes, the sand... I've always had problems being assertive, I could never talk like that to someone's face, and instead just smile and nod like an idiot. This sometimes leads to complications, like this:

My sister says to me:

'Don't you dare respond to that ad! Some jolly old bloke in a jacket will show up, beret cocked on one side of his head, holding a rose to make sure you recognise him; then he'll come up to you and say: "Michał, I presume?"

'Then he'll escort you, *Michał*, to his Trabant, and introduce himself, and his name will be Ambrose!'

I always feel rotten about turning people down, especially when they're angling for a date. But then everything turns out just as expected: a senile, groveling old git shows up with his flowers and his avuncular sense of humour – Ambrose – and asks me if I like *The Cabaret of Elderly Gents*. And I say I do, to be polite, and dream of assertiveness. Of assertiveness, which comes out when I'm writing, when I don't have to see anyone, and at night I churn out my letters to the world and slap people right across the face with them – though I can't imagine talking like that to anyone face to face.

## The Old Dears (Cont.)

'I don't like it. It's not that I'm intolerant, but I just don't like it when those straight blokes come here with their tarts and bugger off into the dunes to relieve themselves, absolutely clueless as to what sort of place this is. What, isn't your straight nudist beach enough for you? I say to them. Isn't the normal beach enough? Isn't the entire straight normal world enough?!'

One Old Dear put on a pair of large, horn-rimmed glasses and did the crossword; of course she'd later be sending it in in hopes of winning a prize. They were always happy to take part in competitions. They sent in whatever was asked for, peeling and rubbing off code after code, forever dialling the number on the screen. One of them, somewhat younger, won a whole month's pass to a solarium once, with unlimited access. She practically fried her skin. Which was a miracle, since that was in the early nineties, when the lamps weren't as strong. Another one got a trip to a spa from some mineral water company (the code was under the bottle top). But when she arrived, they told her:

'This competition was meant for women...'

But she went ahead and milked that vacation all she could

regardless; she joined the ladies for aerobics, and in the mud bath, and for the makeover. There were two other gentlemen there as well, so she had an excuse: she wasn't the only man…

Those two gentlemen and our Old Dear (Wiesław) always sat down to eat in the same dining hall as the ladies on the 'Diet Boot Camp'. Only they got to eat whatever their hearts desired, while the ladies had to make do with a lettuce leaf, half an orange, a crust of stale bread, maybe a bit of fat-free kefir. Two in particular were going crazy with hunger; they hadn't eaten anything since morning, and the trainers had driven them up and down the mountains all day. In the end they couldn't take it any longer; they kept looking over at the men's table piled high with food and they attacked it all, devoured everything! Puddings, ice cream, everything! The two men came back, looked and said: 'All gone.' That's how our Wiesława recounted it, standing there, fanning herself with her bodice-ripper.

'*All gone* – can you believe it, Michał? And those men always sat together, and they were so well-groomed, the one with highlights, the other one with highlights…'

I was succumbing to slumber, the sun's hot tongue lapped at me, the waves glinted blindingly. I nuzzled my face in the blanket and felt hard sticks and pine cones bulging under the fabric… I felt languorous, sated… I wanted to fall asleep in the sun, amidst the drone of flies and sough of waves, and later I would get up and have a swim and go back to sleep. Then Old Dear No. 1 shows me what a wonderful, orange windbreak she'd got, with the Kolastyna logo on it; they were giving them away free at Rossman's with the purchase of any sunblock. I open an eyelid, That's really super… What time is it? Only three.

'But we're supposed to have good weather till Sunday. Sunny and warm tomorrow.'

There's a howling in the distance, like a motorboat or a coast guard vessel. I look over: coast guard. What's even funnier, the Poznań team have changed into some tight special clothes and are trying to surf, only the sea is as still as a lake… I shut my eyes. I'm dying to smoke, but can't be arsed to reach into my bag for a cigarette; and among other things, my watch is in there, and I'd like to avoid getting sand in it…

…

'They've forecast thunderstorms and a drop in temperature on Monday. They said on the weather it'll affect the whole country, but only after Sunday…'

…

'Well, excuse me, but Robert got her everything from that wholesaler, everything she wanted. I went to Łódź to get tomatoes from my allotment, but when I came back, my flat…'

…

'It was Kunicka who sang that, not Jarocka. And it was Laskowski who sang "Beata of the Albatross" – I remember.'

…

'Evidently she had a mammogram, but who cares?'

…

'Look how worn out I am, I don't know, maybe it's blood pressure, but I've already had a cup of coffee or two…'

…

'Those queens always did go gaga over him, one of them had her gold teeth removed…'

…

'I've seen that one's flat, what a place the old harlot had, with those paintings that are just two lines crossing each other, but they're awfully expensive… what did she call it? "Contemporary art", makes it sound really brainy…'

…

'What do I know? Not that long, just enough to get them a bit browned…'

'Ooh, but don't you have pretty swimming trunks…'

'I paid dollars for them.'

…

'So I says to her, "Listen here, you dumb cluck…"'

…

'A UFO like that, how much petrol would you need to run a UFO like that? Oh, but you know they have their contacts, the top brass in Israel…'

And the last thing I saw through my heavy-lidded eyes was an aeroplane flying past, leaving behind it in the sky a big slit covered with cotton wool.

## Private Styling

...

'Twenty-two down: seven-letter word for *attack*, starts with *a–s–s*... – Ooh, *assault* fits...'

I wake up slowly, try to turn on to my other side, and feel a searing pain. Pain, sunburn: my whole side, there and there and there, from my ankles to my shoulders. It burns. The Old Dears put away their crossword and offer to rub cream into me; but even the lightest touch hurts – it hurts. It stings and burns. I stand up, walk by myself into the shade, over to the dunes, the Bois de Boulogne even, but my head is spinning, black shreds float past my eyes. I drape a shirt with my face printed on it over my shoulders and keep walking. The bushes are aquiver in all directions, despite the protestations of the team from Poznań (I recognise a few of them), everyone's naked, and a certain Zbigniew (queen or no? it's hard to tell...) says to me, Girl! Come on! You need to shave! Don't be such a peasant!

When I return to my digs at the Deaf Hag, the nearest guesthouse to Lubiewo, I bolt my door; she's always so inquisitive about me: the minute I walk out she starts going through my stuff, sticking her fingers in my creams, reading my journals; now she knows everything about me. I decline her offer – she wanted to make a sour milk compress for my sunburnt back – so she leaves. I try to create a little atmosphere, put on some music, turn off the lights, take off my briefs, grab my scissors and comb and begin cutting, because it seems a better idea to trim everything down before starting with the shaving cream and razor. But all that hair, black and curly, is now all over the pillow, as I'm sitting on the dishevelled bed, resting against the kilim – a straw mat covered in postcards. I blow at it, it scatters all over; and when I cut too close, in the space where my thighs meet, it stings, it really stings. Now everything down there is stinging, everything feels different, as if it wasn't mine. Genitals. That's not a cock any more, I've made a penis out of it; and my balls – they're just testicles now. Caught off guard, naked, stinging, looking like a shameless, crooked mushroom. Then I think: I'll be really original and give myself an asymmetrical shave down there. Once when I was in Germany I saw a sign for an *Intim Friseur*\* – who did bleaching, piercing, punk-style, in green, with sugar… But then I examine my pubes more closely, I even grab the lamp I use for reading my academic books off the table and hold it up to them, and what do I see? White and black and microscopically tiny dots, practically a powder of them covering my loins – my loins! Ungirded, deforested. A powder, Lord help me, please don't let it be lice! Lice! I've been infested with lice! I'll have to cut it all off, shave everything, depilate! And burn my knickers – or maybe I don't need to burn them? Hang on! Where are they?

---

\* *German*: personal stylist

Thrown in the corner. What about washing? Then they'll drown, but oh fuck, maybe they're waterproof? And my trousers? And the hair on my head? Maybe they got transplanted there, maybe I touched my hair too… Now I understand why all those slags are shaven from head to toe! I look around – everything's covered with my cut hairs, accursed locks! And now I'm getting obsessive-compulsive disorder: wherever I look, pubes, lice! Whatever I touch: infested! I grab all my sheets and dirty clothes and shove them into a bin liner, and wearing clean clothes pulled straight from my suitcase take off into town to buy new ones. But it's already dark out, night. Only the chintz dealers on the board-walk are still there, selling their chintz. White jeans with silver stripes and the word LOVE stitched in pink across the bum. D&G knockoffs, knockoffs of knockoffs. As if the whole world had been left at home, in whatever cities people came here from; and the things here, just as in Plato, were but echoes of it. What would the Style Queens say if they saw me wearing that crap tomorrow? Tinsel Tina! Oh, she'd be the queen of good taste on that prome-nade! But they don't have knickers here anywhere. Playboys aren't interested in what gets worn down below, it can't be seen anyway. No luck, I'll just have to buy something at the shopping centre tomorrow. And stop by the chemist's for whatever shite. But how will I do it? What will I say? There are always such queues in Międzyzdroje since there are only three chemists; people all stand-ing there, waiting for their antibiotics, and I'm supposed to go up to the lady and be like:

'Excuse me, do you have anything for pubic lice?'

…

On the other side of my door is a television room, where the other guests of the Deaf Hag congregate. I lie naked, cradled in the sound of their chatter:

'*07 Do You Copy?* is on tonight after the news, with that Captain Borewicz... I can't wait...'

'But you do know that Captain Borewicz is...'

...

'All they do is line their pockets... Send them down the mines...'

...

A gasp goes around the TV room at the report about bonuses of the former executive board of Orlen, the huge sum, two and a half million zlotys. Knowing whispers, glances, sighs. Then comes the paedophile case. A statement from Lech Wałęsa. Everyone has it in for the priest. One of the ladies says:

'I'd rip that bloke's balls right off.'

Then came a toothpaste advert. One of them turns to me:

'Of course it whitens them, but with what...?' – I return to my room, doze off...

...

'How many autographs have you got off the boardwalk so far?'

'One from that queen from *Clan*...'

'I saw Błaszczyk yesterday, she was sitting very discreetly in a café, all in black, very discreet, no bodyguards or anything, you'd never know she was a big star.'

'I saw Jacek Cygan...'

'All I can say is that to be an actor you've got to be part monkey or something, to put yourself out there like that for the public...'

'Well, I for one would...'

## The Deaf Hag's Complaints

Knock knock! Who's there? The Deaf Hag.

'Ooh, Mr Witkowski, how lovely of you to come and stay with us, to rent a room. But you do know, don't you, that we only ever have lonely, single gentlemen staying here, renting rooms from me, from May to October?'

'Like who?'

'What?'

'Like who!!!'

'I beg your pardon?'

'WHO, FOR INSTANCE?!!'

'Well, for instance, that man from Bydgoszcz, the one that famous artist always comes to see...'

'Which artist?'

'I'm sorry?'

'Which artist?'

'Which what?'

'Who?!'

'You know, you're all tarred with the same brush, you all go to that nudist beach of yours… You think I don't know… Artists, the lot of you…'

'Excuse me, madam, but I really am an artist, you know.'

'I know, that's what I'm saying, you're all *artists*…'

'No, I actually write *books*.'

'What?'

'I'm an artist because I write books!'

'Oh, this sort of book, right?' And here the Deaf Hag gesticulates with her hand as if she's jerking off!

Exactly, this sort of book…

# Virgin

Virgin worked for the city, in a branch of local government. All through communism she'd set up queens with jobs and, when things got bad and they had no money, free meals.

'Those girls would wolf down chops like there was no tomorrow.'

She was a good woman, but fairly mercenary when it came to things like that. Often she would pull her strings pro bono, but just as often she'd want sex in exchange. And that's how her friendships with Desirée and Radwanicka worked during the communist era; she was always arranging something for one or the other of them. For example, she got Radwanicka a job with the Gypsy folk orchestra (Radwanicka: 'I sucked off each and every one of those Gypsies, but they never wash! I mean, *really*!').

Virgin was killed by grunt in her own flat. Seventy-seven knife wounds, tied to a chair. Half the picket line was at her funeral (a whole busload drove by the town hall), everyone sobbing, because she was such a good person and all, but when they started singing 'O noble and blessed Virgin…' and 'immaaaaaculate Virgin,' the queens lost it and totally cracked up. Some immaculate virgin!

## Radwanicka

I'll tell you about Radwanicka, Michał. But if she finds out I was talking trash about her, just promise you'll pay to get my teeth done! Tell me you'll pay for my new teeth when that whore beats the shit out of me, let me go to Germany and get new porcelain ones!

In *The Great Atlas of Polish Queens*, on the page dedicated to Radwanicka, there in the lower right-hand corner, is a grinning skull. A deadly poisonous toadstool that might seduce you with its amiable, appetising looks, the looks of a smiling, spruced-up old gentleman – but that will lay you out on your bed a month later! A truly villainous queen, worse than Doctor Mengele! As a little girl, she used to heat the water in the fish tank with a heating coil, and she enjoyed it so much she boiled the fish and even ate them too, for all I know.

She strolls through the park in her white coat and hat, and everyone thinks: what a high-class dame. Then an hour later you see her queuing up at the soup kitchen, waiting for a cheap meal.

God help you if she latches on to you while you're walking through the park on the arm of some young grunt. First she'll come on sugary as a communist-era sweet; then she sends you off for cigarettes, for whatever, the latest issue of *Nie*, batteries. Then she starts interrogating your grunt, and when she figures out he has no idea who she is she'll say to him: 'Are you really hanging around with that banshee?' (she means you). Then she pulls a long face and leans into the grunt's ear, as if she had some painful truth she needed to tell him against her will, in order to save his life:

'I'm so sorry to have to say this, I mean, you came here with that person and all, and now he's gone off for batteries, the newspaper, but...' – she leans in even closer – 'don't throw your life away, lad. Don't ruin yourself. You've no idea; you'll have a hard time finding a slapper worse than her. A slut like that, sick and poor. Why, back in the seventies she infected everyone around her, laid up with syphilis three times before you were even born, lad... You're better off hanging around with me,' she says, all so she can toss off a young lad that night. And then, when you return from the errand she'd so perfidiously concocted, she's all milk and honey again, because she's already seeded her poison in the grunt's ear.

The whore sits on the bench, smiles affably, talks about Fredka:

'What a good soul our Fredka is. It's so important to be a good person!' And the young grunts, runaways, gaze at her as if she was an altar piece, and it doesn't occur to any of them what kind of old slag they're going around with...

Radwanicka was living with Desirée then, biding time until Desirée kicked it, because she was hoping to inherit the flat. Whatever gave that slut the idea that Desirée was going to leave her her flat – which was dilapidated and mildewy, but had a good layout– when her family would never let Radwanicka get a thing? It was enough that she dressed up as Virgin at night, counting on Desirée's weak heart, appearing before her saying:

'It's time to come to me. Come to me...'

Wearing a sheet, or not... I'm not sure any more how she pretended to be Virgin's ghost, but she was a dreadful old slag anyway. She came here from the East. Someone I know once went there, came back talking about the mud huts, the poverty and hunger, God help them! First Radwanicka escaped to Warsaw, hitching a ride on a logging wagon. That's how the movie about her might start: Radwanicka riding the logging wagon, escaping the famine of the countryside. In Warsaw, she stole, went to jail, stole again, then things got too hot, and that's when she bloody well had to come here. She'd been shacking up with this one bit of grunt there, see. One day the grunt pretended he was going out, but instead he hid himself so he could spy on that trollop, and of course she immediately started rummaging through all his cupboards and drawers! So she buggered off back east for a bit, then landed here, to get away from the police. All those shoes she stole in Germany. Even today, even though that whore lives in utter poverty, with nothing at all, not even claiming benefits, she always wears the most expensive clothes and shoes. The poofs all wonder how she can afford it, but only the ones who don't know her. Anna once said to me:

'Why, she can nick any pair of shoes she wants, ha, even a coat, walks right out of the shop with them! Long as they don't have those security tags, and I suppose there are still quite a few shops that don't tag the expensive stuff, right? Of course that tart knows to cut the tags off with scissors, but she's of a different generation (unlike Poontanga, you know), and she's no good with those electronic tags, doesn't really understand how they work. Well, Radwanicka isn't exactly rolling in it, but when she goes shoplifting she always ends up with the most expensive things... But when she goes to social services for the free lunch (she can't steal that), and her benefit cheque, do you think she wears those stolen, high-heeled, shiny crocodile-leather shoes of hers? Heavens, no! That whore dresses up like a beggar, in a little beret with a pompom, and rags... An actress if ever I saw one!'

Valentina came round the picket line the other day and says to me:

'Radwanicka's gone off her rocker. Radwanicka's delusional, she keeps thinking someone's calling her name, keeps saying Fuck off! to everyone. She's been tearing leaves off the trees in the park and eating them, hanging up little pictures of saints on all the tree trunks. What a nutter!'

'That's right, it's because she wants to get her pension increased.'

'Oh, right... her pension...'

'Because she has benefits for the mentally ill, and they're about to run out.'

Then there's Jackie, who sells kebabs under the viaduct. Some-times Radwanicka will go round at lunch time, and you know those gloopy bits that drop off kebabs and fall on the floor? She scoops them up, makes a sandwich out of them, and eats it. Then she chats with Jackie for a bit, camping it up, because Jackie gets bored selling those kebabs all day by herself. Radwanicka says to her:

'You think this is normal, the way we live? This constant drifting and running around?'

'How should I know why I'm like this? You think I've never

thought about it? Maybe because I'm the youngest, and the seed had already lost its vigour, I have no idea... No idea why I turned out this way...' – entertaining a primitive form of genetics. Because Radwanicka was bourgeois at heart, even if she was a queen among criminals. You just had to listen to the crap she was saying under her breath, about how guilty she felt for being a poofter, how she dreamed of having a family, a normal life...

She'd bring back cheap, knock-off perfumes from the Reich and sell them at market here for ten zlotys a pop, but she always wore the most expensive perfumes herself. She was an old floozy; once she even got caught. Of course, she found a way to work it to her advantage – and how! The police treated queens like shit, and the feeling was mutual. The police, back in the day, would make the queens get up on a table and harass them, talk to them as if they were women, saying if only the normal citizens had all made complaints long ago, and so on, and those queens would simply laugh through their tears and might even go down on one of the pigs. Because the queens would be imagining themselves describing it all in the park later on, thinking about the added aura this would give to their bios.

Years later, when they let the whore out, she was skinny and poor, utterly poverty-stricken, as if she wasn't Radwanicka at all any more. As if she was sick. Until the queens passed around the hat so she'd have something to eat. And that's when Virgin showed up with those free lunches of hers. Then she pulled some strings and got Radwanicka a job as a case worker. I once even got to go along with her to see some deaf, blind and bedridden old lady. I suppose I don't have to tell you that those old tarts would take their grunts along and drink wine (always unbranded, from a bottle just labelled

'Wine') in the kitchen with them, without the old bag in the next room knowing a thing about it? No doubt she cleaned the whole flat out, too, because it was ages before anyone saw her in the park again, until all of a sudden she hit the big time with 'Tabor' or one of those other Gypsy ensembles. One time, when the compere got too drunk, she just walked out holding a rose and started talking! And could she ever talk, that Radwanicka!

The orchestra struck up! The high-hat warbled! And out walked that harlot in tails and says:

'Ladies and Gentlemen, may I present: *Tabor*! What woman doesn't dream of meeting a handsome Gypsy! What man's eyes don't light up when a Gypsy girl enters the room! But what is it really worth to love a Gypsy? Because in the end…' (and so the old tart blathered on, but when she said 'to love' what she really meant was 'to service').

The Gypsies in the group said:

'Fuck me! This old slag's better than the compere!' But of course she diddled their books and got banged up again. People would come for the show, look around for their seats, and it'd turn out there was more than one person with a ticket for the same seat! And the whore would be standing in the wings, sniggering.

Then there was the time when the whore nicked a huge jar of preserves from the Supersam (this was back in the deepest days of communism), put it in her net bag and kept walking. And this one bit of grunt there, no doubt an old trick, shouts after her:

'Ya poof, ya fuckin' poof!'

And what does she do but swing her arm round with all her might and smash him on his head. The grunt was covered in blood, glass in his face, walking round that shop half-conscious, and the old ladies with their shopping backing away from him like the plague. And she says:

'That'll teach you to get cheeky with a queer!'

What happened later on? Well, later we had the eighties, and the police came up with their 'Operation Hyacinth', which they merely copied from the East German Stasi and the Romanian Securitate. The queers all started grassing on each other like mad to the vice squad, though they always got the shit knocked out of them, too. They had a need, which they usually satisfied by gossiping, to tell stories, to make things up, and now they'd found even more attentive listeners. More and more queens had files; Grasser Grażyna was bursting with reports. And they put Radwanicka away for good. When they started making up things to add to her biography, the police could hardly believe who they had in their hands. And that's how Radwanicka, who was always the first to gossip, was felled by her own weapon.

For instance, at night, in the park, police vans cruising around... Radwanicka was still on the wanted list, ever since her Warsaw days. So she'd take some grunt into the night and go down on him, and of course his trousers would be down around his ankles while he was getting sucked off, and she'd be emptying his pockets and he'd never notice. The grunt would shoot his load, go. Soon after, he'd notice that his wallet was missing, keys, everything; the bitch had cleaned him out. Since the park at night was practically blue with policemen, he quickly found a patrol car and said:

'It's like this, see, I'm a homosexual, I admit it. And this bloke [Radwanicka] was giving me a blowjob in the bushes, and he pulled my trousers down and took everything out of my pockets.' Uff. You couldn't get me to say that to the police. But he did. So they asked him:

'Which one?'

They looked, and there was that whore, sitting pretty on a bench along the path, in the dark. They put her in handcuffs and into the patrol car. Your papers, they say, and she hands them over, and the police say:

'Fucking hell, man, you're wanted over the length and breadth of the country!'

Flashing lights twinkling violet in the darkness of the park, siren wailing, cops, Radwanicka in handcuffs. And so the whore was taken away, but first she stopped, threw back her head, and belted out her valedictory aria to all the queens in the park. She paused theatrically at the door of the police van, in handcuffs, on the running board, as if it were a stage, and shouted to all the queens her grand communiqué. Enunciating every word. Slowly, her voice, small at first, accumulated volume and so much expressiveness that she almost had to whisper so as not to shatter into tiny pieces. In a single exhalation. Her voice low, gravelly. Seeming to speak only to me, but in fact addressing a whole world she was about to leave at the siren's wail:

'Huh? What? You stupid slag, you, who in cunt's name do you think you are? You think that just because you get to stay out there, free, that you're less fucked up than I am?' Here Radwanicka broke off, like she had so much to say she didn't know where to start, like she was bursting at the seams with it. The cops weren't forcing her to get in either, they were just keeping an eye on her, waiting apprehensively for what she would say next. They were giving her permission, like granting a condemned man a last cigarette – this was Radwanicka's last cigarette!

'We're all of us fucking pervs, you know… Look how people live their lives; they have families, they have each other over for coffee or dinner, buy furniture, watch the telly. And us? Neither snow nor rain nor heat can keep us from chasing after a bit of rough cock. Like the hard-up, accursed slags that lurk around here – and you call that normal? That's what you call normal?! This flitting and flying about we do?'

I don't say a thing. No one says a thing. But eventually, I open my mouth:

'Yes, that's what I call normal!' I say. She bridles:

'You! You always had a screw loose! Here you have it, the life of a queen: once a year you get to grope something drunk on a bench, in secret, illegally; to suck an anonymous cock in the bushes, in the wind, in the snow. That's the life we lead – the life of a pervert! Admit it! You poofs are all mental, you are! Really, who do you think you are?!' At that she proudly raised her already handcuffed wrists as if she were only now expecting them to cuff her. Enormously impressed with her speech, she turned and said to the officers:

'Gentlemen, do what you must.'

And so Radwanicka was escorted away. The stern officers, the romantic stage, Radwanicka the heroine. The trollop was beaten, packed into the police van, and taken away at the siren's wail to be arrested.

## Fredka

... sits on a bench in the park in the morning and sleeps. She sleeps because she's old, cradled and lulled by the golden autumn of her life. Beside her is her net shopping bag, and in it is an old vinegar bottle full of tea. The next bench along is empty. The bench after that is empty, too. And somewhat further along, Radwanicka is sitting with a bit of young runaway grunt and some queens. As soon as Fredka's old, tired head begins to droop and then drop, Radwanicka winks at us, points at her, and quietly creeps up behind her. WHAM! She frightens Fredka, whose vacant and terrified eyes fly open. The queens burst out laughing.

And every spring, when they give the benches a fresh coat of green paint, Fredka inevitably sits down on one of them, falls asleep, and gets stuck. Then the queens have to unstick her.

She comes to the park every day from one of the villages outside Wrocław. From Oleśnica or Oława, Milicz, Dzierżoniów, even Środa Śląska – it doesn't matter which one. What matters is that she comes in on the morning train for three zlotys, and by ten she's on a bench, tanning herself in the autumn sun. It's not as if she'd be doing anything different in her Milicz or Środa, she'd just be doing the same in a regular park, imagining it was the picket line.

Once a month, though, the postman brings her her pension, and Fredka freshens herself up, puts on her brown jacket, and catches the train in her customary way, but now with a degree of ceremony. Because she never usually brings money with her, but she remembers them. And she has a grand total of sixty zlotys in her wallet. Three twenty-zloty bills in three envelopes. And with three different teenage grunts, runaways who need the cash, she'll head into the ruins. Three blowjobs at twenty zlotys a pop. This month at least she can afford a little Indian summer.

But Fredka in the old days – what a star! She and Golda would party all night at the Hotel Monopol. They'd slip under the table where the moneychangers sat and take their pick. Then Golda would take out her dentures and give him a blowjob. The thing was, the moneychanger couldn't let on that he'd been chosen. Stony-faced, silent, the lads would play cards, watching each other's faces for the least sign of bliss. When the chosen one broke down, they'd all start laughing, and Golda and Fredka would ask from under the table: 'Keep going?'

There's an addendum to Fredka's story: it turns out she wasn't from one of those villages after all, but from the outskirts of Wrocław. Radwanicka the whore was exaggerating as usual. That one never spoke a word of truth in her entire life.

## A Room With a View to the Promenade of Stars

Straight people have their quirks, too. I'm sitting, after dark, at my window. Before me the promenade courses past, a river of boys, each one lovelier than the last. Under the corrugated roof of Club Neptune, some ringmaster is announcing the next song, sung by so-and-so from who-knows-where, and a disco-polo hit starts up. 'O, o baby, did I ever cheat on you?' And then 'White Roses' comes on, which moves me to tears. Outside my window a group of about eight boys walks by. Actually they're somewhere between being boys and being men, about twenty-four years old. Coming at a clip towards them is a group of women around the same age, though they're definitely already more women than girls. Everyone's dressed up, perfumed, cologned, peroxided, all in white, as people are on the promenade. A woman with a pram, a man with a shaved head. The woman with the pram lunges at the bald guy:

'What are *you* doing here?'

And she kisses him. The bald guy submits, but he's clearly bewildered. It turns out she's mistaken him for some other bald man, her own man. Everyone has a laugh about it. But they've all had a few beers already, too, so it's no big deal; if it had happened on the street in a big city, there would have been a riot – but here at the seaside, it's a window of opportunity! The woman with the pram says to her friend:

'Hey, who'd you think he looks like?'

Her friend nods her head. Whispers the name into her ear. Laughter. The gentlemen try to get to know the ladies better:

The gentlemen: 'Join us for a drink?'

The ladies: 'OK, maybe tomorrow, if we run into each other again.'

The gentlemen: 'Why don't you girls give us your numbers now?'

The ladies: 'Uhh. Dunno. If we run into each other, then definitely. But not like this.' It's mainly the bald one who's pushing the point, the other guys standing on the edges of this conversation. But all of them are drooling. They'll have to make do with slobber tonight. As for my role in all of this, I'm suspended above them, invisible; though all they'd have to do is look up, and what do you know: why, that's a camped-up, cynical, pubeless poofter up there. Quaffing their saliva and watching them, as if we were in a public toilet.

Suddenly all hell is breaking loose outside my door. And it shows no sign of stopping. I slip on my knickers and fling open the door. It's the Deaf Hag, my landlady, sitting there with *Dynasty* on the telly at full volume, so she can hear.

## Now I'll Never Straighten Out!

'Oh! There've been some changes round here!' one of the Poznań lads says, staring at my crotch; fortunately it's not the skinhead. 'Things are looking up. Why, whoever saw someone with thatch like that, it's like you had a beard down there!' These lads even shave their armpits. I always felt that it made me more physical, that being shaved gave an armpit a sudden materiality, a life of its own. That when one of those Rambos laser-depilated himself, his whole body began to clamour, to be. With physical lads like these, sex meant nothing more than bodies fucking, no soul, nothing metaphysical, just thrust in and slide out – body sex, necrophilia! Two unpeopled bodies rubbing against each other. All head, no emotion. First a little snogging, then a blowjob, then sixty-nine – everything in its own compartment, discrete. They have sex with their heads, but they're corpses – what is a human being without a soul after all? And they slather themselves all over with lotions, so their bodies don't even taste like bodies any more, just chemicals and antiperspirants. Fucking plastic. From a distance it's enticing, promising, but when you start doing anything with it, it's like eating a gigantic chemical strawberry coated with cotton wool.

And they're surprised at the falling fertility rates in the West, in Poznań.

As for us – us old, hunchbacked intellectuals, reading newspapers in cafés, in our grey jackets and glasses, smoking our pipes, us unshaven literati – our bodies are practically see-through, inconspicuous. We forget about them. I have one inside myself, too, of course! You just need to dig a little. But when someone gets butch with me, I ebb to femme, and when they're too femme, then it's the other way round. It's all in motion, and even as I write my queer magnum opus here – seriously! – I have my shirt tugged down around my shoulders in a kind of decolletage, and I ring up my queeny friends, giggle giggle, and talk about how my sentences have grown so camp I'm a lost cause: it's curtains for me, Lucretia, help! I'll probably never straighten out now, never go back to being the unshaven intellectual... People have even started giving me looks on the street when I go out on my daily cigarettes-and-pizza run.

I ring them and say:

'Talk to me, Patricia. Talk to me, Lucretia! Tell me something, anything.'

'OK, how about that time Zdzicha got up on that gravestone so the attendant at the cemetery would see her, and started wanking, and then the gravestone collapsed, and she said to the police: What're you arresting me for? I'll be punished when the ghost whose grave I smashed up starts tormenting me! And afterwards Zdzicha went to that fortune teller, but refused to pay her the five hundred zlotys. Anyway. OK, I'll slow down the narration now, take a deep breath. So time moved on, and back then Zdzicha used to have a wank all over the place. Whenever I was on the train, passing by the landfill, I'd hear someone yell:

'"Abomination! A pervert! People, close your eyes, look away!" And everyone would crowd against the windows, except for me: I knew that was Zdzicha's turf... But what was I saying? Oh right, Zdzicha wouldn't give that fortune teller the money, and strange things started to happen... There was a fire at her flat, blah, blah, blah, silly little things, and finally she put those five hundred zlotys in an envelope and sent them to her by post; and things calmed down after that.'

'And then?'

'And then... what? That's all, Michał. Will you be putting it in?' Queens are seriously mental.

'Let's get serious, I'm certainly not going to write that Zdzicha's psychotic, and spanks the monkey everywhere she goes, and has the police chasing after her. No...'

'But when you start at A...'

'You don't need to jump right to Z.'

Brrrrng! One of the two Kiosk Sisters is ringing.

'Hey ho, did you write about that time in 1988 when you came by to show us how big your willy was? You know, at our kiosk, inside...?' Queens are always tenderly calling each other things like 'slag' and 'tart' and 'bitch': it cheers 'em up.

No... The way you lot would write this book, there'd be nothing left for me to add... Whatever... I never thought it would come to this, Flora writing my book instead of me! Isn't it enough that half the Wrocław picket line is writing my book for me? Like all I have to do is proofread it?

So the Kiosk Ladies do remember me from back then. Nothing has changed. Except that now they're rich and go on holiday to Tunisia for the Arabs.

'You know, you have to bring vodka for them, and you really have to be careful, because they've certainly all had their fair share... They're all prostitutes basically, I mean, not the way we are, but same thing...'

'Oh, wouldn't it be great to run into Grasser Grażyna...? But she hardly ever goes out any more, only to Szczytnicki Park. You really should talk to her, though. She used to keep files on all the chanteuses there, you can ask her anything...'

# The Perspective, Not the Human

Old Dear No. 1:

Those wild beaches, where I used to gather amber, they're gone,
all gone! It all happened back in the eighties. No one had heard of
AIDS yet; they were all spreading it like crazy. Nobody used condoms. Why would they? And then, around 1988 or so, people
suddenly started talking about it. It never occurred to anyone that
anything like that could happen in Poland: it was a product from
the mythical West, like pineapples; it was chic, a little bit like drugs,
I guess. It was exotic; no one ever thought that we might get it, too.
And no doubt everyone was completely convinced that if communism hadn't ended it would never have happened. AIDS under
communism? Some bloke with a red star-shaped blotch on his forehead queueing in one of our dismal shops? AIDS was all scarlet and
crimson, and communism was grey through and through. And even
if we had things like that under communism, no one would have
spoken, let alone written, about it. The West came to Poland and
brought its diseases with it, its rotten pineapples. Who asked them
anyway? Or was it really so bad on Lake Wigry, those nights in
Augustów, the delicate thread of cormorants, dances on the wooden

pier... The mosquitoes. The fare at the cafeteria was superb, oh, it really was... On holidays we always had our BLUD, which was our acronym for Breakfast – Lunch – Dinner. In the morning we'd have milk soup, an apple, a hard roll with a pat of butter, jam, and we'd often get cheese slices as well. Later, we'd have a proper lunch, no junk food or anything, just soup (tomato or cucumber) and for the main course a cutlet, mashed potatoes, cucumber salad. Compote or even liquid jelly to drink, and dessert, too: cream cakes, stuff like that. Then at teatime, there'd be sweet rolls, apples and pears, and compote. And for dinner, well, they had just everything: slices of yellow cheese, sausage with those little blobs of fat, herring salad... Kiosks with souvenirs. We used to travel, but now a pensioner like me only gets a couple of hundred zlotys, so just to get up here once a year for a shag you've got to save your coins in the vase all year long, the one on top of the television, the crystal vase (whatever I want now, I need to fill a new crystal vase). Back then everyone had a right to his holidays, and that was that. We had a right to go to the spa. Time was when you had really lovely books from the enterprise lending library to read, sitting on a bench, in the park, in bed. And young people today? Then, they joined the scouts and provided a service to society by cleaning up, planting flowerbeds, all those little pansies and petunias. And now? *Please* – the dunes are completely covered with rubbish, plastic bottles, and tattered newspapers – because they use the gay press for wiping their bums. All I'd like to ask is: 'Queens! *Stop* littering like that, think about what it looks like after you've left!' You can write that down, Michał.

I used to go to Ciechocinek, to the spa... People would dance in a café near the Mushroom Fountain… The compere encouraged everyone to dance… People would sit on benches around the towers, inhaling and gossiping, and at the spa, too, with the pump room and peacocks and coal black swans with their red beaks wandering about… It was so pretty! Ciechocinek water went by the name *Krystynka*; I think it's known all over Poland. In the pump room you paid a pittance and you could drink the water all day from a spout shaped like a little frog. Of course the queens would meet each other in the spa as well. Did they ever! It was a cruising ground, with all the frills. Peacocks in enormous cages, at the centre of the park. You wanted mountains? Krynica-in-the-Hills. The beach? Krynica-by-the-Sea, which was somewhere else. All you had to do was go to Krynica; there was something for everyone there. I'd sit my arse down in the train and be whisked away to wherever. None of that stress, that rushing around. You could spend your whole day at work just gossiping, sipping coffee, smoking cigarettes. I had a job in a cloakroom, and no one is going to tell me that was bad work! My friend Kangaroo would come round early in the morning since I worked right across from the picket line. All I had to do was take people's coats, and my work was done. Except for the door, that heavy, carved wood door the tossers always left open. I made a sign: 'Closing the door is the mark of a civilised person'. No luck. So I changed it to 'Shut the door!' But to no effect either. I put up a third sign and shouted my head off. But no matter: they never shut the door; it was always left open. I asked them to put up partitions, from the counter to the ceiling, made of glass, so it would be like I was sitting in a kiosk, and they could pass me their coats through a little hole. And this smart-arse, some professor, an architect (ugh!) says to me:

'No, it's an historic interior, it would spoil the perspective,' or something along those lines, to make sure I understood why. And then I told him that for people like him it was the perspective, not the human, that mattered. As for the counter, when they were renovating, the handymen asked me how high I wanted it, and I gave them special orders to keep it just a bit lower than the crotch so I could take a good look while I was there.

You could buy suntan lotion at Baltona if they had it, and if they didn't then you were out of luck. Queens were always rubbing their faces with whatever they could get their hands on, not lotion but things like oil or yogurt. And the music back then was wonderful: Wodecki, Sława Przybylska; the songs had melodies, and the lyrics were classy, they rhymed and had a beat. Now they listen to that rap music… The wild beaches are gone… And let's say, God forbid, you fell ill at the beach: you just went and saw a doctor, no questions asked. You could get treatment anywhere. And now if there's something the matter with my heart, God forbid, they tell me I've got to go back home. I'm telling you: Puppy Pancratius and Floppy the Bear are dead… The wild beaches are gone, the wild beaches are gone…

Old Dear No. 2:
Well, life wasn't always a bed of roses. One time, I remember (we had a centre here and one on Lake Niecko), everyone got sick from the bigos. Everyone loved the bigos, couldn't get enough of it, and there was this waiter who took a shine to me, pulled me to one side, and said:

'Listen, Wiesław, it's like this. Don't eat that bigos; the sausage meat is bad. This morning it was green, rotting; but the cook said that no one would notice after it had been fried.' And everyone stuffed their faces; and that night the news went round like wild fire: 'Food poisoning!' Queues to the toilet, people in the queues vomiting. They only had that one little cabin there, with a hole in the ground and flies buzzing around... Or that other time when I went with a girlfriend to the kiosk to buy ice cream, and the lady says to us:

'Not right now. What I got was thawed out when it arrived, and I haven't had a chance to freeze it again. Come back in an hour...'

Can you believe it? Or when you went to the post office: back then, Michał, you had to make your phone calls in a little booth, and during the call the operator would interrupt every few minutes and ask:

'Still talking?' You couldn't even camp it up properly because that old slag could break in any moment with her 'Still talking?' That's how she checked to see if the caller was still on the line, and all you could do was answer her with a blasé 'Still talking, still talking...'

But under communism everyone talked all the time. We had nothing. The shops were all empty, so what could we do but make things up? When the queens talked behind each other's back, it wasn't out of malice, but just because... everyone needed something funny to talk about...

'Before we left I washed the curtains and the windows, vacuumed, and took the plants over to the neighbours... Uff. I can breathe now.'

'I moved the sofa. But I don't think I got enough bread for Sunday.'

# THE GREAT ATLAS OF POLISH QUEENS

## Style Queens

I grabbed my cigarettes and went for a walk through the dunes towards Świnoujście. I looked over and saw that Apothecaress from Bydgoszcz lying there. She had her umbrella with the Vichy logo opened up and was slathering on sunscreen as usual. I bowed politely, proffering my respect, and started to pester her about lice: how could I get rid of them? She gave me a long lecture, explaining how I had to shave my entire body, even my legs and armpits because there's no place they can't spread, and in extreme or chronic cases the little bitches can even infest nose hair and ear hair and eyebrows. Finally she told me to go the chemist and buy a bottle of Lindane, without saying anything about the lice. Just say:

'Lindane, please'.

I thanked her and got the hell out of there quickly because she said that if I had lice I might have probably picked up something even worse, and I should go to the STD clinic for a battery of tests… Again she tried to persuade me to buy a webcam and give up my real-time depravities. Even though she was rich, she still lived in the very room where she first drew breath, with her aging mother in the next room, her first girlhood ponytail, instead of a plait, pinned to a tapestry as a memento, the whole thing looking a bit like Auschwitz. The ceiling was covered with porn, the peeling wallpaper was a backdrop for old movie posters from the eighties, kung-fu films, *E.T.*.. And smack dab in the middle of this hole was the computer. Dear children, please make sure you never, ever answer this man's private messages in a chatroom, even if he tells you he's thirteen and still plays with dolls! He's the fat bloke in the poster, the one warning kids against talking to strangers on the internet. He has a one-track mind. He's a client of the Hottie Tot escort agency and the Whippersnapper travel agency. He'll swallow you up entirely, bones and all. He'll stick out his tongue and start licking. He'll get at you through his state-of-the-art camera. Just imagine his enormous, red tongue clambering out of the camera and licking you all over! The internet – that's where the real depravity takes place, that's the real libidinal Lubiewo, the real lewd beach!

'My neighbour came over, installed everything, totally professional, explained how it all worked, started up Windows, and what do you know: There on the desktop was one of the nude photos of Mr Poland 2003!'

The sun in its golden chariot had already covered half its course, and the buzzing of bumblebees slowly gave way to that of mosquitoes. The sea was calm and silvery, the air still, the flat water inhabited by half-immersed, motionless figures, like a picture of the baptism at the River Jordan. But there was no sin any more. Up above, on the dunes, stood a corpulent queen I had always admired. She was making a toga for herself out of a silk towel printed with enormous white flowers; crouching, she wrapped it around her breasts and knotted the corners. She was old, but the hair on the back of her head was long and dyed red. I once overheard her talking Russian on her mobile. Another time I greeted her from a distance, and she responded with a dignified nod, like a cultured matron from Germany.

Sometimes she would walk along the edge of the woods here with a cane, like a wraith, her curly hair shimmering all these shades of vermillion at the back, the rest of her head bald. She always wore a skirt, made out of a blanket or that floral-print beach towel, anything as long as it wasn't trousers... And she never, ever showed her breasts; she always knotted something over them. There was always another man at her side, stocky, elderly – her husband. An old married couple, one the man, the other the woman, her in her floral-print beach-towel dress, him with his fishing rod and cigarette...

I walked past her, past a series of hollows inhabited by naked, fortysomething men tanned almost black. There were a lot of them. Each on his own, each with his own designer rucksack, fashionable cigarettes, expensive tanning oil, his own designer sadness permanently plastered across his face. Suddenly I happened upon a hollow that was entirely in the shadow of some peculiar bushes and occupied by two young, fashionable damsels – one with enormous glasses and a woolly perm dyed purplish-black, the other gorgeous, ginger-haired, the face of an eighteen-year-old ephebe... They at once whistled after me, so I called back loudly:

'Hey ladies! What are you doing hiding in the shade? Is our little bit of sun too hot for you?'

'Well, it certainly is too hot for my Eugenia. Her complexion is so delicate...'

I was certain these were Style Queens, which is to say they lived in the big city and earned more than three grand a month, but they seemed very nice regardless. In order to find out for sure, I gave them the 'hair straightener' test, which involves merely mentioning at some point in a conversation the fact that one has recently purchased a straightener for one's hair. If the queen under examination responds with 'What's that?' then she fails. But if she asks, 'Ceramic?' then you have a classic Style Queen on your hands.

'A ceramic one?' Eugenia asked earnestly. Yes, of course it was ceramic, I informed her; it isn't worth buying metal ones since they totally ruin your hair. Then there's the question of whether to get a dual straightening and curling iron. And there are all sorts of other complications, too. Straightening, fine, but with what? With those professional hair products you can find for a hundred zlotys in only the most expensive salons? Very well, but now: which brands leave a sticky residue in your hair, and which don't? Then there's the question of whether or not to colour, and if so, whether to colour the whole head or just have the top spiked and highlighted – which is in again now, part of that wave of eighties nostalgia (which Limahl's autobiography has certainly contributed to as well). But that's just the head, there's so much else. Nails, for instance. Is it better to go to a salon for a manicure, or do them yourself at home with nail clippers and special sandalwood sticks? You can buy everything in the shops these days. And then: will generic cosmetics do, or should you get them from Sabon? Well? Who knows? Because every Style Queen will tell you something different. And then: is it better to whiten my teeth with that crap from Rossman, or get something from the dentist? And my hair: when the ends start splitting, is it better to fix them with Kerastes or Wella Professional or L'anza? Who the hell knows. And clothes:

'Should I run them up myself or not? Are retro and second-hand still OK? Or maybe it's better to buy fewer more expensive items rather than to have a whole wardrobe full of shite I'll never wear...'

Suddenly Eugenia glances at my Zara shoes, which I was holding in my hand and now toss on to the sand, and says to the monkey next to her:

'Oh look, remember *those?*'

They both giggle.

'Oh, the trouble I had with those shoes!'

So, she had had the same ones. The problem with Style Queens is that whenever Zara brings out something really nice, all the Style Queens in Poland will be wearing it the next day; it's the only place in this country they dare to shop. Unless they have something tailor-made by Arthuretta, of course, but that's really upmarket. Then later at Scena and Scorpio and who knows where else, suddenly everyone's wearing the same thing, and they all swear how they're never, ever shopping at Zara again. Well, maybe a blouse from the ladies' department – these queens are so skinny, with their long arms, long necks: a new type of human that can actually fit into those super-tight, super-short tops (a diamond in the belly button!). And jewellery, too, for decorating their fingernails and toenails, wrists and ankles... A whole market of footcare products spread out before them, those affluent queens, bored silly at the end of the working day.

All the young Style Queens I knew had read at least one book,

*Dangerous Liaisons*, and they all identified with its protagonist, the Marquise de Merteuil.

Eugenia: Darling! I'm the Madame de Merteuil!'

Monkey: 'No you're not! *I'm* the Madame de Merteuil!'

Later, they would start their text messages with things like Cher Vicômte… I, for one, always write my diary like that, in the form of letters to my girlfriend Paula, a.k.a. Madame de Merteuil… My handwriting is neat and sloping, with all sorts of parenthetical asides revealing my various little intrigues, most of them invented, though some really do happen, and generally embellished with this or that juicy, cynical snipe or archaism or other.

'Unfortunately, the majority of Polish queens,' Eugenia lowered her eyelashes, 'are entirely too brand-conscious. They act all excited about something you're wearing, but when they notice that it does- n't have a label they stop liking it. It never occurs to them that it might not be from the high street, but made to measure.'

While they were explaining this all to me – although it was hardly necessary, my being a Style Queen myself – I simply nodded and fantasised about sending Monkey off to Świnoujście on a long walk – ideally one-way – so that Eugenia and I could have a bit of a snog again, suck face to our heart's content. What would Madame de Merteuil do? What would the Vicômte de Valmont do? So I con- tinued nodding, but we weren't really having a conversation, because they were saying the same things I was; we were on the same intel- lectual plane (in the Hair and Fashion department, of course); we were in unison, not dialogue. They had been sitting on the pier at Międzyzdroje the day before, people-watching at Café Paparazzi. Men were promenading past the café like on a fashion runway, but not one had anything decent on – designer knock-offs, discount items, tracksuits. One of them, the proprietor of a tanning salon in Świnoujście, was tanned coal-black and wearing all white, even her hair was white, a right mess. And there were some other young things in for the day from Świnoujście, real heifers. Two blokes had slipped away from their wives to have a few beers 'like we did in our bachelor days'. And so on. All their factory seconds were showing!

Think, think – I thought – think of some way to get Monkey out of here… Start some Vicômte de Valmont intrigue… Oh, I know!

'Look,' I said to them, 'just look at this ring.' I held out my silver-and-titanium ring, which I'd had made by a silversmith I knew in Wałbrzych. They enthused.

'Super! Where did you buy that?' Oh, she was mine! Eugenia was mine! Mine the ginger-haired, fair-skinned genie… And now my Eugenia retrieved from her bag an Alice band made of plastic, like the ones good girls wore in those old primary school textbooks, *Ala Has a Cat*, etc. She combed her hair back from her forehead with it and set it daintily in place on the crown of her head… Later, at the dentist's, I came across a weekly magazine with a photograph of David Beckham wearing exactly the same sort of hairband. She must have got the idea from him…

'Hurry,' I said to Monkey, 'hurry along to Świnoujście! They still might have some of these rings there – I saw a man selling them next to the ferry stop earlier on. He had a few left. Go and get one for your Eugenia!'

At that, however, Genie piped up: 'What? Buy jewellery without me? Never! He'll choose the worst one!'

Nothing remained for me to do but to retreat graciously and wish them a sunny – though not too sunny, given Eugenia's delicate complexion – day. But before walking too far, Monkey suddenly turned and pointed at Eugenia and squawked the following at me:

'She's seen aliens, you know!'

'You're the one who saw it, not me!'

Like little girls squabbling in the playground, they start screaming at each other over who saw what, each embarrassed to admit it in front of me.

'Really? What did they look like?'

Eugenia and Monkey start to get all excited and shriek. Suddenly it turns out that, in fact, they both saw them.

'The one had on a Galliano waistcoat...' But Eugenia interrupts her girlfriend:

'I already told you, that was Arkadius. Galliano has different buttons, like this' – she traces the shape of the buttons in the sand – 'and those buttons looked like this' – she draws the other ones.

'He had on Kenzo sunglasses and the most faaabulous Prada shoes!'

'I don't know why you bother opening your mouth, 'cause you don't know the first thing about fashion. I saw everything with my own two eyes, and I even know what he smelled like as well.'

'I saw everything! I did! He didn't smell like anything!'

'He smelled like Rosi Braidotti, if you really want to know!'

Screams, a mayhem of shrieking, they hit each other, struggle on the sand, tear each other's hair out, and out of the chaos I hear the occasional shout:

'Donna Karan!'

'Galliano!'

'Hair straightener!'

'Diesel!'

'Estée Lauder!'

'Anklets!'

'Nail extensions!'

'Hair straightening!'

'Body art!'

'Permanent makeup!'

'Belly-piercing!'

'Galliano!'

'Alexander McQueen!'

'Arkadius!'

'Toni & Guy!'

'Vidal Sassoon!'

And they'd be screaming like that to this day if a torrential rain-storm hadn't blown in and flooded that whole luxury boutique of theirs. The mood took an abrupt turn, as if summer had come to a sudden end. My Style Queens and I fled the beach. From out of nowhere the Old Queens disinterred some very communist-looking plastic hoods. Plastic scarves on their heads, like old women in the countryside. The Apothecaress toddled past with her Vichy-advert umbrella: *Health is Vital – Start With Your Skin*. The Style Queens with their designer umbrellas – the fashion this season was for ones so transparent they couldn't be seen: it's like they're not even there! The gays from Poznań were calling each other to their Puntos, their motorcycles and bargain-basement cars, because what else would a small-time businessman drive? The beach emptied, and the water's surface, which had been as still as that of a lake, was broken by large rings of rain.

Only one – some madwoman or other, some middle-aged queen, though obviously D-list, all totty and no knickers – stayed behind in the rain, dancing, shouting, and gulping the rain as it falls down from the sky, writhing in the wet sand, inspired. She yelled out something about innocence regained, how the rain has revived her youth, added years to her life, how her blood was flowing faster again... And then a few other old queens went back as well, at first uncertainly, gathering up the rain in their outstretched hands, then scooping up the wet sand, smearing themselves with it, lying down in the sea, loudly proclaiming their regained youth, that the rain has purified them. In the throes of inspiration, in some mystical rapture, they shouted:

'Rain, o rain! I'm a virgin again! Purifying rain, sent by God to wash away the evil...'

## The Others

And that was it for the rain! The sun started shining again, the way
it does on the Baltic Sea. So I continued walking. The dunes became
less sheer and above them the forest with its bunkers full of stag-
nant water and flies gave way to meadows. Suddenly this old thing
from Stargard popped up (that's how queens describe others, by
referring to them not as 'old person' but as 'that old thing'; and
instead of saying 'I was with someone', they say 'I did this thing', or
'There's nothing around today' or 'Maybe we'll find something').

'Are you a student? Do you have a job?'

'Good heavens, there really is *nothing* interesting around today,'
I said, trying to let him know that it was pointless. But he grovelled:

'*I'm* interesting...'

I managed to discourage him with banal chatter, his excitement
dwindled, and he went away. I passed a couple of Germans. I can
always identify naked Germans by their tiny, flat-lying ears and
handsome, intelligent faces (not a single ounce of that Lech Wałęsa
mix of grease, moustache, and beer belly), and by their slim, expensive wristwatches. Also by the fact that they always put their
cigarette ends back into the pack so they can throw them out later

in special containers made for recycling. I always say 'Ciao!' to them because they're so cultured and speak English so well, and you can talk to them about literature and the environment. There's only one thing you can't do with them. There's something so methodical, so calculating in their eyes, something really grunty about them… But grunt has to be more Russian, bigger, and completely unpredictable in its behaviour. Grunt throws its vodka empties into the bushes – recycling is an alien concept. And of course it doesn't shave or pierce its balls. Real grunt doesn't exist in the West. It starts appearing east of the Oder and continues all the way to the other side of Russia.

I walked on, looked around, and realised that the Old Dear was right: queens always leave such a mess on these dunes. It makes you want to wring their necks.

I carried on walking, and suddenly, from behind a mountain of condoms, empty water bottles, and old glossy magazines, emerged one of the stars of the open-air theatre and music hall, a pre-war diva of sorts. All in black, a scrap of fur across her shoulders… Later I realised that it was Madame de Pomme de Terre. Or her ghost, rather, since she'd been a regular at the Little Fairy back in the six-ties. Madame de Pomme de Terre was a Queen of the ancien régime.

It's important to understand that in addition to the Style Queens (an innocuous and cultured sort found mainly in metropolitan areas) there is a great variety of other species of queen. The Old Queen, for example. Age will not make of a Style Queen an Old Queen, because the latter is old to begin with. Even at birth she breathes a pre-emancipatory air of railway stations and grunt, and embodies in equal amounts the twin pathologies of skinniness and obesity. Old Queens generally originate in small- and medium-sized cities and may be found at railway stations and bus depots; they're an endangered species. There are also Demi-Queens, a particularly interesting variant. The Demi-Queen is likewise alternatively oriented, and that orientation lurks in every gesture. She does not, however, refer to herself as a lady, nor does she speak in a high-pitched voice, and she dresses in unassuming garb. But just watch how she puts her mobile phone back into her shoulder bag: she leans over a tad too attentively, opens the bag a bit too deliberately... and *voilà*, the bag becomes a purse! She radiates her orientation unconsciously – all would-be ostentation is concealed. Ninety-nine per cent of those emancipated upstarts from Poznań are in fact Demi-Queens. They shave their heads, but shake their arses when they walk. Muscle-bound, they rub their faces with skin cream just like any diva...

But let us proceed to the next page of our atlas, where we shall find the Goth Queen and, farther on, the Mall Queen (a frequenter of shopping centres, her distinguishing feature is the whitewall haircut, shorter on top than the Style Queens wear it, and never coloured), the Show Tune Queen (and her permutations: the Ballet Queen, the Opera Queen, the Pantomime Queen), as well as the Cloakroom Attendant Queen, the Academic Queen, and the Queen of Everlasting Cosmetics Sales. On the next page of our Atlas we find a rare species: the Press Spokesperson for the Lesbian, Gay, Bisexual, Intersex, Transgender, Queer and Questioning Community Queen, or LGBITQQ Queen for short. Newspapers and TV stations contact her whenever there's a public demonstration against homophobia or when they need a soundbite on Gay Culture. As soon as an LGBITQQ Queen shows up and outs herself, the media quickly acknowledges her for the rare and useful specimen she is. She generally speaks on behalf of all other queens, though many of them would probably disagree with every word she says. But as they rarely end up finding out what that is, nothing happens. This species naturally combines with the Activist Queen, creating a more or less stable, but erotically unappealing, hybrid.

Mall Queens, similarly, can be found crossed with Style Queens (the 'all for beauty' model of consumption), and there is an Ikea variant, as well (the 'all for home & garden' model of consumption). In general, Style Queens will cross with all subtypes except Old Queens. For example: Art Fag + Style Queen = Gallery Queen.

Blackie was an example of this last category. As the name implies, Blackie always dressed all in black, draping herself with new silver jewellery. She worked in an art gallery and regular went to the theatre, gallery openings, and poetry readings. She was all about pretense and snootiness, long-filtered cigarettes, silver cigarette cases… She never took off her hat in cafés, but would sit there with it on like an old woman in a beret, shovelling down her slice of cake and prattling:

'We had a concert of ballads, you know, which is why I couldn't make it any sooner. I was having drinks with Krystyna and Olgierd… We're doing a play with Stanisław, you know.'

But that's nothing compared with what you get when a Style Queen is crossed with a Stylist Queen. Any hair salon of note is filled with the sort, and there's no one who can cut or style or colour your hair better than they can. They know whole storylines, whole *Nights and Days*, by heart. Skinny, tall, beautiful, indolent… They smoke and have piercings all over their bodies. They know all the latest hairstyles. They know which way the wind is blowing, and what happened yesterday on the catwalk in London. Sometimes a gaggle of them will get together in someone's fabulous flat, all equally fabulous themselves, and sit there among the old armoires and vitrines full of trinkets, wallowing in their ennui like decadents. Instead of books their antique bookshelves are stocked with an assortment of vaguely extraterrestrial hair product containers and stacks of neatly folded, black, terry-cloth towels.

Karen, for instance. All the way through school Karen would doodle cartoons of women in various poses in the margins of her textbooks; each one she signed with the moniker 'Lady', a whole army of stiffly postured females. In class, while the teacher was talking about wars and kings, Karen would put her bag on her desk and set up her own little 'corner' behind it, her 'cottage', her private, miniature world. She had her mirror, her antiseptic ointment, pimples to squeeze... Outside were wars and uprisings, and there she was in her corner, her little cottage, her private retreat...

At home she covered the canopy over her bed with hand-drawn portraits of weeping Pierrots, drawing lips and tears and flashes of light on his black turban. Her boss at the salon where she worked complained that Karen was a lazy and lousy boy. She daydreamed while shaving the customers, and as a sign of protest dyed her hair blue. It's no fun at all having to wash hair all day, to hear how lazy and lousy you are, and to have to spritz spray on your hair during your breaks. She read all the magazines in the waiting area from cover to cover – they were her escape! The Toni & Guy catalogues, too... It was a whole other world! A black-and-white world on slippery, shiny, white paper fragrant with perfume samples. A world that appeared to Karen only in fragments, shreds of a photomural that someone had ripped apart. In this other world, the coffee was strong and came served in elegant cups, the men looked like movie stars, horses reared up on their hind legs, and cooking had nothing to do with the pierogi from the canteen. One day she realised that this world existed in its entirety somewhere far away, and she left to seek her fortune in Paris.

'She upped and went to seek her fortune in Paris! Well girls, if you don't kill me, that will! So, Karen left to go glue together that photomural of hers... No way any good will come of this.'

# PAULA

Suddenly my mobile starts ringing. I pick up: Paula.

'Guess what, Vicômte. I'm at the other end of the beach. Come on over.'

'Where are you?'

'In the straight bit. Wait, let me cover myself up; all I have on is a black thong. I'll be right over…'

She's forgotten everything again; and again I have to explain it all to her. So I tell her this:

'Dearest Paula, did you really purchase those, how shall I say it, *spectacular underthings,* just to go and hide in the bushes every time a spectator happens upon your charms?' Paula had to concede that I was right, she told me I'd utterly emancipated myself (which is true), and that she wasn't covering herself, but putting herself 'on display'. But the problem lay entirely in the displaying. Emancipation means showing off, and there's nothing you can do about it. If you're not hiding yourself, then you're displaying yourself – but you're not *being* yourself. All of this will vanish anyway in the post-emancipatory phase; there'll be no more gay beaches, no more gay bars, or gay newspapers… And no gay ghetto either. Queerness will be so transparent that when two lads start kissing on a regular beach, no one will take any notice. But fortunately, Paula, we won't be around then to see it.

## How Paula Took the Piss Out of a Pseudointellectual Queen

On my way here, Vicômte, I ducked into a hollow for a lie-down and this Pseudointellectual Queen latched on to me. Tinsel Tina I think was her name. Just imagine! Oh, there she goes! Look! There, on the horizon! She's probably walking back to Międzyzdroje!' (Paula points to someone strolling along the water's edge.)

Well, I guess I really did give her what-for. She ran off with her tail between her legs. I was spreading out my blanket when she came over... But I have to describe her for you: bright-coloured scarf on her head, string of Buddhist beads around a weatherbeaten neck, and clogs, just like our Poontanga. She spread out her blanket a few metres away and started reading a book. She kept glancing over at me, wondering why I wasn't chatting her up, seeing that she was so important and all with her book and beads. Finally she says to me:

'Mind if I join you?' And without waiting for my answer, she 'joins' me, like we were sitting in a café or something. And she was so full of herself! Says to me:

'So where are *you* from?' She was talking down to me like I was some chump on the street. So I said to her:

'I'm from Wrocław, basically.' By now I had her number.

'Basically? Oh, you mean, you're from *outside* of Wrocław?' She was pleased as Punch to have found a country boy, thought she'd be able to do whatever she wanted with me. If she had any idea she was dealing with Madame de Merteuil in the flesh, she wouldn't have taken the bait and wouldn't be running off in a panic now either. That's what people are like these days, Vicômte! No style, no taste, no class, and no panache! No sense for ruling by the sword, no feeling for the cloak and dagger, for intrigue, for love – nothing at all! All they do is consume, consume, consume! Everywhere you look, fat slobs gorging themselves on chips! Anyway, having provoked her question, I answered it:

'Umm, more or less means I spend half the year in Paris.' Well, she screwed up her nose, but continued talking down at me:

'Oh? And what do *you* do *there*?'

A chump, Vicômte. She was asking me what a *chump* does in *Paris*. So the *chump* replied:

'I'm *doing* a Ph.D.'

Well, at that she retreated into herself entirely; it was clear that the furthest her intellectual ambitions had ever taken her was a few poems published in the journal of the Proletarian Cultural Workers' Club, Zgierze Section. But then she asked me, flamboyantly:

'Huh. Really. So what is your topic?'

At which point the chump took a deep breath and rattled off the topic of *your* (unfinished) dissertation, Vicômte:

'Well, it's a deconstruction of the Cartesian subject in light of Derrida's early work, with special consideration given to Rosi Braidotti's deconstruction of the feminine subject!' There, eat that!

Eat that, intellectual! What more can I say? With all the wind knocked abruptly out of her sails, she threw in the towel and slunk off...

## St Mary of the Relics

'We have another saint on our hands, I'm telling you.' Paula is talking about Mary of the Relics, whom she ran into before her trip and whom they sometimes call the 'Lover of All Priests'. Another saint? Rolka may be a saint, but her? 'Her of all people. Just imagine: an ordinary young queen, eyebrows plucked, a collection of old relics. Her life is entirely bound up with the church, her speech larded up and down with Latin and archaisms; she knows everything, and she's no stranger to carnal desires either... Oh, honey! The things she's told me! Heavens! But she told me never to tell you. What she said was:

'"If I'm ever really down on my luck, I'll sell it all to *Fakt!* That little princess Snowflake will have to scrape my uterus six times before she gets anything out of me..."'

'Brrr!'

'But I will say this, Michał: we were stupid, we were so stupid, not to have entered the priesthood ten years ago. What we could have had there... I mean really. Of course, there'll always be some beastly prioress around, some chubby alpha queen wearing glasses who just happens always to have the whip ready, and if you cross her you're done for. But so what? Get her off and it all blows over. Just think: the highest ecclesiastical dignitaries, and so on! Maybe she was making it all up. I really don't know. Queens will tell you anything about anyone, for them nothing's sacred: insert name of politician – oh, *him*? I did him. Or of some well-known paragon of virtue – I'll give you *paragon*, girl! That slag had the run of the picket line, dishing out her honour to all comers! I did him a thousand times! The higher the position, the more obvious it is that he's a queen, a queen, with a cruising-ground history. That's how they talk, Vicômte, and it's hard to hear. After all, as you know, I was raised in a country house, in an ancient, patrician Jewish family. With respect for values.'

'Oh, they're just making it up! They see everything in their own image.'

'Mary told me about two queens, priests from Poznań, who lived in the presbytery. They would fuck the night away in dark rooms (dressed in civvies of course), then rush back to the presbytery early in the morning to prepare for matins. But in order to avoid performing mass in a state of sin, they'd go out to the balcony and take turns saying and giving confession to each other. Typically one of them would bow her head as if deep in thought, a distressed look on her face, and listen to the (for her very familiar) catalogue of the previous night's sins, before giving her friend the blessing. Then they'd switch. They even did penance. And then the two clergymen would put on their vestments and go out to perform, their eyes lowered devoutly.'

Mary herself personified the hypocrisy of it all. She'd sewn herself a black and white habit, the kind worn by nuns, and put it on when she was at home, just like putting on a hairpiece. 'If you ever saw her with that thing on her head, you'd crack up! She has that look of a jolly old soul about her, plus she's a fatty, and then there's that habit she made, looks totally realistic, and her eyes turned heavenward, wearing those horn-rimmed, old-lady glasses of hers... She laughs at herself: "This here psycho queen's gone and made herself a nun!"

'She keeps her money in an old eucharist wafers bag. It has the words *Eucharist Wafers prepared in full accordance with Canon Law under the Supervision of a Priest Chaplain* printed on it!'

'Eucharist wafers?'

'You know, for communion, the... umm, host. It says *A CHRISTUS Co. product* on it. And that whore keeps her money in it.'

And she collected religious relics, too.

'She buys them?'

'No, you're not allowed to. Since the Middle Ages the trade in relics has been strictly regulated.'

'So how does that tart get them?'

'You have to write a special letter to the Vatican, a really long one, and write about your beliefs in it... And you have to describe how you're on your knees begging for a relic in order to boost your lapsing faith. Saints are multiplying like rabbits these days, as you know, and when someone is canonised there's a whole procedure, relics categorised A, B and C... The C's are the worst. All you need is for the saint to have touched an object, and even part of it, a rosary bead for instance, will count as a category-C relic. In any case: the Pope makes someone a saint, or a blessed. Then they pull him out of his coffin and cut him up. The thighs are distributed to parishes around the world, parishes that have been on the waiting list for them for years; the head goes to Rome; fingers to some important place or other; and slivers of the various remaining bits go off to private individuals. Some parts of the saint are considered holier than others. For instance, Mary has loads of category-C relics and blesseds, but only one category-A. Among the Polish saints, she has a small patch of St Faustyna's clothing and a wood chip from the coffin of St Rafał Kalinowski, and then there are the bone fragments of the two Spanish Carmelites in that gold double medallion. She has a Joan de Chantal and a St Mary à la Cock... I asked her about medieval relics, Michalina, so I could maybe get you a St Alexis for your birthday, you always loved the *Legend of St Alexis*... but unfortunately, the really old ones, including all the St Alexises, no longer "circulate", they're not available any more. The Renaissance is the limit.'

'But wait, maybe you could still get me a Renaissance...?'

'And that whore' – here Paula laughs – 'got all conspiratorial with me, she was like, "I'll show you something, but it's a secret." And out of her shopping bag she pulls out that double medallion, which was inscribed with some kind of flowery script... "Here, take a look. Bones of Spanish Carmelites..."'

'Where did she show it to you then, at her flat?'

Paula chortles: 'No, guess where...'

'No! Not there!'

Paula nods, stifling her laughter.

'No, you must be kidding! She showed it to you on the picket?'

'On a bench, on the picket line. She was like: "Well, I know it's a sacrilege to show holy things in a place like this, but you've got to see it." And she reached into an ugly plastic carrier bag from the supermarket and pulled out the gold medallions. She didn't have a problem with it. She'll end up like Rolka, our Mary will, just wait and see.'

'Did you look inside the medallion?'

'What are you talking about? It's locked permanently! No way to open it.'

But when I ask her if Mary is still collecting relics, if she'd acquired any of the old ones yet, she tells me that that sinner was tempted by a snake, and ever since she ate of the forbidden fruit she's given up collecting, which is to say: Mary still had an ounce of decency left in her.

# Trash Queen

Brrring-Brrring! It's Anna:

Oh Annie, what I went through yesterday... You know how I'm from a very good, old Jewish family, to the manner born. Even if I *were* poor, I'd still have class, which is not so much about money as about breeding and good taste. I always buy Hutschenreuther china from Niskie Łąki... And you know I forbid the use of certain words in my presence; I simply refuse to acknowledge ever having heard them. Like that word that begins with 'b', which everyone's doing in the parks now, smoke billowing all over the place... That's not something I do. I will, however, consent to a *ball*, with a glass of delicious French wine sent down from the château by our very own Nadya Nadyeyevna Yepanchin...

Which reminds me, there was this fellow I went to meet, a straight man, who used to come and see me every now and then for the obvious reasons. He said to me: My wife is out of town, come over. Somewhere out by Kowale. I really had no interest in taking the train out there; I'm thinking, what good is a bachelor in Kowale to me...? But I went; it seemed silly to refuse. It was dark, cold; I was afraid to walk the streets of Kowale. Of course the street went on for a whole kilometre, and *nada*: there was no such address. Finally it turned out he lived in an old schoolhouse that had been converted into cheap flats. Oh, Annie, that place was like a chicken coop! The way some people live! Just imagine, the minute you walk in you're assailed by mustiness and decay. A tiny, depressing cubbyhole... but what depressed me most was the old television set, and this big, dusty, plush dog on top of it, its paw drooping over the screen. I thought I'd faint. Of course, you know that even having a television is suspect – but a stuffed animal? Utter kitsch! If only he'd get on with it... But he must have watched too many American movies; he'd got it into his head that we were going to have a romantic evening together, just the two of us (his child was sleeping in the next room). He clutched my hand and offered me a glass of wine...

'Fancy a glass of homemade wine?'

I told him I had no idea what that meant – 'homemade wine'? What is that? *Aucune idée: 'homemade wine'? C'est quoi?*

His response:

'Well, I made wine from grapes!' See, my dear Michalina, the things one gets exposed to by associating with the proletariat!

My response:

'I was not aware that they produced wine in this sorry country... *Je ne savais pas que dans ce pays triste on fabrique le vin!*'

He became upset. Of course there had been no mention of sex yet. But the way some people live! That place simply stank, it was *vile*! And all these dusty posters for American films everywhere. Of course: filth and squalor everywhere, but he still had time for a DVD! He offered me tea in Duralex (I'm not kidding, in *Duralex*!), but those DVDs, that was really the last straw... *Figure-toi ma petite*

*il existe les maisons dans notre pays triste où on sert le café dans une
tasse, o! Non, non, non! Pas dans une tasse, mais dans une bidule
qu'ils appellent 'Duralex', mon Dieu! C'est vraiment horrible!* The
atmosphere was stuffy, like in a dusty antique shop, like the window
display in a pawn shop; there were some dusty artificial flowers,
roses made of dirty, coloured foam rubber... And in the midst of it
all, his little one was sleeping in the next room. I was a wreck; how
on earth would I get back home from Kowale?

And there I was, straight from Paris, where among other things
I'd been to the premiere of Almodóvar's *La mala educación.* I'm
telling you, *mon ami:* it was a tiny cinema, a typical Parisian premiere, the hall packed with queens, and all of them acting simply
scandalously! They were swooning and simpering, asking each
other for the smelling salts. They insisted that the film was all about
them, and that they couldn't bear to watch any more. They were
camping it up in French, copulating, singing! I'm telling you – compared with them, we're just a bunch of girl guides!

## Paula and Her Men

'You have no idea, my dear Michalina, what a huge role has been played in my life by the gesture of a hand being taken. My hand, that is. How my entire life is shaped by it, how it returns in the most extraordinary moments. A man, taking me by the hand, leading me somewhere.'

Paula is sitting on the blanket, wearing her enormous white hat. We're telling each other things we've always avoided before, despite our knowing each other for fifteen years.

'The first time it happened to me I must have been six years old. There was a real rascal who lived locally. He had jug ears, red hair, freckles, protruding shoulder blades, bulging eyes... Everything about him was bulging and leering... He was the worst student; he was already going to school, in fact. The little queen who was the caretaker at the school once told me how this rascal climbed up the tall pole they used for flying flags during assemblies, in the middle of the sports field. Crowds came and begged him, Get down from there, Andrzej! Get down! The school nurse, the teachers, nothing worked. All he did was dig in his heels and laugh through those yellow teeth of his, the huge gaps between them, his shoulder blades sticking out, his ears sticking out, everything sticking out all over! The pole swayed to the left, then to the right. He refused to climb down. That's how he was. Later he told me the story from his point of view, how he'd watched them all from up there.

'I recall that time in my life as being truly remarkable. I remember the marshes and some crossroads with the Virgin Mary. That was when I committed the sacrilege – I took the statue off a roadside shrine and it turned out to be hollow, like a "Virgin Mary Bottle" with a screw-on head, attached to the floor by a rusty wire. Good, good, I thought, the spell is broken... Then suddenly a lizard scurried out of the statue right into my hand...

'Well, getting back to the story. Hands. Right. So anyway, the rascal said to me: "Listen, let's run away." And I had this picture I'd cut out of *Przekrój* or some other magazine of Antarctica. So our plan was to run away to Antarctica. He asked me if I by any chance knew where Antarctica was? And I said, probably not far. But where? On the other side of the marshes, no doubt.

'We had to run away at night. I must have felt subconsciously aroused to be running away to Antarctica with a rogue like him. I brought a half-kilo of sausage, a warm sweater, and so on. We agreed to meet near the shrine, the one with the lizard. I slipped out of the house. And we started off, unnoticed by anyone, for the woods, and all of a sudden he offered me his hand – a gesture that brooked no resistance – so that we'd make it through the marshes faster. The woods were on the other side of the marshes, which I was horribly afraid of walking through. But he gave me his coarse and furtive hand, and was my guide. Then, when we reached the very middle, in absolute darkness, he told me that we probably wouldn't make it to Antarctica; we both knew we weren't really up for it and were having second thoughts. So we started heading back. And all of a sudden he told me that he'd brought me there to kill me. I stood there, petrified. He wouldn't let go of my hand; he kept squishing it until our fingers were slick with sweat. And so we stood there, for a very long time. And he said:

"'It's going to suck you in. We'll wait until the marsh sucks you in." I started to cry. It seemed like it would never end… He said:

"'Now I'm going to drown you…" Then, when I began to sink into the marsh, he said once again:

"'Give me your hand…" And he clutched my hand tightly, as if he wanted to both drown me and reassure me at the same time.

'It wasn't until day started to break that search lights came towards us, and they discovered us just standing there in the marsh, which doesn't seem dangerous at all to me now… Maybe people just called it a marsh, but actually it was just marshy terrain, not anything you could get sucked down into. Who knows. Later on, I was at this camp in Czechoslovakia…

'It was one of those communist camps with barracks made out of plywood. But it was paradise for me. I was fifteen by then, and the entire boys' side of the camp was in a homosexual frenzy. Constantly. They'd go up to each other, for example, and just start rubbing each other and groaning. They'd organise these mock orgies every night. Everyone paired off with someone else, and every night it was someone different. We slept on the floor, on pallets, and on the 'bunker', that is, on the very top bunk of the bunk beds. And just as I spent that summer sleeping by turns with a bit of rough on the ground, with a nobody on the first floor, and with a metaphysical poet up top, so too would all the men who would later come into my life belong to one of those three categories. You know, from the monkeys – the pure, standard-issue grunt libido – through to something more or less quotidian, all the way to the acme of romantic love. Naturally I remember the one from the ground best; the one in the 'middle', the ordinary one, I've forgotten entirely. So anyway, that first day I was sleeping with the one on the floor. He said to me:

"'Hey, you're the one I'm fucking today." I didn't say a thing. He lay on top of me and started rubbing. Everyone laughed; it was all a kind of in-joke. There was a certain young queen there, too. My God, was there anyone she didn't do! And how she protested! She was wearing white briefs from Pewex. And this is how it was: I was lying there on the ground with that young grunt, in a sleeping bag, with a quilt under us, and she was right across from us on the lower bunk. And the things she was doing with that arse of hers! Twisting it left and right, so the grunt on the bottom and the poet up top could see, too.'

But wait, what was it that Wojtek kept saying to her? Paula falls into her thoughts and pulls out a cigarette; she rests her head in her palm. 'You know what, I can't remember. But she blathered something about turning the lights out; maybe she thought it really would lead to something? Now I remember what happened, but you can't write this down. Please no! Don't! Cross it all out, I mean it! Now I remember everything, of course.'

'Yes?'

'Well, that Wojtek with the poofter was more my… than my lad on the floor, who was already groping me; so I pulled a little maneuver, fired off some aphorism or other, and we switched. The little

231

queen in the white Pewex briefs went down to the ground floor, and I went up to the first-floor bunk with Wojtek. Eventually everyone fell asleep and lights out. And what happened with Wojtek, well, that was for real.'

'Are you serious?'

'Of course, you loon!' Paula laughs. 'What do you think? The true course of our life is love, but our element-engendered body… Those top-shelf poets didn't stand a chance against the first floor…

'Everywhere it smelled of youthful sweat, of plywood, and paint… The odour of grunt. The next day I slept on the first-floor bunk. With a "mid-level one", a "middle of the road". A nobody. And the third day – I was up on top with a lad who read his poems to me all night! Exactly as expected. You know: long hair, sensitive… *Nix*. I even experienced that gesture of my hand being taken, too. Since there was going to be some recitation competition or ceremony in someone's honour. I was singled out as a star, of course, because I'm a humanist. But I rebelled; I refused to memorise the poem (by Gałczyński). I sat in the cafeteria, furious at the world, my soup getting cold in front of me; everyone had already left, and my tears drizzled into the bowl. Then that grunt from the floor, the big, uncomplicated one with the broken nose, came up to me…

'"Hey, what's wrong, Paweł? What happened? Don't worry, everything'll be just fine." And he stroked me. I sat there, upset, so he'd keep on doing it. My nose was running, a tear welled up; I lowered my eyes and prayed in my heart of hearts that he would take me in his arms and console me. He continued:

'"You don't have to play football with us if you don't want to; I'll look after you…" Then he took my hand in his and talked to me like I was his tart:

"'Come on Paweł, let's go to the woods and rehearse…'"

'I just sat there, sniveling and looking at my nails, since a growing girl needs that kind of manly warmth and tenderness. And just so he would offer me his coarse, masculine hand and squeeze me, hard, oh so hard! Come to the woods! With me, to the woods, maybe even to the marshes…

'Eventually he led me to the rehearsal, by the hand, like that redhead did when he took me to the marshes, like he wanted to both protect me and kill me… All the queens in the schools and summer camps were scared shitless of those butch studs from down on the ground. They'd belch at us and bully us, but then, after we'd had our little cry, they'd gather round, like they would round an affronted tart, and take us in their arms…

'Anyway, I won the competition; I was the star of the camp. The lad from down on the ground walked round me like a bodyguard, so proud that "our team" had won; that's how they are, those straight bits of rough. He didn't have a clue about poetry, but he honestly felt that "our team" had won something; after all, I was from his house. As for the middle one, I don't remember what he thought about it; but the one upstairs… Well, he swept his hair out of his face with a preoccupied air:

"'Oh right, right… Gałczyński, definitely; he's rhythmic, easy to memorise. Right" – and here he swept back his hair again; oh, how he was always sweeping back his hair! – "*right*. But have you ever tried reciting Stachura, for example?" Exactly.

'The third time, the gesture happened in my lodgings. It was the early eighties, just after I left our manor in M. for school. I boarded in a house that was probably built in the eighteenth century, all red brick. A very barracksy atmosphere. What strange characters lived there… In the toilets for example: mildewy walls, no bathtubs, just shower bases, everybody washing at the sinks. Everybody – except the queens! There was this one queen there. And since there was no bathtub – oh, you'll get a kick out of this, Michał – she'd run water into two of those shallow tubs and lie down in them, legs in one, back in the other, and her dry torso and naked arse in between. And then she'd read a book! She absolutely needed to have a bathtub, with bubblebath and a book, like in the movies. A makeshift Holly-wood in the dormitory! We'd be washing at the sinks, and there she'd be lying, reading in her tubs, every inch the star.

'There was a lad in those lodgings who went to the fine arts acad-emy; he had long dredlocks, piercings up and down his ears. He was always painting me. Then once he squeezed my hand in his and said:

'"Listen, Paweł, how about we don't go to school tomorrow, but instead you sit for me…?"

'Here was a lad from the highest bunk of the bunkbeds. Long hair, makeup. To me, my hair was blonde, but he said he saw plum in it, and I said, "I'm sorry, but there are no plums in my hair…" And he started to laugh and kissed me on my hair; and he smelled of turpentine and mulled wine with cloves and cinnamon!

'But there were the ones from the first floor, too: the ones who washed themselves at the sink, splashing about, the ones from the Railway Mechanics Workshop… who'd fling soap at each other.

'When I was little, our teacher took us on a "career education tour" to that railway workshop. We had to get up at five in the morning for it. I remember the roar of the factory siren, which was absolutely unbearable at that time of day. We were all freezing our arses off; it was late autumn. I rubbed my bloodshot eyes and thought I must still be dreaming. I had visions of grubby men fiddling with the machines, amongst the sleepers, in the grease, in the frost, all morning long. It was still dark, as if those lads had come to work in the middle of the night. With grimy hands they peeled the paper from their ungainly sandwiches of fatty sausage. When they rolled up their shirt sleeves, they revealed deep scars, in rows, as if they'd been made on purpose. Their nails turned black, transformed into little clumps of earth, and disappeared. Somewhere in the foreman's office a radio was quietly babbling some important speech or other. As long as the morning appeared to be night, sleep seemed unnecessary, and it was exciting, such strange things happened at night, but what would happen once the the boring, humdrum day finally broke? That's when I decided to become an actress, and that nothing could make me become a railway mechanic. I enrolled at the House of Culture. The teacher told me: if you study hard, you won't end up in a place like that. The people you see here were all trouble-makers; they bunked off lectures, smoked cigarettes behind the school, and never learned to play piano. But they winked at me not to listen to her. Grimy lads daubed with their Tuesday like a coat of grey dust.

'Then, years later, that gesture came again. I was sitting together with my Filip on All Saints' Eve by Szczytnicki Bridge; we'd lit candles and were drinking vodka. We were looking into the water, which was rising. Over and over a ship's siren kept wailing. Filip hurled the empty bottle against the Odra's concrete levee, and I rose unsteadily to my feet. I said we should walk along the bank, not on the embankment, but along the levee, the sloping levee that leads down to the water. And then (but is that what I wanted?) he took my hand in his, and holding me tight, he began to lead me. Our feet kept slipping on the moss covering that old German cobblestone levee; but we made it to the next bridge, which was too low to stand under, and then we discovered a manhole leading to a cellar under the bridge, and then… and then he took my hand in his once more.

## Paula and Her Phone Calls (I)

Paula still in bed before her first coffee of the day, reading.

Brring-brring-brring!

Who's calling? Oh, it's Rotunda!

'Hey Paula! Inez is here, over from the States!'

'Inez who? Don't bother me, you old bag; I'm in bed reading about Greta Garbo.'

'*Inez*, you nutter, Inez who went to the States before martial law, the one who robbed Jurka from Krzyki. The one who lived with Daria from the Pewex...'

Paula fumes:

'I don't remember her.'

Rotunda responds:

'She's invited the old gang to McDonald's for lunch tomorrow!'

Paula puts down the receiver and gets up, mumbles something under her breath, and goes off to make coffee. She turns on the radio to Channel One. Classical music fills the kitchen.

Paula with her first cup of coffee behind her. Sunday morning, in the distance the sound of bells ringing. Brring-brring-brring! It's Anna.

'Your line is always engaged, Annie. What a chatterbox you are!'

'It's always engaged because I've been ringing up all my friends. But listen, I've just got the new ranking of the Wrocław queens at Stage. None of the old names are there. What happened to them? Where are they now? The names are all different now – Esthers and Pamelas… You and Michalina La Belletriste aren't even mentioned! The only consolation is that your sister here came in thirtieth. And now, listen to what the cards told me this morning: Cruising Central will undergo a renaissance. Except it will be the same old faces meeting there again. Everyone will come back. It'll be like the old days. I can't say any more about it. And the cards don't say when it will happen either… Paula?'

'Yes?'

'Can I come visit you in Wrocław?'

'Of course, Andrzej. Come! By all means!'

'You know what, dear…'

'What?'

'I'd like to rob you… You and that slut Michał…'

'Ha! Ha! Ha!'

'I'd slip truth serum into your soup and rob you blind, I'd say: Bitch, tell me where you hide your money…'

'Ha! Ha! Ha!'

'Tell me or I'll kill you, I'd say! And you'll go off to the picket line in Szczytnicki Park afterwards and go up to one of the biggest gossip whores there and say, "You still remember Anna who went to Bydgoszcz?" And one or the other of them, Grasser Grażyna or the Owl, will say, "Uh huh." And you'll say: "Turns out she's a thief now, emptied out my house and robbed me of a hundred thousand zlotys... The bitch even stole the eggs from my fridge." And then the others – I bet you anything – will all say, "I always knew that one was a thief; that whore had the look of a thief in her eyes! Call the police right away, don't think twice, no mercy for that slag!" How happy that'll make them!'

'Ha! Ha! Ha! Oh God, Annie, the things you come up with!'

'Paula, you know why that whore Michał is writing a book about us, don't you?'

'Why?'

'Because he thinks the grunts will read it, that they'll be moved by our story and feel sorry for us, and kindly offer to let themselves be sucked off. They'll say, "So much fuss over that cock of ours! Well, here you go, Michał, have a go..." And that slag will go off on reading tours on military bases, and she'll be doing grunts all over Poland, and we won't get any, even though the stories are all ours! She's a high-class lady now. She won't be joining you on excursions to the park like she used to, oh no, that would involve her getting herself dirty... Come on, we'll rob her for it or drag her name through the mud...'

'Since when does grunt read books... I mean, the book's supposedly all about blowjobs.'

'Right, a thousand poems about shelling peas... But you know she's already counting her money, just look at her profile; even though the Witkowskis converted, why, she could just as easily be a girl on the streets of Tel Aviv... There's an ahash – racha – bash for you... She can count her money, all right. Can she ever!'

'Michał's a Jewess?'

'Just smell her breath sometime... There's no question about her nationality. If you don't drop dead first! She reeks so strongly of garlic it'll make you hallucinate… I'm serious… An absolute slag, that one.'

'Annie! You know what, I ran into Radwanicka on the picket line!'

'May heaven help you!'

'I think she's very nice.'

'Well, I think that slag already found out you have a huge flat and rooms available, and now she's going to butter you up – and down!'

Paula hangs up the phone and begins to brood. Cruising Central, that was one of several picket lines. What were the others? The Beaux Arts, the General Bem… And now they're back in fashion? Paula rolls her eyes and shakes her head.

# Mock-Grunt

Paula says:

What is the world coming to? Everything's going to the dogs. There I am walking in the park, I look over: a grunt. This one was a real bull, his face, arse, everything. You wouldn't figure him for a homo in a million years. Just your typical straight man, but he's walking through the bushes, so I follow him. After all, a stud like that doesn't come along every day; there wasn't an ounce of the poofter in him, as far as I could tell. Right? Classic grunt. He unfastens his fly and I kneel down. All well and good. But then I felt something touching me, and there he was, pulling me out and crouching down too – he wanted to go down on me. But I'm the woman here, the bleeding queer, right? And he's supposed to be the grunt! And then he pulls his trousers down to his knees and there… Red lace stockings…! I thought I'd die laughing. I couldn't keep it up of course, but I did make sure I got a good look at everything so I could describe it all for you in detail. I said to him:

'You know, the police are all over this place, it's too much, I'm getting out of here.' And I took off. Really, grunt wearing hold-ups, who ever would have thought…

Now of course everybody knows her; they call her The One With the Stockings. No one could be bothered to invent a special name for her, just The One With the Stockings; sometimes the simplest solutions are the best. But the first time that anyone who didn't know him saw that grunt walk by, they'd all start tailing him immediately; then, later on, after The One With the Stockings started cruising the park officially (top half skinhead, bottom half slapper, like a mermaid or something), they had all already figured out his number and would just say:

'Ha ha ha, what a psycho queen. *Psycho queen!*'

# How Paula Pretended to Be a Grunt in Szczytnicki Park

'Night. I'm sitting there on a bench on the path in the park, smoking a cigarette, pretending to be a grunt. But in my winter cap I looked more like an old woman with a scarf on her head. You would've laughed your head off, Michał. In any case, I stretch out my legs in my jeans as far as I can, dig my Adidases into the dirt, and put on my best grunt face. Like this.' Paula mugs for me; she doesn't look anything like grunt, though she does look a lot like a big old poof…
'I didn't want people to see my cap, so I pulled this very grunty hood over the top, from a shirt with a sports logo on it. So I'm sitting there like that.'

'And exactly why were you pretending to be a grunt, you freak?'

'Anna from Bydgoszcz told me to over the phone. She instructed me to conduct a study of the culture of young queens. I had to sit there a long time because most of the queens already knew me and weren't fooled, but just had a good laugh about it…

'Eventually this young thing turned up, probably straight from the country or a small town. She said she was a student, first-year. Just a bashful little thing, looking up at me like I was the sun, squinting her eyes. You could see right away she took me for grunt! I saw

a caricature of myself, the way I am with grunts, bowing and scraping… And I started to hate her! The more queens are alike, the more
they can't stand each other; and that's why I should have risen above
it, gone back to my normal self, and squelched the hatred inside me.
But princess was absolutely clueless, and she simpered at me with
her girlish voice:

"'You were here a couple of days ago… I recognise you… You
were walking with someone else, a friend… I recognise your
hoodie…"

'She took me for someone else, genuine grunt, which was probably why she didn't look at me very closely. She must have spent her
nights groaning and rubbing herself raw for that bit of rough! Eventually she said:

"'I live in the halls of residence, know what I mean? I just want
you to know… so I can't host."

'Goodness. I had to stifle my laughter. I mean, who says things
like that to a grunt? What school does that belong to? Whose style?
Not ours, that's for sure!

"'Gotcha…" I said in a low, manly whisper. Her resistance melted,
and she asked me:

"'So what are you into?"

'Well, that was clearly going to get me to confide in her, Vicômte!

"'You'll see," I said. "What about you?" Oh, Michał, that *What
about you?* I only asked that for your sake, so I could tell you about
it later and see you split your sides laughing. For you. I mean, as far
as I was concerned that little queen had already failed the test. But
her answer… Well, she really outdid herself, Vicômte! She recited it
so quickly, and under her breath, as if she was at confession, you

know, like someone embarrassed about something and talking too fast, everything all at once:

'I like kissing on the lips, sucking a penis (only reciprocal, though), nipple play, and all-over body contact...'

'Nipple play! Heavens...! All-over body contact! I told her to go find someone else, picked my arse up off that bench, and got the hell out of there.

'I rang Anna to tell her all about it, and she says to me:

'"This happens because they have no one to teach them... All the old queens have either been murdered or don't go out any more. Who is that little puppy supposed to take as her mentor? How is she supposed to learn? Where are the textbooks? Girls like Baker's Roma and me, why, we had to learn from the ground up; we trained with Uterina, with Poontanga, Culinaria, Zither, all the old mistresses of the art. But young queens now, they don't realise that if that lad really had been grunt, not only would she have never had a chance with him, but he'd have landed his fist right in her face! They don't understand that you just can't say things like that to grunts! Grunt couldn't care a rat's arse about our Brabant laces! You walk up and immediately train your eyes on ground zero, then without a word you open up the grunt's flies, and Bob's your uncle! But this one, with her 'body contact' and all her requirements, 'only reciprocal though'! I'm telling you, Uterina must be spinning in her grave!"

'Anyway, I rang up Zither with the Broken Nose, ancient, emaciated Zither with the Wall Eye. She's poor; she has thyroid cancer; she sits at home all day, taking care of her memories. She goes about like a duchess in a little periwig, the hair all combed upwards. She once performed in Florence at the operetta. With her crooked, broken nose. She spent her whole life dancing, singing, and ambling through Warsaw on her way to Café Amatorska (that must have been during the Stalinist years). She danced with Mazowsze under Madame Sygietyńska. A very cultured girl that one. The younger generation could learn a thing or two from someone like her...'

Paula extinguishes her cigarette with a look of distaste and puts the end in the packet. She purses her lips. Then I begin to tell her about Giselle, so I can contribute something from my own youth as well – except my youth happened in an entirely gay milieu: hardly the place to search for hidden desires, like that taking-by-the-hand of hers. Just flagrantly open ones.

# Giselle

'No-ohhh!' says Giselle, emphasising the second 'o' like a little girl.
'No-oh! This can't go on! We have to do something about it. We
should find some kind of sponsor!'

Her hair was blonde, German: long in back, short in front,
permed, peroxide. In addition, she had a remarkably pretty face, the
face of a sixteen-year-old. She loved Papa Dance and Modern Talking, and dreamed of being famous. She would hang out with me on
a bench in the park, smoking extra strong cigarettes and prattling on
for hours about the band she was going to start, Magic Talking...
And suddenly she 'changed faces' and started singing in a high voice;
she sounded like the background singers, echoes of Modern Talking.
In English. And then it was Dieter Bohlen this, Dieter Bohlen that.
But the truth was an entirely different matter. And she was running
away, hiding from that different truth in Dieter Bohlen.

Giselle was destitute and scrawny, and lived in that part of town
called the Bermuda Triangle. Her boyfriend, a bricklaying lout
named Lech (with a moustache), used to beat her. One day we were
sitting by the pond in the botanical gardens, and she had her prized
possession on her lap: a large, brightly coloured, battery-powered

cassette player. We were listening to her Modern Talking, and she was singing, because at the end of every cassette they had the so-called 'reprises', the instrumental versions of the songs. Hey! Let's all be stars! She was more interested in being Thomas Anders; I had to sing Dieter's part. 'Romeo and Juliet' and other hits. She was always retreating into her dreams, into unreality. How she'd rake it in at the market, or one day just happen on a fat wad of cash. Or how we should go over to the Hotel Wrocław, where we might meet a German or a millionaire. The pinnacle of her dreams was a stereo tower, large as a wardrobe, with the turntable on top; this was back in the eighties.

'And I'd have all my records alphabetised, too, the whole lot of them. Dieter Bohlen, Modern Talking. There, behind glass doors.' All of a sudden Giselle starts making sounds like a train, which is what one of the songs starts off with. She could reproduce a whole disco with her mouth! Boom boom boom, eeh eeh eeh, ooh ooh. Fuh fuh fuh. Ooh – ooh – ooh. Her face changed completely when she started playing her mouth, its drum and bass.

Then all of a sudden that awful Lech turned up, the lout, and he really let her have it, right across her face. He ripped the cassette player out of her hands.

'What fucking time were you supposed to be home, you fucking slag? What time? What fucking time where you supposed to be home, you slag? What fucking...'

He slammed her down on the ground, then threw her into the pond, which was blanketed with water lilies; we'd been sitting the whole time in the botanical garden. But she wouldn't leave him; she loved him. And you couldn't tell her a thing.

A million times I must have said to her:

'Giselle, come to your senses, dump him. He hits you, he beats you up...' And she'd always say:

'But he can be really gentle, too. When he's sober.'

There's a queen for you.

Eventually she said to me:

'We have to scrape some money together somehow; I can't do this any more!' We walked through the night. Back then, it was always night; we only ever hung out at night, wandering around Wrocław, straying into unknown neighbourhoods, ducking into courtyards. She came from a bad family, and I was from a good one, but I was sick of school, of family dinners, of reading. Of having to hear how I fraternised with the dregs of society and was sullying myself in the gutter. She lived in Traugutt Street; I was in Baciarelli. Another world entirely. I spent the day in school, she in her broken home. Nights we spent together. I'd tell my parents I was off to the discotheque. And with Giselle it really was non-stop disco; she couldn't help but sing, make noises. And in my memories of that time it was always and forever night. The night of my youth, of my fifteen years of age. So we needed to scrape some money together. But where? At a hotel, of course; where else could you do that in 1989, when communism was already finished and capitalism had yet to begin? At the Hotel Panorama, which has since been demolished to make way for the Dominican Shopping Centre; at the Hotel Wrocław. The get-up she had on, all second-hand! A green jacket and a sweatband made of brightly coloured rags on her head. Pink leggings. Blue eyes. Scars on her arms and her angelic little voice and blonde eyelashes. We would sit in the lobby. We'd sit there, smoking Extra Strongs, and maybe Carmens, too, which we'd buy just for the occasion… Elderly German lady pensioners would walk by with their leather bags, grey-haired, no makeup on, a far cry from the world of the disco. A far cry from 'Strangers in the Night'. We pressed our little noses against the glass wall of the drinks bar; we must have made a fine sight. But there was nobody inside – the German lady pensioners weren't interested in partying. Defeat across the board.

At least we knew a queen who worked at the Panorama. She was a toilet lady, so you could always have a slash for free, fix yourself up. This fashion designer was supposed to come by. Hey, Giselle, let's tell him we want to do an article on him for the school newspaper… He was gay. He started buying us drinks at the bar… He'd say things like:

'One more shot for Babycakes here!'

Giselle clambered on to the bar stool, which was much too high for her. But nothing came of it. The designer had to catch a train that night to get to a show in another city. Giselle let herself go, went about unwashed, drunk. And she had such an innocent little face, I still remember it clearly; such blue eyes. And she could make such amazing noises. And all those times she played Alexis…

One night we met this bloke who told us he was going to start up a wholesale company in Legnica; back then everyone was starting up something or other. He told us we could work there, we'd earn three million a month, it was a sure thing. Three million – that was a leather jacket every month! Something none of us could even dream of. I saw one at the market once, leather patches stitched together, a patchwork jacket. That's twelve jackets a year!

'You're a lost cause, Giselle. Are you stupid or something? If each of us buys a jacket the first month, you won't need to buy a new one the next – get something else, cowboy boots or something!' And we looked at each other, grasped each other's hands and squealed in delight: only now did we realise what we had to look forward to!

'Right! Cowboy boots! And later on we can have gold bracelets!'

'Swear to me,' Giselle said one night, in the park, 'swear to me, you silly goose, that we'll always be together and that life and everything will always be really amazing! Swear on your mother's life!'

We went with this bloke to his flat, an old, ugly flat crammed with dusty antiques and rubbish. In an old building, in a shabby part of town, not far from where Giselle lived... In the morning, he sent us out for vodka with coins he'd shaken out of a little vase, to which we had to contribute our share. I still have this image in my head: Giselle that morning in his bath. In the bubbles. She was calling me, covering herself with the bubbles, and which shampoo would you use, if you were me, to wash my hair, this one or that one or that one. Oh, go and listen at the door, silly, and see if he's standing on the other side. No. Then she went all gasps and giggles, spraying herself with whatever she could find, rummaging through everything.

And then for a long, long time, nothing. The bloke never called. But he'd given us the address for the wholesaler.

'He fucked us over.'

Giselle was eating candy floss under the stars.

We were sitting on the back of a bench. We kept fiddling with a sunflower, nibbling on this and that. Giselle scratched a scab off her knee and licked the blood, I spat tobacco and poked at it with a stick.

When she gouged under her long fingernails with a match to get the crud out, I chewed mine. When she bit and tore the skin off her lips, I didn't even notice because I was busy sticking a wad of gum under the bench, then scratching. Then she pulled out a little bottle of counterfeit perfume called Made in France and sprinkled herself with it. Then I started to scratch my thigh.

'Maybe everything really will be different. Think about it: cowboy boots, leather, gold necklaces, L'Oréal shampoo!'

We took the train to Legnica, or was it Trzebnica. To the address he'd given us. We wandered about in the sweltering heat. We sat on a low wall and drank mineral water; we blundered between the garages…

At last we found it! An old villa, stairs. A woman in a tracksuit opened the door.

'Does Mr So-and-So live here? We were expecting to find a wholesale company.'

'Yes, he lives here, but he's not here at the moment; and it didn't work out with the wholesaler's. Maybe next year. Would you like to leave a message?'

'Umm… Umm, maybe you could tell him… that Grzesiek and Michał were… 'cause of the wholesale company…'

We hitchhiked back. It was raining, pouring. Giselle laid her head on my shoulder and fell asleep, rocked by the swaying lorry. I never saw her again; I stopped hanging out with her. Not just her – with all of them.

# The German Old Dears: The Revenge

What? Like I'm going to bother! I'll be fucked if an old whore like me has to *hunt* for a chemist, one that hasn't any customers or tourists or queues, or that's out of the way; I'll go to the biggest one in the very centre of town, right next to Neptune Square. Hello, excuse me, I desperately need something for my pubic lice, something strong, to nuke every last one of those little bitches off my fanny! Chuck together a bit of this and a bit of that, and make me a mix of pine tar and spices, medicinal lovage, pharmaceutical rue!

No sooner do I reach the promenade than some Old Dears from Germany sink their claws into me. Vicious. Every last one of them wearing cream-coloured orthopaedic clogs, cream-coloured anoraks, brown trousers… All individualism scrubbed out of them with soap and water. Hair cropped short, grey. No makeup at all, just daubed with affectation. Naturally they came from the former GDR. Jolly, elderly ladies. They'd had it drilled into them over the years never to stand out, always to obey power and do what the bosses at work told them to do: no talking back, no thinking for themselves – just perform! After work, it was off to the allotment graciously provided by the Party. It would be hard to expect any individualism now in their clothing, in their behaviour. All they care about is whether they're normal. Are those pearl earrings she put on too large? Maybe she should take them off in the toilet? Maybe they're inappropriate? It's especially hard to expect them to change now, in their old age. Which – because of the high standard of living in Germany today – has been prolonged. But it's even more hideous and conspicuous as a result.

It was just such an agitated group that waylaid me on the promenade and asked, in German, about a Hotel Grunwald.

'Have you heard of it?' They'd been searching since morning, had already reserved the room and paid the deposit over the phone before they left. They repeat it, loudly and clearly to make sure I'll understand: 'Hotel Grrrrunvald!' – boiling the 'r' in the back of their throats.

I knew there couldn't be a hotel by that name in Międzyzdroje because most of those types of conveniences were actually meant for Germans. Someone was taking the piss out of them, and was having a little joke with the name, too. Not the first time Grunwald had spelled bad luck for the Germans...

## Lindane, Please!

But they couldn't get it into their grey heads that somebody could do something like that. When I turned away, they immediately started grilling the next passers-by. Who merely shrugged their shoulders. And I was off to the chemist's. A queue of holiday-makers; it was clear at once that the straights had sent their birds off to stand in a queue while they watched the football. A few of them had screaming brats in their arms; others, it was clear, were childless, and had only come for some tanning oil. 'I'm here for tanning oil, I'm here for tanning oil, too!' I shouted to myself, but repeated, so I wouldn't forget: *Lindane! Lindane! Lindane!* Unfortunately – I said to myself – you already have more than enough tanning oil... A sizeable queue had formed behind me, a potential audience in case I blew it. A young, bleached-blonde thing behind the counter. I was seized by dreadful anxieties: how to make sure no one else overheard me; whether for her the word 'Lindane' meant only one thing: you have crabs, you're infected! And her all pure and hygienic like that, like an Apothecaress. But I concocted something, and when I arrived at the front of the queue, I said in a relaxed voice:

'Lindane, please. It's for my child...'

She wouldn't give it to me. She insisted that for head lice in children another remedy was needed, a kind of shampoo. I bought it without arguing and left. I walked to the next chemist's.

'Lindane, please!'

'What for?'

'For lice.'

'Head lice?'

'Y... yes...'

She gave me a bottle of shampoo, the same kind as before. I bought it. I went to a third (and last) chemist's shop. A queen I knew from the beach, one of the Poznanites, came in and stood in the queue behind me. I was like:

'A bottle of suntan lotion, please.'

I bought it, and walked away from the queue. Then the queen behind me goes up to the counter and says:

'Can you please give me something for pubic lice?'

'Lindane?'

'That's fine.'

'Here you go. Sixteen zlotys, eighty-five.'

# Oleśnicka

Just as boredom was setting in, when my Old Dears were starting to repeat themselves, I glanced over and: Oh, I hope that's who I think it is! A little dog in the distance was waddling towards us, all dressed up, a Pekinese, and farther on, a limping little roly-poly. I'm thinking: I hope to God that's Oleśnicka, I'm not asking for much, just please let that be Oleśnicka's Pekinese!

Please let that be Oleśnicka! Please let that be her – fat, crippled, short, simultaneously bald and bleached blonde – and her dog, a dog who'd broken the record for pissing on trees, having spent his whole life in parks, on picket lines. That dog had urinated on every single picket line in Poland, on each and every tree, and here he was pissing on all the plants on his way towards us! Please let that be Oleśnicka's little dog, who had done his time in the cruising grounds of Bydgoszcz, Toruń, Kalisz, Suwałki, Zgierze, Wrocław, Warsaw, Poznań, Olsztyn and Kraków, everywhere peeing, pissing, passing water, piddling, relieving himself, urinating, micturating on the trees; because if it *is* him (or rather: her, since she was all dressed up in a bow tie and rhinestones – a little queen-dog), then that roly-poly human companion would have to be Oleśnicka, and that would spell hope, a light at the end of the tunnel, an end to this boredom, to this ennui, because then our story would get a shot of new energy!

And indeed, it was no other: Oleśnicka in the flesh.

'Hey girls, having fun? I flew in on my broomstick when I heard Kangaroo was in town, that bitch! Have you seen her yet? You know, they call her Kangaroo because she used to live in Australia, and still gets an Australian pension...'

My Old Dears blanched; they'd realised they were talking to none other than the infamous Oleśnicka, whose name was known throughout Poland from the graffiti in trains and railway station toilets. Who was gossiped about in the cells of prisons. Trash-talked about all night in the wards of hospitals, where the chanteuses did their national service. Throughout the years of communism she'd been second in line, right after Lucia La Douche. But now, ever since that grunt killed Lucia with a curling iron, she's the No. 1 Queen for life in all of Poland. The Old Dears fell at her feet. I, too, fell. With a majestic gesture Oleśnicka bade us rise and asked us if we hadn't seen that tart Kangaroo, because she'd nicked (an uglier phrase was used) twenty zlotys from her.

'She was here at the start of June, shagged herself out, and left.'

'What about Georgette?'

'That banshee hasn't shown her face around here yet.'

'We haven't seen her since last year. She's stuck in her parish.'

'Earned a reputation round here, must be going to Rowy now... They don't know her there yet.'

## The Toilet Lady from Oleśnica

And then Oleśnicka takes a bottle of vodka out of her satchel and in the good old park-bench tradition wraps it in a plastic carrier bag. Then she offers us some, maybe with a Popular or a Strong, and maybe another sip; she wipes the neck off with her fist and drinks with us. For the chaser she pulls out two litres of artificially coloured and flavoured shite, the cheapest thing she could find at Frog Mart. For her, getting drunk meant escaping into madness, escaping her miserable fate. She barks:

'Angelica! Get over here!'

Angelica is off rooting in the dunes, looking for a shag. I hustle Oleśnicka for a story, and in the shadow of the afternoon, sipping her vodka and chaser from mugs emblazoned with the face of Old Dear No. 1, she tells me the following:

'Times certainly have changed... A few nights ago I went out cruising on my own, back home in Oleśnica. I gave the toilet lady two zlotys and wrote graffiti about myself above the urinals: "Bożena is a whore. Bożena is a slut..." and signed it "Bożena, age 40". I walked out and whispered to the toilet lady:

259

"'Excuse me, ma'am, do you realise that three homosexuals are sitting in there?'"

'And what do you think she says?

"'Oh, I know, they warned me when I started working here, I know all about it. I have so much trouble with them…" And after a moment she shooed the air with her hand. "They can sit in there all day, for all I care."'

# The Lorca Expert

Save your breath, the blankets have already been pulled together; ours is the main one, making a Bald Mountain of sorts, a sabbat for all the witches tonight, ooh, it seems they're preparing for St John's Eve... For the moment, however, it's still daylight, though we're all sitting there listening to Oleśnicka as if we were gathered round a bonfire, or rather, as if the fire itself had summoned us there with its story...

Then Madame speaks up:

'I was on the bus, on my way back from Sobótka to Wrocław, and this boy gets on, cultured, young, nice-looking. Not drop dead gorgeous or anything, but a nice lad. Well, one thing leads to another, and after an hour he tells me he's gay.

'"I'm telling you," he said, "because I feel as if I can trust you." I hadn't said anything to him, but he already knew. We got to Wrocław, and he says:

'"Come on, let's go to a bar and have a beer."

'"No, why do we always have to sit in bars, drinking beer, with all that smoke. We should just go to Ostrów Tumski if all you want to do is chat. We'll buy some beers, find a bench with a view of the

Odra." They've renovated all those nineteenth-century benches; it looks like they've even put up gas streetlamps there.

'So there we were, sitting, drinking, him going on about poetry and Lorca (*Lorca*, remember that), you know, a cultured lad. *Nix*. I go off to have a slash in the bushes and come back, we drink another beer, and I start feeling a bit drowsy; I still remember saying something like "This beer is making me really sleepy".

'I wake up to the phone ringing. I'm in my own bed, it's Małgosia calling. I was supposed to be at her place for lunch – three days ago. What happened to me? I'm thinking:

'"Just a second, just a second… There's something I need to get sorted here…" I sat up in bed. All at once everything flashed before my eyes. The whole sequence of events. Good Lord, he must have slipped something in my beer when I went off to pee – I'd left my beer on the bench! My flat had been cleaned out, of course. Later on, the police found out that he'd cashed three cheques for a thousand each under a false name, an identity he'd also stolen. Naturally he signed them all with my name, but nobody at the post office bothered to verify the signature, even though they had mine on file in their computer.'

## Kangaroo

'Kangaroo once took this grunt home, a bloke named Shogun, who stole her passport. No big deal. She reported it to the police, blah blah. They got her a new one, and she forgot all about it. All of a sudden, years later, Kangaroo was taking a trip to Turkey, to meet Turks. As a rule, the worse off a country is, the better the cock. The more they violate human rights, the less they violate the right to cock. Cuba's the best as far as that goes.

'They detained her at the border, your passport please, blah blah. She handed them the new passport. Oh the looks they gave her! "Oh. My. God! Me. Kangaroo. Wanted for murder. An international criminal! That is, until I started camping it up and said to them, 'Oh beat me! Beat me, Mister Customs Officer!'"

'Later, when she'd got back from Turkey, she says to me:

'"Can you even imagine what this means? I shared a bed with that passport-stealing grunt, and that means I slept with a murderer, an internationally wanted man! An Al Capone! A mafioso killer! He was amazing; I couldn't be any happier about that matter of the passport!"

'Back on the Ukrainian border, they tackled her to the ground, and dragged her off the coach. The other tourists all looked at her in horror, of course, and the things she must have been spouting, swishing it up as usual (if I know her, she'd been knocking it back a bit on the coach). All those stories she made up about being in prison, and went around telling everyone, how all the convicts raped her, and so on (that she was locked up, I know is true). Anyway, the story was that the grunt was some kind of big shot among villains, and he'd been using her passport; he got caught for something, escaped, but they had a record of it, to search for so-and-so for such-and-such. But that's not the least of it. You know what Kangaroo is like, what a diva she is, what a madwoman. The scene she made during the interrogations... Just imagine:

"'I fall at your feet, I beg you! Please don't kill me, for I am innocent! It's Kangaroo, Kangaroo from the picket line! I let that grunt into my home, and he stole my passport...'"

## Kangaroo's Prison Tales

'That much may have been true. The rest was probably all made up: how she languished in prison for three weeks before the truth came to light, how an unknown woman in a niqab passed her cosmetics through the bars in her window so that Kangaroo wouldn't go to pot during her confinement. You believe that?'

'No.'

'Oh sure, she was in a cell with a murderer who drank her perfume, and sure, she gave everybody blowjobs – all she wants is to make people jealous. But you know how she is. She goes off to Turkey and comes back saying things like:

'"I did the Turks, all of them! They're so desperate for it there, their women have to be virgins until they are married (and then, on their wedding night, once they have their cherry well and truly popped, the men hold the bloody rag up for all and sundry to look at). They can't even ask women out on a date, so all we had to do was stand on the hotel balcony, and there on the next balcony across some Turkish workers were busy, so we gave them a little show" – here Kangaroo demonstrates: she licks her finger, preens herself, pokes out her tongue and pulls it back in – "and they made gestures with their eyes towards a shack. We looked out on to a narrow court-yard; shops backed on to it, there was rubbish, leftover flowers, fruit and fish – a regular Campo dei Fiori – and there was this shack there, and they kept looking over at it, they wanted us to go there that night."

'And everything would have been fine, and we could have broken open our piggy banks for the trip and had something to live off, but unfortunately there was a flaw: the story was coming from Kangaroo, and you can't believe a word she says, and it's not worth dragging your arse all the way to Turkey to check, only to find out she was lying, making it all up, having us on with that nonsense of hers… And now the little crook's nicked a twenty from me.'

Madame: 'But let me finish my story about that bloke with the Lorca…'

'All right then.'

## The Lorca Expert: Part 2

'... As soon as I got to the police station they drew my blood to analyse it – "Ah yes, that Lorca expert put 'truth serum' in your drink, sir, the stuff used by Americans in their interrogations; it's against the law. It'll make you do anything." I was terrified: how had I got home? I might've committed acts of murder during that time, and without knowing what I'd done I'd have denied it! The investigation also showed that first he found out my address (I must have graciously blurted it out to him on that bench), left me there, burgled my flat and left the door ajar. I'd then found my way home on my own; the neighbours testified that they'd seen me outside the gate, dumping out the contents of my bag as I looked for my keys; they thought I was drunk. Then they let me in – they looked, and the door to my flat was open. I don't remember a *thing*! Naturally I didn't get one penny of my money back and even had to pay overdraft charges. And then, what a nightmare, those neighbours of mine being interrogated at the police station, a fat lady with an even fatter wart sitting behind the typewriter, not an ounce of understanding or tact, just sitting there with her scratched nail polish, just like during communism, and the whole time she kept saying:

'"Please just stick to the facts, sir! So, you arrived home at ten p.m.?"

'And I said: "I don't know. I was unconscious. That's what my neighbours said."

'And she would say: "So did you or not?" – And then more rubbish, and she writes: *homosexual, Lorca expert.* I say to her: "What?" "Well, that's what you said, sir…" And although the police themselves discovered that "truth serum" in my veins, they hadn't told this woman about it. She still didn't understand a thing I was saying, just that I had "arrived at the premises at or around ten p.m.". Later on it came to light that the Lorca expert had taken almost all of the chanteuses to the cleaners. Flora Trattoria, for instance… And then there was that thing Flora and I called the Mystery Spot…'

'Mystery Spot?'

'When I woke up in my flat, although I'd been robbed blind, the first thing I realised was: he'd been there. And then: I had no clue what had happened. I mean, he could have murdered someone and hidden him in my sofabed. And in the middle of the grey carpet in the hall there was this conspicuous, damp spot. Flora found one on her sheets.'

'Oh my goodness!'

'Exactly! Those idiot police dusted all the doorknobs with white powder as they looked for fingerprints, but they paid no attention at all to those spots…'

## The Man Who Nicked Kangaroo's Passport

It all started very romantically... She picked him up in front of the young offenders' home. Beautiful. Simple as a flick knife. Kangaroo rang me up after the romance had already progressed some ways, happy as a lark. Bah! See what those lads are capable of? He used to write her poetry! Just ordinary little poems, on cards, in long hand, maybe not quite like Lorca, but all the same... Anyway, it turned out later that he really was a major league criminal, a murderer. They called him Shogun; and this Shogun, this murderer, used to write poems about flowers and little birds and butterflies and love to our very own Kangaroo... All they can write about is flowers. Well, it made that whore happy to show off her poems; she'd read them aloud to me over the phone: 'Love – Springtime. To my darling Kangaroo'. I understood everything after she once told me when and where she was going to meet him, and how I should go and watch them from a distance. The essence of grunt: legs up to the heavens, great big bulging packet, straight Roman nose, gently receding hairline, biceps. Words can hardly do justice... He walked over to where she stood under that needle in Szczytnicki Park with a swagger, like a sailor. Right, just like a sailor! Like a tank would walk if tanks had legs! Ten generations of certifiably proven heteronormativity! Eventually I could bear it no longer, and I left my hiding place and said to her:

'What, don't you recognise your girlfriend, Kanga? Why don't you introduce me to your friend here…?' Like it or not, she had to introduce me, and that's when I met him. What was it about his face, his eyes, about the form of him, that had us all fluttering headlong into the flames, even though we knew he was a criminal? I mean, his eyes were almost bulging out of his head. And below each eye protruded the most delicate ridge of flesh. On his cheek he had a scar, and his beard was patchy, and he had such extremely varicose veins on his hands; everything about him was extreme, like something out of a comic book. Exaggerated. For instance, he had sideburns like some Russian Ivan, right out of the nineteenth century; huge ones covering half of his face. Oh *honey*! And how did it all turn out? We ended up at Kangaroo's place. The usual: vodka, beer, I started acting like a rich queen from America; something in my subconscious told me that the more I showed off how much money I had, the more he'd be interested in me. So I took out a hundred zlotys and started squishing it on the floor under my heel, but he shouted at me instead – how dare I throw money bearing the Polish eagle on the ground. He was… what was he now? Some kind of nationalist something or other. Something about respect for our country, our land, our national emblems. But I was wankered, and I ripped up that hundred-zloty note and set it on fire with a lighter, like Nastasya Filipovna. The moment I saw him, those mammoth legs of his, there under the Needle, I had this fantasy: me in the bath, him standing over me, so I could look up at his legs towering like two columns, and pissing. All over my chest and face. And spitting on me. So I whispered in Kangaroo's ear: 'Come on, Kanga, lock the bathroom door, let him drink all the beer, but don't let him in. Don't let him come in! Lock it shut for me, if you've ever liked me even a little bit, if you've ever been my girlfriend! Just lock the fucking door, don't let him near the toilet, don't let him set one foot through that door.' I put the keychain around my neck; Kangaroo lived in an old building, the toilet was in the same room as the bath, and it was all locked shut with a skeleton key. I hung the key over my heart and returned to the living room, where he was taking off his boots. We explained everything to him, and he said:

'OK,' and chewed his gum.

O-K… Two letters that could only sound like WC to me. Now to get him well and truly pissed. Drink up, drink up. What can I say: my dreams were coming true. Kangaroo stood in the bathroom doorway smoking a cigarette, utterly jaded.

A short time passed. I ran into Shogun in town. He was nice enough, I invited him for a drink, offered him a cigarette. I happened to have a fair bit of cash on me. He instructed me to buy him boots, a pair of knee-high combat boots. He led me to the top floor of Podwale, already knowing which ones he wanted, they cost three hundred zlotys, a lot of money at the time. Stupid me, I wanted to impress him so I started throwing my money around, buying both him and myself this, that, and the other. Until I confided in him that I was being called up for army service. He told me not to worry, but to pay a visit to his uncle at the command post; for six hundred zlotys he'd pull some strings and get me passed as unfit for military service. We got in a taxi and rushed off to see the uncle; I was completely pissed, because every time we'd bought something we celebrated with a drink in another posh bar. The taxi turned into an old street in the Bermuda Triangle. He said:

'Wait for me here in the car.' He took my military card and the money and disappeared into the building. I waited, waited. After half an hour the cab driver, who was beginning to squirm, said to me:

'Excuse me, sir, but I don't think your friend is coming back...' Only then did I realise that he'd gone into the front of the building and out the back; but what can you do, those big eyes of his, those big raccoon eyes of his... And after all that he actually had the audacity to go and see Kangaroo and ask her how I was getting on. And to nick her passport. And use it. Years later he slipped this letter under my door, about how he was waiting for me with my military card at the Needle, and only if I came and brought such-and-such amount of money with me would he give it back, and if I didn't show up he had a syringe full of infected blood he'd stick me with... But what can you do, those raccoon eyes of his, those scars on his cheek... I completely ignored the letter, and there were no repercussions, except that I can still see those thighs of his towering over me even now, and I don't regret a thing. So as it turned out, I, too, went with a major thug, a mafia leader... It's just a shame he never wrote me poems, because even today Kangaroo keeps that doggerel of his stored between empty bottles on a shelf in the bar, reading them aloud to anyone who'll listen...

## Doctor Mengele

A deadly poisonous queen, from Oświęcim, she looks like a beaker full of cyanide. And on top of that beaker someone had stuck a pair of round wire spectacles. Skinny, tall, ruddy-freckled. She'd done time for murder, was released early. Now she's here visiting us.

Right away a whole circle coagulates around her on the picket line. The cream of the criminal crop: Radwanicka, Crooked-Nose Jadwiga. I look over: who's the new local saint? Then Patricia whispers in my ear: *Poison!*

'Watch out,' says Patricia. 'Watch your step. That one on the bench over there, she's a horrible, pernicious queen; they call her Doctor Mengele. She's staying with Duckie. Go and have a look, but don't say a word, just listen, because you never know... she gets into your head, I mean, she can really fuck you up.' She was wearing glasses and really did look like Doctor Mengele, blonde hair – a Nazi on our bench! She was telling a story, sorting out some business with Duckie there, something about money, about cock...

Then that Stallion, that Shogun of yours, came over, the lot of you creaming your pants over him, and started whispered something to Doctor Mengele. Psst-psst-psst. In her ear. Then she stood up and said:

'Excuse me, but I must leave now. I must go to the railway station.'

A saccharine-poisonous smile spread across her face.

Patricia whispered to me:

'See, they've arranged a rendezvous. And now he'll follow her there. Oh honey, if that Shogun of yours knows Doctor Mengele that's even more reason to give him a wide berth!'

## The Mysterious Blond in the Black Sombrero

Those words revived Old Dear No. 2, who then came out with a story about something that happened to a chanteuse she knew from Tczew, who met a beautiful man at the train station, a blond, dressed all in black, a swashbuckler even, with a black hat on his head…

'They call it a *sombrero*. Of course that queen started straight off trying to seduce him. He walked over to her (which was already creating suspicion, a lad like him with that old queen) and gave her a sob story, something about just missing his train and how there wouldn't be another one until the next day, so maybe they could buy a bottle of vodka and sit on a bench in the park and drink it… She was beaming, of course, absolutely smitten, and – just as he planned it – she said to him:

'"Why a park bench? Why on earth a park bench, when I live right around the corner?"'

We all laughed; Old Dear No. 2 curtseyed and, satisfied, continued.

'Of course he agreed – going to someone's home was just what he was waiting for. They bought the vodka and headed back, an old building, like the ones they have on the wrong side of the station in

Tczew. Just picture the two of them: him, young and beautiful; her, old and utterly flaming. They drank. Later, they had coffee. She pulled out some cake and offered it to him. Super. He ate the cake, drank the coffee. He said:

"'Wow, this coffee's great!" – at this everyone laughed – "What kind of coffee is it? Could I beg another cup?" That chanteuse was beaming from ear to ear, not only was he beautiful, but he fancied her coffee, too: oh I really made a good call there, she thought, from now on I'm only ever buying Celmar. So she went to the kitchen to make another pot, and did herself up again. She came back with the coffee, beaming from ear to ear. They sat and drank; and of course she fell sound asleep, because he'd slipped some crap into her cup while she was gone. She fell asleep; it was some kind of sleeping pill, not truth serum or anything. And as soon as that queen was completely out of it he punched her in her face with all his strength, and broke something; she flew out of her chair into a corner of the room, and only then did she lose consciousness. That was it. When the queen woke up her flat had been cleaned out of course. She went to the police and they laughed at her. (We did, too.)

"'Oh, not him again, we booked him for theft in '85 and again in '90... Hey, Wacław, Krzysiek, can you go over there, I somehow... I don't feel like it... It's that bloke again, the one who's always getting robbed...'"

We split our sides laughing – although we were laughing through our tears, because this was our fate, too, this was our fate...

'But "Blackie" had made a mistake. Because the first thing the police did was order a copy of the telephone bill, and there it was! In plain sight! Calls to number such-and-such on such-and-such a day at one in the morning, two calls to Ełk! What happened was he'd rung up his *wife*. Right? Maybe he'd wanted to tell her the operation was a success or something. At any rate, there was a confrontation down at the police station; they presented our queen with ten blonds all dressed in black, standing behind one of those two-way mirrors. Anyway, the queen goes right up to the second to last, that one there. Right. He got three years in prison. But the queen moved away, she was afraid he'd retaliate. She was so nice, too; really lovely that one...'

The Apothecaress had had quite enough:

'Well I, for one, would absolutely love it if some nice bloke saw me on the street and came over and fell in love with me on the spot. Where's the harm in that? It happens to plenty of people... Why shouldn't it happen to me too? A bloke who'd stand there and be overwhelmed with emotion! And not rob me blind... I mean, to hear you talk, you'd think that as soon as someone shows any interest at all, I mean someone nice, the minute he flirts with you, flatters you, it's not because he loves you, but because he's just a thief or a murderer...!'

## The Nice Guy

I'm walking through the dunes again. I look over, and there on top
of a hill my Nice Guy is standing, the one who disappeared on me
when he committed Mistake No. 18. He's put down his rucksack,
taken off his jeans, and is brandishing his stick, smiling at me, oh,
what a beautiful smile! So I cast a sympathetic glance at him and
continue walking leisurely down the empty (it would seem), well-
trodden path between the dunes. And then I hear that Nice Guy
walking behind me, step by step, catching up. So I slow down, light
a cigarette. And all of a sudden, what do I see walking down that
track between the dunes towards me? It's Eugenia with her monkey
friend, shouting in the distance: '*Alo! Salut! sunt eu, un haiduc...*'
and so on, like in the song. I'm thinking, what do I do? They'll scare
him off, they will. But if I don't stop, don't talk to them, they'll figure out immediately that I'm trying to pick up the lad behind me,
my Nice Guy. But it's not like I can just whisper 'Begone!' at them.
And then my Nice Guy passes me by with a stony face; he keeps
walking and vanishes over the horizon together with the sun... o
my Sun, my Helios! The two gazelles start up:

'Hi! We're on our way back to Międzyzdroje, we went to Świnoujście, but they don't have those rings any more. They say it'll be sunny and warm tomorrow…'

Ah well:

*Que sera sera…*

And so instead of an orgasm, all I got was a bottle of warm Pepsi.

## Jessie

'But that's just the beginning,' says Oleśnicka, rubbing her hands together. 'Now it's time to light the bonfire, because today is St John's Eve and I'm having a witches' sabbat here, like on Bald Mountain.' And she orders her decked-out little pooch to go and gather twigs and sticks from the dunes and bring them back to our hollow. We, too, spread out, and one by one return with blackened logs so we'll have something to sit on. Thank God the night's going to be warm, tranquil; even the sea is like a mirror, and a swim would be nice. Hey! I'm swimming in the water, it's warm, I'm skinny-dipping! The water's amazing. Lying on my back, I can see that the fire's been lit, and they're all flying in now, maybe even on broomsticks. The air smells of salt, my hair is wet, Oleśnicka's dog is splashing on the shore, about to swim out to me… Suddenly I feel something in the water! I feel something in the water! Something strange, a slimy body! I feel something. A ghost? A drowned body? Angelica starts howling like a queen who's been cursed and turned into a dog! Christ, it's Jessie! She's come back, surfaced from the depths of hell!

Of course. Jessie's back to avenge herself. It's because, though she's played an integral role in all these stories, she hasn't been mentioned for, um, polite reasons. So it's hardly any surprise that Jessie's bleached her fringe, put on her best blouse, the one with the palm trees (almost new, straight from the USA), laced up her Adidases, the ones with the big, jutting tongues, and headed off for the ball uninvited, a thirteenth fairy godmother.

'Jessica! Old mate!'

'Ibiza! Mallorca! Fat English tourists! What on earth?!' Jessica is beside herself with indignation. Jessica's about to explode. 'Why everything's plastic, American clichés! Look: beaches full of tattooed prettyboys! I'm telling you: plastic, plastic, plastic! Bodies tanned at the solarium, inflated at the gym. Clone faces, they're all identical! Now listen to me: Night, November, the nineteen eighties... Raining, Wrocław-Psie Pole station... Well, this was an entirely different world. Some drunk soldier comes walking by...'

'Ooh, *honey*!'

'... walks into a building in Bierut Street. Entryway reeking of urine, the murky light of a dirty lightbulb. He walks down into the cellar. That was the life! And here you are with your Ibiza! Fun in the sun! Why have you made me come to something out of a travel agent's advert?'

'First, Jessie, this isn't Ibiza – you must be seeing things; it's the Baltic, Lubiewo. And second: get out of the water, will you? Come and join us at the bonfire...' We start walking, and just look at the crowd of people who've gathered! A genuine witches' sabbat! Cora, Anna, the Countess, Baker's Roma...

## Baker's Roma

… was very common and very fat. She worked as an announcer at Central Station. One time she was announcing the train from Wrocław to Kraków and forgot to turn off the microphone. And since Babette was sitting right next to her up there, she was swishing it up to high heaven; the passengers certainly got an earful that day… Those girls were such spoilt brats: they'd see a queen they knew walking through the station and decide to have some fun at her expense, so they'd call her by her (male) name through the megaphone, requesting that she 'come to the station master': paging passenger Jan Kowalski, please *come* to the station *master*, passenger Jan Kowalski…

They'd sit there drinking tea, coffee, vodka, sweet brandy, smoking cigarettes, announcing the trains. And it was as if all that travel rubbed off on them. Oh, look – look who's walking through the hall. They had a camera, and the monitor gave them a perfect view of the entire main hall of Central Station and all the queens traipsing about with their shopping bags. Being envious types, the moment they noticed one of them cruising some grunt or a soldier, ready to chat him up with some folksy pick-up line, they'd page her in a solemn voice. As long as they knew both her name and surname, they'd get on the microphone and say: 'Passenger Jan Kowalski, your presence is requested at the train dispatcher's office. I repeat: Passenger Jan Kowalski, your presence is requested...' And eventually they'd run out of vodka, thanks to partying with all the queens they'd called up there. Every now and then a queen would come up to see them with some grunt she'd just met, and Roma would announce the trains while the grunt fucked her. People used to say, wait, listen to how Roma makes the announcement. If she does it quickly, then nothing's going on, but if she speaks really, really slowly, pausing before every word, then it means her eyes are travelling up and down the text of the announcement as she gets it in the arse.

Roma was so plain and so common that grunt would go with her without hesitating. They understood each other, not like us intellectuals. With us, whenever we talked with a grunt, he would tell us how different we sounded, how we talk like an actor, or a radio announcer, how they felt that they were listening to a radio programme, with all these proper expressions... But Baker's Roma would see a soldier on leave, a guy whom someone better educated would have been incapable of chatting up, and since she was on his level she'd walk right up to that grunt and lisp:

'Eh, soulja...'

'Huh?'

'You from Bsheg? You thtationed in Bsheg?'

And he'd say no, that his unit was stationed elsewhere. And she'd say, Uh-huh, I been there. Then she'd say:

'Hey soulja,' – the way they say it in the country – 'hey soulja, wanna getta drink wiv me?'

And he'd reply, for example, that he was waiting for someone, but that someone wouldn't show up, so she'd take him home, ply him with a sea of vodka, and say:

'Hey soulja, you eat yet?'

And she'd make him a sandwich, heat up some soup, do her laundry... She'd say:

'Soulja, you want I wash sumfin for ya?'

And when she'd got him good and pissed up, she'd say to him just like that, no qualms about it:

'Oh, soulja, soulja, now that you've eaten and drunk your fill, well, you know... I'm a... I'm a ladyman, you know...' – a fat ladyman, she forgot to add, that Roma of ours. Then she'd pop on a DVD and say, 'So maybe I can service you, huh?'

Of course there were many times when Roma got it right in her face, but there were plenty of other times when she got it right down her throat.

Once Roma and Babette got all dressed up in white trousers, white blouses, and gold necklaces. They went off to the barracks to see the Russians. They climbed up the wall and landed in the coal, in the soot, because the coal heap was just on the other side of the wall. The soldiers laughed about them for years afterwards; for years they'd recount over glasses of vodka how they'd hauled the two of them, like two she-devils, out of the soot, smeared all over with coal dust, looking like something the cat dragged in. It took a military intervention to get them out.

And then Romek died. He'd spent his whole life with a railwayman, and maybe it's just as well he didn't live to see these terrible times… Goodness, how that girl could talk! She'd talk your ear off! Towards the end of her life, when she was living in Opole, she'd ring up me and Patricia to gripe and moan:

'Sister, what a fine woman you are, I love you so much 'cause you love the army too, just like me! Listen, I was out walking, looking for some action, but there wasn't nothin'! Eight o'clock, the Opole train station's empty, I'm shaking my hips, my little net bag, couple a beers in it. I look over, and this uniform walks by. I says to him:

"Hey soulja, how long you got left?" And you know what he says to me?

"What the fuck you care?" Can you believe it? Young people these days! That's what I get in my old age… Oh, sister, come and see me, you and Patricia both. I love you both so much, come and see me in Opole, we'll go for nice long walks, the whole town knows me, they know I'm a queer, an actress… Did you ever go to Szczecin? I used to serve in a unit in Goleniowie, and to get to Szczecin all you have to do is take the tram out to Jezioro Głębokie, the last station on the line, and once in a while out there… you might find something to shag…'

Roma (from a distance):

'Lukey, Lukey, honey, you're looking so fine, where you going, what a fine-looking woman you are! Come here, don't leave me, take a break from studying for once, come on, let's go and see the soldiers! Lukey, come on, I'll tell you who I shagged last night.' We sat down on a bench and she tells me, 'Lukey, he was this army pilot. I go up to him and say, "Ooh, what a handsome soldier you are! I'm one of those ladymen, you know, I go with lads, come and have a drink with me, screw them, have a drink, come on, I got half a litre here, come on, drink up, no problem, and presto!'"

And that was back when you could only buy vodka with vouchers, and only after one in the afternoon, any earlier you had to run around looking for a *melina*. So the soldier walked over, Roma explains:

'And pulled out this fucking cannon. I went down on that, I did, and then I gave him the rose petals, he had no idea. "What are you trying to do to me?" he asked me – he thought I was trying to suck him off – and I says, "Naw, I'm just givin' you some rose petals."'

That Roma really was something. And when Radwanicka gave her the what-for, years later, Roma was already on her last legs; that was the second-to-last time I ever saw Romy. She was already in Opole then. The three of us were having tea at Bolita's place in Jama Micha: Radwanicka, Roma, and me. And Romy was giving me this look, and then she says to me:

'Lukey, you sure were pretty back in the day. I sure had the hots for you, even though I'm no lesbian. But my, you've aged...'

Well, Roma was already on Radwanicka's shit list, because she'd been spreading the rumour that Radwanicka came to Opole to sponge off her. Though it was in fact true. Radwanicka came to visit, and later on she told everyone that Roma went out and bought a chicken, tossed it in the pot, a whole pot brimming with broth, and for the whole week they kept reheating that broth, and that's all they ate. Carrots nicked from an allotment, free bread (Roma still did a couple of shifts at a bakery somewhere). I was actually planning to visit her with Patricia, but Patricia's too tight, it would've meant buying a ticket to Opole and some little gift or something for Roma...

In any case, Radwanicka was itching to lash out at her, and she said:

'What? You fucking minger... And what do you think you look like, you old slag? Lucretia here's an educated girl, she's got manners, but that doesn't mean anything at all to you, does it? Listen here, I'll smash this ashtray in your face, I'll fuck you up, I will, the way you look, you old mutton face. You bloody whore. Freak! Come on, Lucretia...' She stood up and said to me, 'Let's go. Come on, Lulu, let's get out of here.' And we left poor Roma all by herself at Bolita's, sitting there with her tea in a plastic cup.

Out on the street Radwanicka says to me: 'Can you believe that! And she'll be talking shit about me now, how I only eat processed cheese nicked from the Supersam! That old whore... I can't understand why the earth hasn't swallowed her up yet!'

Heavens, and then Romy went and died, having spent her whole life with that railwayman. She never stopped believing she'd one day come back to Wrocław and bring the old days back to life. Sometimes I think it's better she's not around; it would've crushed her to see how things are now. She was a legend, a mega mega legend! But my god, how she could talk! How she just talked and talked!

## How Anna Cruised Józek the Lorry Driver

Back in the nineteen eighties the biggest star in all of Wrocław went by the name of Anna. She'd find some stick in the park and start singing songs by Anna Jantar on her microphone:

'Anna Jantar was the best!'

'How come?'

''Cause… 'cause "jantar" means "amber"!'

She'd phone you and right away start making up stories:

'Fuck me if there isn't a crowd at Cruising Central tonight!'

'A crowd *there*? That's a load of bollocks!'

'Like hell it is! They've set up a scale model of the picket line, Radwanicka's there walking about in a white coat, sucking off grunt left and right, a great big commotion, cameras, lights! Except they repeat the scenes like twenty times, and they can't do the take as Radwanicka's eyes keep rolling back into her head the minute a cock goes in her mouth. The director wants to get a shot of her looking, of her eyes, and that's the moment they have to keep doing over and over! Queens all walking about in high-heeled shoes, tight white trousers showing off their bubble butts! Wiggling their arses!'

'Did you get my card from Ciechocinek?'

'That was *you*?! *Warmest regards from sunny Ciechocinek – Regina, Roman, and the children?*'

'Yes, we were doing a training course there… I heard Michalina La Belletriste is writing a book about us… God, what a *comeback* that girl is having, a cover photo and everything. I remember back in '88 when the queens at the Nellie Bar and Cruising Central were already saying how she was on the slide… 'Cause back then if you didn't show your face for any length of time, rumours would start flying round about how you'd been locked up. They'd say things like:

'"Snowflake's either in the slammer or she's finally met her maker in some poorhouse, destitute, just like Norwid." And here I come down from Bydgoszcz and that whore Michalina's all tarted up! What a star, with a cover photo and everything! Talk about marketing! And how young she looks, like a punk rocker. I bet the queens are all making Instant Whip over that one.

'And did I ever tell you girls about the time I went back behind the Novotel for the lorry drivers? No? Ha ha! I went back there…' – and here she starts singing *So much sun all over the city, you've never seen anything like it…* 'Just a second, girls…' In the background she says something in English, in German, muffling the mic with her sleeve, but not so much that we can't hear her. 'Listen, I've got the Scorpions here visiting me… Just a second, I'll be sending them off, they're going into town…' And again she says something in the background. 'OK, I'm back.'

She's been living the last few years in Bydgoszcz, our Anna has, in a working-class area. She's all alone, doesn't know a soul…

'But don't you know any other queens there you can swish around with?'

'I do. If I draw stick figures of them. *Day, memories of summer, day...*'

The Scorpions have evidently left, and now Anna pretends to be her sister on the phone:

'Anna's at her dressing table putting on her face, shall I call her?'

'Anna, Annie... come on and tell us about the lorries...'

'Anna! The gentlemen from *Gazeta Wyborcza* are on the phone.' And then a moment later: 'Hello? Yes? Oh, it's that whore Michalina. Get out of here, you really think I'm going to talk to *you*, so you can make money off me and smear your cunty Lancôme balsam all over my stories? Is that it? Well, whatever, I'm only joking... Anyway, so listen, I was down in Wrocław not so long back, and I'm thinking to myself: the barracks are gone, and I'm not going anywhere near the young offenders' home cause I'll run into Oleśnicka there, and I've owed her fifteen zlotys since time immemorial and that slut won't have forgotten... So I'll just go to the lorries and compete with the vice girls, I think. But I'll be damned if I don't run into Patricia there. It was winter, bitter cold, steam coming out of your mouth, and how on earth am I going to get out on to the highway, way out by the turn-off for the Ikea carpark?

'But I set off anyway. I can always manage at night, just like when I used to wander around the railway station, spending half the night trailing a soldier, or a railway guard, or some nobody, until he found a woman, and I'd follow them: they'd take the night tram out to Biskupin, and I'd be there with them with; they'd head off for the bank of the Odra, into the dark of the bushes – and I would follow, too, and when he fucked her I'd be standing six feet away, and then I'd crawl on the ground towards him, and in a fit of jealousy I stole the handbag that whore tossed on the grass. She didn't notice a thing. Where he was standing, I could have reached out and touched him. The infamous chanteuse Anna in action. Sometimes they would take their women into the front hall of a building; sometimes they'd just go into the park behind the station, but I knew their routes. One of them said to his woman:

'"Bend over. Show me your cunt."

'And then he slapped her on the arse! I was speechless. I told my Zbyszek to slap me like that, too, and talk to me in that way. Something else I used to do was go to the porn cinema at the railway station. I'd sit down next to some conscript wearing a scarf printed with naked women, and watch while he masturbated. It was only worth going there on Scarf Day though – undergarment-washing day for the whores meant general mobilisation for the queens. Word always came through the grapevine. The first to walk through the railway station at six in the morning on her way to work would blurt it out: Fuuuurrrrloughs! Once I tried to pick one up. Heavens, he didn't half make a fuss! The lights went up, all these men glaring at me, the manager and the usher leading me out the door. I felt so *humiliated*!

'So one night I headed out past that Novotel, a bit further on, a couple of stops on the bus, a greenish-yellowy petrol station on my left, lorries up and down the road on my right. I headed over to the shop at the petrol station so I could pretend to be reading a German newspaper. But there in the distance I noticed Patricia standing in the window, and I was overcome with a fit of laughter at how old and fat she looked, with that fat belly of hers (second trimester, at least!), and hair dyed black with purple highlights. Goodness, how she'd aged during all those years without me! But Patricia didn't have a clean conscience where I was concerned, so when she saw me in the distance she slunk off behind the McDonald's and peeked back around the corner. Aha, I thought, go ahead and peek all you want, I'll fix you!

'I'll fix you, all right. So I looked over, and there in front of all those parked lorries the female prostitutes from Russia and Romania were milling about, carrying cardboard signs that said things like: "*v ruku\**: 20 zl, *v pashtshu\*\**: 50 zl, *v shopu\*\*\**: 100 zl." One of them, hair cut short and bleached blonde, was eating chips; that's all she did, she just kept eating them, sticking chip after chip into her mouth with the same repeated gesture. So I sashayed over to that Russian, all dramatic like, and at the top of my voice, loud enough so that trollop behind the McDonald's would hear, started to ask:

"'So where's that whore, the slag, the fat one? You haven't seen a whore with dyed-black hair moving in on your patch, have you? A whore who does it for free, who does it *v ruku* for free, and positively adores doing it *v pashtshu*?" The Russian just kept eating, and between one chip and the next, chewing, she pointed at the McDonald's:

"'She's hiding in there. Over there. Look at her hair standing on end. She's hiding over there." And she kept chewing. "She's hanging out over there." And chewing. "You can see her *pashtsha*." And between one chew and the next: "There, there, there!"

'Girls, don't laugh. I love Patricia like a sister, but running into

---

\* *Russian*: in the hand.
\*\* *Russian*: in the mouth.
\*\*\* *Russian*: in the arse.

her like that, Lord help me! I had to keep a straight face so the Russian wouldn't figure out that me and that tart had known each other for years. So I acted like I only just noticed her:

"'Oh, I see her now, I see that slag!" And I said to that Russian: "Thank you. I'll just go and chase her away now… Keep on working. That whore won't be giving her *pashtsha*, her *ruka*, or her *shopa* for free to anyone. No way anyone's going to pay a moron like that. I'm here from the tax office, and that stupid twat hasn't paid her taxes in forty years, so I'm shutting her shop down for good." I had a plastic bag with vodka in it to bribe the lorry drivers and get them drunk. I went over to her, behind the McDonald's, and she raised those chubby hands of hers to her eyes and said, "No! No!" and "Forgive me!" and I whispered to her: "Act like you're shielding yourself, bitch, scream like I'm beating you black and blue," and I pretended to hit her over the head with the bag, and although I was laughing to myself, I screamed out across the entire parking lot so that *prostitutka* could hear:

"'I've found you out, you stupid twat! So I found you slinking your way back behind McDonald's? Take that! Take that! You haven't paid your whoring tax, you whore! Giving it away for free, you were! Take that!"

'So I pretended to beat her, and out the corner of my eye I could see the Russian calming down about her and her friends' fortunes that night, realising La Brunette over here wouldn't be giving them any competition, giving it away for free and all. Right.

'And then somehow we fell into each other's arms there behind the McDonald's. But that old slag quickly got fed up of me and grew irritated about me competing with her. So she said to me sweetly:

"'So are you staying at Paula's? Really, Annie, this isn't Bydgoszcz, we're in Wrocław here, everything's really spread out. I'm just worried you won't find a bus at this hour... I mean, public transport has become so unreliable even during the day; they seem to have scrapped the night bus altogether... You should get going, go on home, put on some cold cream and your night shirt, the way they do at your age. I think I'll wait here a bit longer, though I suppose I should be going home myself before long, seeing how empty it is and how cold, the whores all rubbing their hands and stamping their feet, steam rising out of their pashtshas like steam engines.'

'Can you believe that? I left that whore there and went off to the lorry drivers by myself. I ran across the busy motorway. Since they sleep at the wheel, you need to climb up the little ladders on the passenger side to see who's in the cab, because it's really high, like they're sleeping on horseback. They sleep. And on their windscreens they have pieces of cardboard inscribed not with *v ruku*, *v pashtshu*, *v shopu*, but with their names: Rafał, Wojtek, Big Shooter, and... Józek!

'Oh, Józek, Józek! I could've washed your socks for you, what do you need an old slapper for? Heavy-set, fortyish, a little belly, fast asleep, exactly the type of grunt I go for. I climb up, knock on the window. Nothing. He had these curtains, window-coverings in his cab, and I'm sure he drew them whenever he took in a prostitute. I fantasised about him fucking me as I shouted:

"'Józek! I'm not sparing you tonight! Józek! Harder! Deeper!"

'Listen, Michalina, listen, you little tramp, I know you'll be getting rich off our stories, carting your arse off to catch some rays in

Lubiewo and all. Or maybe Rowy... Probably better not show your face in Lubiewo after this book is published... But, listen, I just couldn't stand it anymore. I pounded on the window and climbed down the ladder. The bloke looked out to see what was happening, and there I was having a wank. Heavens, was he ever shocked! Like he'd seen the Countess's ghost! Or the Virgin's. His face took on – I'm telling it like this, bitch, so you'll write it all down just as it happened – his face took on an expression of terror and incredulity. All at once he pulled the curtains shut, and that was the last I saw of him. And then that tart with the chips comes along and says to me with this smug look on her face:

"'*Vot, spektakla nye budyet!*'"*

'*Nye budyet spektakla*, she says, all full of herself, because now the cat was out of the bag: I'd been planning to give her a run for her money too, and all without charging a cent.

---

* *Russian*: Oh look, the show's been cancelled.

## How Jantar Went Into the November Night For the First Time

'So, tell me, darling, when did you first discover all these places?'

'Well, you know, I really didn't have a clue. This was back during the academic year '85/'86. And it all started because in my first year at university I decided not to return home to visit my father's grave for All Souls' Eve. It was quite a way to go, after all, and I'd have had to come right back, and I was really busy with school, with my classes. I was constantly studying. I thought: if I want to get into the army, I have to finish my degree.

I suppose it goes back even further, when I was still living in my village, and there were these workers, see, fixing the bridge. And at night they'd get pissed out of their heads, and pass out and fall asleep on the ground outside the barracks, their clothes all crusty with mud, you know? And I – I was still a child, I suppose – I'd sneak off to grope them. They were so drunk I could've robbed them blind and they wouldn't have noticed. Their clothes were so shabby, their flies fastened with safety pins instead of zips. I undid them, copped a feel, and ran back home! The dark of night, I'm lying in bed, o good Lord! Did I remember to fasten the pin back properly on that blond, or did I leave him wide open? I couldn't sleep, thinking of him turning on his side and the safety pin puncturing his willy. So I stayed up all night, and at dawn I ran back and checked. Fastened. Uff.

'And thus was I compelled into the November night – into the smoke and into the leaves, into the chill air and smell of bonfires, like Queen Margot herself, everything egging me on, "Go Margot! Go!" Compelled, compelled towards death, Eros and Thanatos at once! Wisps of smoke, there's something moving over there, go on! Don't stay at home, the Devil's calling you! So I went to Hanka Sawicka Park. I'd found out where to go the day before when this one queen in my year had shouted out to the whole college:

'"Fucking Ayyy! Get a load of *this*! You wanna go make fun of the queers? I'm not just talking about Doctor This or Professor That. Fucking Ayyy! Go see for yourselves, the party going on at the Monopol! All the queers are there, dancing on this moving platform thingy, wiggling their arses, mingling, kissing each other, it's lad-on-lad on the benches in Hanka Sawicka Park! Both sides of the paths, right there on the benches!" And everyone in our year heard what he said, and those stupid peasant cunts were saying:

'"Tee hee hee, Gutek! You're impossible! Tee hee hee, you've really got some balls to go to a place like that!"

'And I'm thinking to myself, "That was me you saw there!" But at that point all I'd ever done before was peek at the picket line on General Bem Street, but only in passing, and then I'd run away like an idiot, like a madwoman, 'cause of AIDS, AIDS, AIDS, AIDS, *run away, run away!* Even as early as '81 I'd found out about AIDS and queers from different magazines, like *Razem* or *Na przełaj*. At first I thought you only had to be a poof to get sick, and didn't know the disease was contagious. I was still going through a phase when I prayed a lot, and I prayed that the Lord God would absolve me of this awful curse. Ha ha ha! I looked the word up in German encyclopedias, and when I was in the fourth or fifth form I happened upon a copy of *Tonio Krüger* at the library and immediately sensed a connection. In my first year at university I was looking at this huge East German lexicon and ran across an entry on *Homosexualität, Homosexuelle*. And I was so amazed, because they wrote about it completely neutrally. At the end of the article there was this note: "Frequently such individuals are confronted with difficulties in finding a partner." Oh! But in our university library encyclopedias like that were kept in the criminal law section, which tells you everything. And there was this normal bloke in a photograph, just your everyday face on the street, and the caption under the photo read: *homosexual*. I died of laughter! Back then in Poland there were still people who subscribed to the nineteenth-century view that homosexuals were built differently, had a different "physiognomy", and could be identified by the shape of their anuses...

'The first person who ever came on to me was Duckie the Gypsy Murderess. She was this Gypsy who'd murdered a queen and done time in prison. Hava or Yava was what they called her. The one on Tombakowa Street. Anyway, I fell in love with Duckie, good Lord... But of course it was never consummated, we just kissed and hung around together... Later Duckie gave me a telephone number, pretended it was hers... She spread a rumour about what a lovely cock I had, and all the queers started going after me. But I only let her touch it once, maybe twice, and then I immediately buttoned myself up and bolted. I ran off, and then I fantasised about her later; I kept ringing her up, and this old queen always picked up (I mean, how on earth would Duckie have had a telephone at home? She was just trying to show off). And it was a good thing I hadn't done anything else with her, because Rafalina fell in love with Duckie around then and was broken in by her – her first time – and as luck would have it Duckie gave her the clap! Duckie was basically a crook, don't forget, Michalina. I was so stupid back then, and only later on did I find out who Duckie really was from the queens, from Owl. From Patricia... Well, I didn't meet Patricia until the following spring. I was snogging this one soldier, Andrzej, on the picket, and we were about to have a shag right there, but the riot police were stationed next door, so we went over by the opera house, into the grass, in the shit, and had a roll in the grass, in all that shit, instead. We squirmed about, kissing, going crazy, but we didn't actually have sex. I never wanted to have sex, just kisses. And then, light-hearted and with a bounce in my step, I would return every night from the park to my dormitory.

'I met Patricia one night in May. After the rain. 1985. For about twenty years Patricia had been going around in this Yugoslavian parka she'd got from a girlfriend who worked in a shop, and by this time it wasn't even a parka any more, just a tattered rag, just like Rimbaud's line: *Mon paletot soudain devenait idéal...*

'So anyway, Patty would go about in this threadbare *idea* of a jacket. But she was so slender, with this great black shock of hair, an absolute flamer all the same. So I see this flaming queen coming at me from the lilacs. And she says to me:

'"Good evening, comrade... neighbour... It's quiet over there, you can go on in. It's safe. And you would be...?" She started chatting me up, and I was so open, I told her I was at university, studying German, and she said:

"'Oh, uh-huh… Me too, I finished my studies last year…"

"'Oh so what did you study, neighbour?"

"'Me? I studied medicine, I'm a doctor."

"'What was it like, was it hard?"

"'Oh, it sure *was* hard, especially anatomy…"

'Right. And she didn't flinch a single muscle as she reeled off a list of all the classes she'd taken during her years at university, and then told me how she'd since been concentrating on radiology. And I was young, and I believed everything, and afterwards I walked over to another bench, where some queens I already knew were sitting, Owl and a few other older ones, and I said:

"'There's this really lovely sister here…" Oh, wait, I hadn't started saying "sister" then, it was two, three years before I started talking like a woman. It was only later that I started conspiring with Joanna the Priest's Girl and Bolita, and Bolita talked me into using the feminine. So I said to them:

"'I met this really great bloke over there, so sophisticated, and he's a doctor…"

"'Right, Andie, so sophisticated, but the coat he's wearing is falling apart!"

'But you know, back in those days… And the girls all said, "Which one is it? Who?" And I said to Owl, "The one who was sitting there on the bench when you walked by."

"'Oh! That's *Patriiiiicia!* How did she introduce herself?"

"'Well, he told me that his name was Piotr…"

"'That's just Patricia! *Her* a doctor? Fuck me! Maybe she once

300

*talked* to a doctor!" And then this hideous old queen who rode with the paramedics, who was an orderly, somewhere outside Środy Śląskie, says:

"'That one does it on the x-ray machine, she does it on the x-ray machine! In oncology. I've seen it. One day I was driving up, bringing in a patient, and I looked over, and I couldn't believe my fucking eyes: it was Patricia. That flaming slag was walking down the corridor just like a doctor, in white clogs, swishing her arse, jiggling her keys…" Well, anyway, that's how it all began…'

## How Anna Dealt With a Customer Complaint

One time Anna came across some drunken grunt in the park, and evidently he was so dissatisfied with her service that he started complaining:

'Eh, a blowjob like that, even my girlfriend can do better…'

Anna immediately stood up, got on her bicycle, and from a distance, where she was sure the grunt couldn't do anything to her, shouted:

'Huh! Thirty years I've been sucking cock, from the Don to the Dniepr, from the Dniepr to the Oder, and I've never had a single complaint!' And she jumped on to her bike, and poof! She was gone!

## How Anna Got a Grunt to Pity-Fuck Her

When nothing else worked, when she didn't have a chance in hell, Anna got her grunt by making him feel sorry for her. She made herself appear all manly, and while they were with friends (having already bonded over the masculinity thing), she suggested that they go and drink vodka together. A bench, the park, bottle wrapped in a plastic shopping bag, a pack of Wiaruses, autumn leaves underfoot. And then they started talking about girls, about 'arses'. The hot ones, the saggy ones, how you really have to chat them up before one of them will give in, and when Anna couldn't take it any more she'd blurt out:

'Damn it all, bloody hell, mate, there's something I wanna get off my chest, but bloody hell – it's embarrassing...'

'Spit it out, man, we're drinking together, you and I, we're pals... Spit it out, maybe I can help you.'

'So, you know, I know it's definitely hard and all for you, I mean, I know it's not easy, when there's not a woman in sight, and a man's on furlough, but what can I say, when I have it a hundred times worse...' Then our Anna spits twice, at equal distances in front of their feet, on the leaves.

'What do you mean?'

Here Anna's head drops, and she mutters something, lights a cigarette, and has another shot of vodka...

'I mean, well, I was once in prison, you know, and fucking hell, that's where I learned it, from the others, and ever since then I keep wanting to, well, you know, suck a guy's cock...'

At that the grunt demonstrated complete understanding, sympathy even.

'Whoa, that really sucks, what the fuck, to be a queer, that's like, I mean they screwed you up badly, didn't they... that's not funny at all, a life like that. You completely sure? And you're able to go out into the world like that? I mean, mate, is there anything I can do to help?'

Anna suppressed a smile, but made a grave face and said:

'Yeah, mate, it really does suck.' She spits on the ground. 'Fuck, I mean, when I see someone like that I really want to beat the living shit out of him, and yet at the same time the minute I get a couple of vodkas in me...'

At that point, the grunt said:

'You know, mate, if you've got to do it, maybe I can help you out? Maybe you want to give a blowjob?' (Grunt always forgot that the phrase required both the direct and an indirect object. In the language of grunt, fellatio was always referred to as 'blowjob' or 'blowing'.)

During the act itself he said: 'Mate, you suck cock better than my girlfriend.' And there you have it. But afterwards, he asked for money, and Anna told him she was on a pension, and off she went on her bike!

## How Anna Picked Up Grunt Thanks to Zofia Kiełbasa

The doorbell rings. I look through the peephole. I think to myself, Well, I'm quite a big bloke myself, so even if he has a knife he can't do anything to me. So I crack the door open.

'I'm looking for Zofia...' She had some kind of funny last name, I don't remember what it was, let's just say Kiełbasa. 'Is this the Kiełbasa residence?'

I'm thinking, what a fine piece of grunt he is; even if no Zofia Kiełbasa ever lived here, does it matter? So I pull this sad face, like

I'm going to cry, open the door a bit wider, invite him in – please, come in, take a seat, have you travelled far?

'From Olsztyn. I'm looking for this girl, it's been years, she used to live here…'

'Oy, oy, oy, well, yes, Zofia… Well, you see, she did live here once, but, well, how can I put it… Zofia died a month ago. Heart condition.'

And then I immediately take him into my arms, comfort him, suggest I go out and get a bottle of vodka and… drink to her memory… together… After all, I was Zofia's best friend…

# THEORIES

## The Inviolability of Cars


Among confirmed heterosexuals there is no place for irony, for games, for inverted commas, and stylisation, not to mention swishing and camping it up. That's the biggest difference between us and them. They're serious, stuck up to their eyeballs in the hard realities of everyday life, and all we do is wink at them and tickle them with our airs. But they're so serious that our tickling them (under their chins) only infuriates them; they refuse to come over to our side; they go ballistic, because they see everything as an attack on their serious, heterosexual world. They're up to their eyeballs in their own social roles, and we come at them with our transgressions, our metamorphoses, our primping and preening. We relativise everything. They have names like Sławek, Arek and Bogdan, and we come at them with our pseudonyms, our Euphrosines and Lucretias. They're up to their eyeballs in their local patriotisms, symbolised by their faith in brewery and football team, and we come at them with our trips abroad and lack of Polishness. They always wear the same thing, and we come at them with our dyed hair. Zero postmodernity, zero relativism, zero sense of the constructedness of everything and the conventionality of values – instead they have a handful of basic, unchanging principles: the honour of their city's team, hence the honour of their city, too, because the two are inextricably bound... The inviolability of girlfriends, their own and those of others. The inviolability of cars.

# Theory of Swish

Queens have adopted the same behaviours that women abandoned in the process of emancipation: passivity, the desire to be dominated, reserve, crossing their legs as a gesture of standoffishness, pursing their lips for the very same reason, preying on men instead of practising independence, self-abasement, a hypersensitivity you'll no longer find even among the most feminine women, gossiping, and moodiness ('women are moody'). These qualities, chucked out through the door of feminism, return through the window of faggotry. The rest of the theory goes as follows: why are queens so ardent in their adoption of these old-fashioned female characteristics? Because that's how men see women (and queens are still men after all). To a bloke, an emancipated, athletic woman with her feet up on the table and a can of beer in her fist isn't a woman at all. In his eyes, only traditional qualities – so uncanny when freely achieved – are feminine and can truly turn him on. And now the real question: are straights attracted to femininity or to women themselves? That is, if I'm feminine, will they find me attractive (fuckable)? Is it *sex* or *gender* that attracts them? Because if it's gender, then queens should by all rights be turned on by butch lesbians. But that, alas, never happens...

## Cha-Cha-Cha

So, for example, one of them says to the other:

'I had a straight man.'

'And?'

'It was all right, but he couldn't get it up.'

'What do you mean? Didn't you cha-cha-cha him?'

'I did, but nothing happened.'

Exactly. If theory had anything to do with reality, if our femininity was what turned them on, then cha-cha-cha would always work, but in practice it only works once in a blue moon. Cha-cha-cha involves painting the fingernails on one hand a delicate rose colour or with translucent shellac, donning dainty little rings, and in general simulating the delicate, cold hands of a teenage girl. Not the paws of a transvestite, but the slender hands of a young maiden. And then, with those slender hands, delicately, effeminately diddling the straight man's genitals, whilst saying things like:

'Oh, just look how big you are, and I'm such a dainty little thing, so little, my hands are even trembling! Oh, come on and show us your ginormous shlongadong.' Cha-cha-cha! And then totally work the little Asian girl thing, squint your eyes, straight from the video for 'Macarena'. 'Coo-coo-coo! My pussypuss is so moist, my little snatchkin! Hi, my name is Anna Maria! Who are you? I'm just a girl in my first year at university, and now look how my hand goes from writing lecture notes to rubadubbing that big fat elephant trunk of yours. 'Cause you're so big, and I'm so teensy-weensy. And my panty-wanties are so dainty and white, but they're already all moist, 'cause I'm right out of a Manga comic, I'm totally kawaii, teen category!' Then on the basis of this simple (really, only too simple!) interaction, the grunt bounces back hard into his masculinity, so that he doesn't get inundated, doused, by all that femininity, so that he doesn't himself turn into a woman, he guns it right into being a man, and the intended side effect of the bounce is that he gets a hardon. Like in Kieślowski's *Short Film About Love*, when Szapołowska cha-cha-chas the young Olaf Lubaszenko and says:

'I'm so wet… You have such delicate fingers…' as a way of infecting him with her delicateness, her fecundity, so he'll feel like a man and pull back into his masculinity. With straight grunt it's no use pretending you're not a queen. You need to be aggressive, look them straight in the crotch, and go totally swish on them, because they're looking for the slapper in you, not the lad. And that's how it's supposed to work.

Supposed to.

## The Supermarket Trick

One day Alligatorina went to the supermarket. She left her bag at the bag-check, but lost the number tag. On returning with her shopping, she searched and searched her pockets – no luck.

The world had become a barcode for which Alligatorina no longer possessed the scanner.

'I'm sorry, sir, but I lost my tag, and my shoulder bag is in there.'

'Oh, well, look in your pockets, your wallet... 'Cause it'll cost you...'

Nothing.

The man in customer service called the security guards. Alligatorina withdrew into herself, frightened. People crowded.

She didn't have it.

'Well, then we'll have to fill out the form, won't we, and there'll be a fifty-zloty charge for the ticket. Which bag is it?'

'That one, in that box down there, the second one up, the pink one!' The security guards set Alligatorina's bag on the counter.

'Excuse me, sir, but this is a lady's handbag...'

'No, it's mine.'

'What's inside?'

'Let me see. Keys, tissues…'

'Excuse me, sir, but every bag has keys and tissues in it. Maybe something a little more specific?'

Alligatorina was silent; she lowered her head and bit her lip because she knew she had her makeup bag and a lady's comb in there, and a little mirror…

'A little mirror,' she added quietly, and lowered her eyes.

And then that hulking. Beefed-up. Navy blue-clad. Security guard. Stuck his enormous paw inside and pulled out. Her bits and pieces. Her odds and ends. All that nonsense of hers. Everything that was so intimate to Alligatorina… It was almost like he was touching her, like he was. Rummaging through her privacy. Under her blouse.

'That's not a man's bag, it's a woman's handbag! Come with me, sir. A man's bag, a man's bag? He's a thief!' The crowd of people kept growing, and even Alligatorina wasn't sure any more; maybe she'd been carrying someone else's bag her whole life?

# FLORA TRATTORIA

Ladies and Gentlemen, allow me to present the world-famous…
Flora Trattoria! Hit it, band!

Flora proceeds to tell us all about Tola, the Health Inspectress,
and the Pissoiress of Central Station. Listen carefully!

## Tola

Tola was from Poznań, and she was stingy, really stingy.

'Goodness, that Tola of ours certainly was tightfisted! She would
piss in the sink because she hated to see so much water go down the
toilet! She bought a refrigerator, but kept her food the old way, outside on the windowsill; she never even plugged in the fridge, cause
she was afraid it would guzzle up all the electricity as it was on all the
time. Tola opened the meter box and told that grunt of hers she lived
with:

"'Look, Mirek, that wheel keeps spinning like crazy the whole
time, it keeps spinning round and round! It's driving me mad, it's
eating up all the electricity, just look how that wheel keeps spinning
and spinning!"

'Anyway, Tola lived for six years with this cook, Mirek, who was certainly grunty enough. Tola was such a lunatic and so tightfisted, it's not surprising that he finally dumped her. And I had just made a date with her,' Flora Trattoria sighs. 'We'd made a date to go to Lidl 'cause it's so cheap. So we're standing there in the queue at the till, and I'm getting some of those Knorr soups, you know, the spicy chicken one, and that cheese banquet one? In any case, there were some other queens standing behind us in the queue, chickens the lot of them, with plucked eyebrows, fauxhawks, straight out of the clubs, but really skinny, long necks, all veiny. Maybe they thought I was grunt' – Flora Trattoria can be pretty masculine, and actually she is quite well built (Lady-Grunt is what she is) – 'and they start chatting me up:

'"What are you buying? Soup? Ooh, I think we're buying the same ones – where did you get that one from? Cup-a-Soup... Ooh, we like that too... And especially *those* ones there."

'Cup-a-Soup!' Flora Trattoria raises her eyebrows, rolls her eyes, and wrings her spongy hands.

'And then there was the pair of longjohns Tola had tossed in our cart; the chickens thought they were mine and said:

'"Ooh, long underwear...! The most vital part of a man's wardrobe..."

'And that's when Mirek's text message arrived: "Moving out. Left keys next door."

'And Tola said:

'"Listen, Florie, let's go – let's go back to my place. I have no idea what state my flat will be in."

But you have to imagine Flora saying this sentence while

imitating Tola's Poznań accent, the way an ordinary woman from the Poznań suburbs would say it, the concern in her voice about all her furniture and appliances…

'So I turned the key in the door, we walked in, and plonk! Tola collapsed on the floor in the cloakroom, bellowing like a cow! She certainly had a pair of lungs on her, that Tola. Mooooo! Mooooo! Eventually she got up, still bellowing, and ran into the kitchen:

'"Oh my God, oh my God, Flora, look what he's done to me, after all those years!" and mooooo, she bellowed. But that was nothing, because she had yet to open her kitchen cupboards, and only then did she really let loose and scream her head off, raving in between the howls:

'"Bloody. Fucking. Hell! My china! He took my *china*! Mooooooo…!" And she started assessing the wreckage in the flat:

'"Cocksucker! He took both my saucepans! Mooooo… The only two I had left, oh my *saucepans*…!" Eventually she calmed down a bit, but then she suddenly looked in the hallway and exploded again:

'"Oh my fucking God! Oh my God! He took my *leather jacket*! Now that is really going *too far*, mooooo! That fucker won't get away with this!"'

## The Health Inspectress

'Really, darling, you mean to tell me this is a four-star gastronomic establishment? Good heavens! This was supposed to be a model restaurant, but what do I see? Squalor heaped upon squalor!'

Flora Trattoria tells me about the time this queen from Health and Safety walked into her workplace. Or charged into it, rather.

With her assistant, a young, terrified lass. With her morning fluster, all aflutter, all up in her coffee. She charges in, asks for an apron and a blue plastic cap, then heads backstage, into the kitchen.

'What is *that*?' She pokes her finger into a saucepan. 'You use *that* for cooking meat? Oh oh! And look at this, mister,' she was addressing Flora, 'do I see food residue here…? Oh, *no*… We'll have to take a swab of it. Małgosia! Get a sample.' And now the apron isn't enough for her. Now she's repulsed by everything. Now she really does wish she were wearing a gasmask, even though everyone knows that Flora's restaurant is one of the best in town, even written up in the paper…

'And just what do you keep in this receptacle?' She opens a plastic box with breadcrumbs in it. Flora is so upset that she gets confused and says:

'Flour.'

'Flour? Flour? But these are breadcrumbs! Oh wonderful. Tell me, were these crumbs used in food production today?'

'Yes, they're fresh. I made them fresh this morning and just put them away a moment ago…' To which the inspectress replies tartly:

'No, sir. That is no longer of any substance whatsoever.' And whoosh! She pours the breadcrumbs into a plastic bag and says the bag has to be labelled, for analysis.

Now she was rummaging in the cabinet.

'What kind of containers are these? Where's your permit? Your business licence?' Flora starts nervously turning over the chops. The inspectress:

'You go from handling money to touching food with the same

hands? No, no, *no*! That is simply not allowed, that will *not* be tolerated!'

And now the Health Inspectress dips her entire snout into the glassed-lidded freezer and holds it there, examining the sandwiches. She mutters to herself:

'These sandwiches are delivered. And these are delivered. And these delivered. Expiry date. Plastic. Bacterial *flora*...' Flora can't take any more, she doesn't know if she should be laughing or crying. 'And what are these raw vegetables doing here? Don't you know that raw vegetables are *not* permitted...?'

'That steam dishwasher is broken? Either way, you have no business using metal cutlery, only plastic!'

Flora clutches her head. Christ, *Christina!* Plastic cutlery in *my* restaurant, the best in the city? Oh, if homo were ever wolf to homo, this is it!

For all that, Flora did a wonderful imitation of her. She screwed up her lips, rolled her eyes. The Health Inspectress was already in her forties, and overweight, and looked like she belonged behind the counter in a chemist's shop. And she had a voice straight out of a judge's chambers or government office. She went over to the sink:

'Umm... Do I see *squalor* here? Is that squalor? What in heaven's name is going on here?' She says to her assistant:

'Write this down, Małgosia: "Carrot residue found in basin for sanitation of utensils." And in brackets add: "Sample taken." Now she was running her finger along the tile floor.

'You mean to tell me no one has ever slipped on this? Honestly. And to think I've been singing your praises! This floor is completely slick with grease!'

Flora Trattoria rolls her eyes so that only the whites show, and wrings her hands.

Then the Health Inspectress sees something in the corner of the room. Flora performs a complete pantomime for us: 'O. My. *God! Omigod!* What is *that*! Ugh! Małgosia! Write this down: "Organic residue in advanced state of decomposition"!' The bitch spotted a cherry stone, and that's what all the fuss was about, Flora explains. For her, anything organic was automatically rotten meat, a corpse. From a distance she grimaced theatrically, ostentatiously picked up the cherry stone with a plastic freezer bag so she wouldn't get infected with SARS, and with her other hand she pinched her nose and fanned the air, the whore. But a week later, of course, she walked in and was all like:

'And here, Mr Director...' – arm in arm, as if they were going on a stroll – 'is the model restaurant I've been wanting to show you. Oh, here, look, something new: a steam steriliser for dishes, state-of-the-art, and here are the work stations, ergonomically designed... As for the rest, Mr Florian here will tell you whatever else you want to know in just a moment. But *afterwards*' – she lowers her voice – 'you absolutely *must* try the pastries. The cherry tart is the speciality of the house...'

Cherry tart, indeed.

## The Pissoiress of Central Station

… had it in for the queens.

'Bloody hell! How many more times are you going to come in here today to relieve yourself! This is the twentieth time!'

'Well, it's not like I'm not paying for it, ma'am…'

Under communism, and later, too, she would sit sullenly in the vestibule of the conveniences, at her desk, in a purple apron that went down past her knees, tousled, sipping cold tea from a jar, slurping it, and 'sitting'. Sitting was actually a way of life. One of them would ring up the other:

'What are you doing?'

'Eh, I'm sitting…'

Or:

'You won't find me changing trains three times, I take the fast train. It may be ten zlotys more, but all I have to do is get on board, and me and my arse get to Lubiewo in no time. I can rest my arse, all comfy, and my backside gets to travel in the height of luxury…'

The Pissoiress had a Sacred Heart of Jesus and some kind of Virgin Mary hung up on the window at work. From her cubbyhole she was able to see the pissoirs at the back of the conveniences, but because they were on the same side as she was she couldn't see the cubicles. Another customer would walk in, and she'd say:

'OK, I need the two zlotys in advance. Paper's on the right! No, the urinals are not free. Yes, use of the sinks is included. What? If you're using a cubicle, take toilet paper with you, there on the right. Exactly.' Slurp. 'What? It's occupied? What do you mean it's occupied?' Here she made the face titled *If I Don't Get Up They're Helpless Without Me*. She let out a heavy sigh, set down her tea, stood up and walked around to the cubicle, pounded with her fist, and in a booming voice:

'You must come out of this cubicle at once! Hello! What is going on in there?'

Banging.

'Hello!!!'

More banging.

'Can you believe that! Hello! What on earth are you doing in there?! Excuse me, but you must come out of the cubicle at once! At once!!! Józek!' – she had an assistant by that name – 'Józek, get me the spare key, let's see what's going on in there. Occupying a cubicle for ten minutes!'

And more banging.

Meanwhile, this whole mystery arose from the fact that while there were three cubicles, one of them had the obligatory Out of Order sign on it, so only two were available. And the walls between them had ten-inch gaps underneath. So the more nimble queens would officially enter separate cubicles, but then slide beneath them (on that wet, urine-slick floor) to get their rocks off. Afterwards they had to return to their cubicles the same way.

'What? Sneaking back into the other cubicle on me?! Oh heavens, it's them pervies again! Go back where you belong or I'll call the police! Back to your cubicles! Józek! We've got another slip-through on our hands! We'll have another wedgie in a moment! 'Cause I'm going to clean this floor, and once I get that mop in my hands I'll have you up against the wall!'

Once when Anna was there the Pissoiress grabbed that dirty mop full of shit and bam! lobbed it into the cubicle, right on top of the queens' heads. Just like in the zoo.

Another time there was this queen trying to slip under the cubicle, and she got stuck under it and couldn't budge in either direction. And she'd forgotten to lock the door. So the Pissoiress went to clean the floor in there, and opened the door, and – well, did she ever go after that queen with her mop and rag!

But usually she just sits there at her desk and says the same thing over and over, a performance piece on a loop:

'Cubicle? Two zlotys, paid in advance, paper on the right.'

'Two zlotys? Why so dear?'

'Because you can wash your hands too, see?'

'Cubicle two zlotys, paid in advance, paper on the right, see?'

'...'

'Because you can wash your hands too.'

'...'

'What do you mean they're all taken? Where's my handle?'

'...'

'Hello! Gentlemen! Time to get off the pot!'

Banging on all the cubicle doors.

'There's a gentleman here waiting! Here, sir, go and use my private cubicle.' And with some secret key and handle she opens the door of the 'out of order' cubicle.

'Hello! The picnic's over! Wait a minute, where's that smoke coming from? Attention! Attention! You are kindly requested *not to smoke* in the toilets!'

'What do you need? A cubicle? Two zlotys, paid in advance, paper on the right.'

'...'

'You can wash your hands!'

'OK, gentlemen, shake a leg, or I'll have to get my handle out! Please don't fall asleep on me. No *sleeping*! Are you coming out now?' Bang bang bang. 'Hello! Anyone *sleeping* in there? All finished? Right then, get yourself wiped up, just a quick wipe then! My God, are they all junkies in there?!'

'Good morning! Toilet paper? Please pay in advance, you'll find the paper on the right...'

'You coming out now, sir?'

'Hold on, what is this? *Hold on*! Fancy leaving a mess like that, where's my screwdriver and my plunger! Excuse me, sir? Mind leaving a little something else too? Not an ounce of decency left in these people! Where's my plumber's helper? Fouling the place up like that!'

'Nothing free at the moment.'

'Oh, please! Two at once in a cubicle! *Artists!* Here, there's a free one over here!'

*

Once – this was back in the sixties – a black man paid a visit, but not for the same reason as us. And since the Pissoiress had never seen a real live black person before, she rubbed her eyes and stared at him. So the queens – Frigid Mariola and Uterina – played a trick on her. After the black man finished using the urinal, they poured black ink into it, then ran to the Pissoiress to complain:

'Ooh! Ooh! Look at the mess he made!' The Pissoiress, enraged, grabbed a rag and began thrashing the black man with it:

'Ooh! Ooh! Devil's spawn!' And she thrashed him with her wet rag. 'It's not enough for this demon to be black, but his water's black, too! Now go and clean it up, or I'll report you to the authorities!' And she hit him with that rag, and the horrified man hadn't the faintest idea what she was saying…

## The Storm

'Distant thunder capers – the sky in curling papers'
*– Miron Białoszewski*

Today, Paula, you're telling a story. Even if you don't want to. Yesterday it was my turn, and I'm not wearing out my jaws just for your entertainment. Not on your life, Paula. No fussing; your turn today. There's a storm brewing; the clouds are coming in from Świnoujście. But go on, talk; we'll get there.

Paula purses her lips. OK, so I'll tell you something. I heard it from this one queen, old, educated. From Kraków, rattling on about sucking off the Wawel Dragon, no idea whether it's true or not... I met her on her way to the Dominican Centre, on her way to Albert's cause they were having a sale and she's poor. She tells me how she saw this famous authoress on the picket line back in the seventies. She walked with a cane, bald. Guess who it was (laughter). Yes, exactly, that's who. Oh, go on, Paula! She was just passing through, there was a ribbon-cutting ceremony at a new school or something, and that authoress told the queen, and the queen told Paula, how it used to be – not during communism, but before that, under feudalism, during the interwar years, and back before that. How it would have been for us back then. Better than with any foreign culture as a matter of fact. No one can tell me that this is the golden age of faggotry, because it isn't. In fact it's never been worse. What good has emancipation done me? What good are all the magazines and billboards dripping with homoeroticism? When I get harassed for the slightest thing? What good are gay bars, feathers up my arse, when I have no interest at all in doing it with other queens, only grunt; and just show me grunt in a gay bar now (other than the bouncers). Back then you would have had grunt galore underfoot. Literally and figuratively. You could have got them to do anything you wanted! Nowadays when you're hunting for grunt, nine times out of ten you get a smack in the teeth, and only once in ten get a cock in your mouth. Right?

Come, let's make ourselves comfy and smoke a Wiarus, and I'll tell you the whole thing, how it would have been for us. There's this play by Janusz Głowacki, *Cinders*, where girls in a reform school tell each other stories in bed, identifying themselves with the characters. We can do the same. So let's say we come from the middling or high nobility. Rich landowners. And we're both around thirty. And let's say…

'Baroque!' I interrupt her pleadingly, the way those girls from *Cinders* each introduced her own story into the round. 'Baroque. *The Countess left the house at half past nine.* And under our wigs we have little boxes with elaborately carved little holes in them. Those are our flea traps. Each one contains a wad of cotton wool impregnated with honey or blood (menstrual of course; none of us cares for pricking our fingers), and all the fleas, from every corner of the gown and wig, are drawn into the trap. (Once when Madame de Pomme de Terre got pubic lice – and who for heaven's sake didn't – she fixed herself one of those baroque traps and even put a jar of honey in it; but all for nothing: lice aren't fleas after all, and they had no use for honey.) And you know what else we have in those grey wigs of ours, Paula? I'll bet you can't guess. Little nosegays of violets and lilies of the valley. And to keep them from wilting, we insert them into miniature vases of water hidden in our tresses! And we wear crinolines so that during banquets we can sit on our elaborately sculpted chamberpots and evacuate. That's what Arthurina told me, that's why crinolines were invented in the first place. And if you got into someone's bad books, she might put a live toad in your chamberpot before the banquet, or a rat. And they invented beauty marks to cover their spots. Our entire wardrobes are positively teeming with little nooks and crannies and secret passageways, like Gothic castles, and the folds of our frocks are inhabited with lovers, or letters, or bottles of poison, or some tiny, carefully sculpted *objet* or other. A rococo trap for mosquitoes! And there we sit at the banquet on our chamberpots, our corsets cinched tight so everything we eat passes right through. We sit there, feeling the lice in our wigs making a beeline for the honey or blood in that miniature golden trap. And when I'm bored, I powder my bosom and shoulders with my special powderpuff...'

'Fine then, it's baroque!' Paula wraps a shawl around her shoulders, giving herself a décolletage. She's crazy about the crinolines, the girandoles, the bustles. 'It's Sunday, and we're riding in a *linijka* with a farmhand... No, wait! You live in your manor around six versts away from me in mine. And I'm making my rounds of a Sunday, and my steward or whoever is explaining to me in that *linijka* the numbers for rye and for wheat, and I'm holding my hand to my temple, all framed in lace, because I have a headache.'

'So wait, are we women or are we lads?'

'Lads, lads. Biologically we're boys. But we can play at being otherwise. In any case, we're big old baroque queens. Just imagine!'

'OK.'

Thunder commences beyond the fences, it's going to pour with rain at any moment; let's go, Paula, you can continue your story on our way back to the centre... Take our blanket, shake the sand out of it, take your shoes in your hand and let's go, let's get out of here, because half an hour from now lightning bolts will be crashing down all over the place. All over this accursed place, as if sin still existed, except that no one will get hit. The water those queens are standing in, stationary, rings rippling out from them like from ducks, that water will heave. And howl. But we'll be sitting pretty with our sultan's cream and candy floss, our cartons of *oranżada*, our Wiaruses. For a lark we'll feast on a piece of cake, and later promise ourselves that never, ever again will we eat *so much*! Let's go, Paula, let's get in the carriage and get the fuck out of here.'

'Anyway, there he was explaining to me, that ploughman, what grew where, and I was bored to tears, had to lean on something, kept yawning. Finally I say to him, "Be a dear, Janek, and drive me back to the mews, my head is positively killing me today."'

'And there I was, waiting for you, all in tight-fitting black attire, with a jockey's cap and a riding crop...'

'Uh, right, a *baroque* jockey cap... Anyway, so you're there waiting. And then: we pick out a couple of stablehands...'

'But I think I'd rather have an ordinary farmhand...'

'OK, so we pick one stableboy and one farmhand, and we say to them:

'"Off to the pond with you. Go and have a bath in the claypit, then hotfoot it back here to the palace, fresh as two altar boys!"

'And they take their caps from their heads and say:

'"But sire! We already bathed at Eastertide..."

'"No matter, dear Maciej, dear Łukasz: off to the swimming hole with you."

'Then, in the meantime, the first thing we do is give ourselves a fashionable enema.'

'Can enemas be fashionable?'

'They can if they're sculpted... Emblazoned with laurel-leaf ornamentation... I mean, we're not talking bulbs and syringes here, like in the nineteenth century, but those sculpted enemas where the water runs through a tube like an IV-drip right up your arse. Back then an enema was the best cure for all manner of ailments, though it was useful for other reasons, too. For five hours, five litres of water, wine, and a medley of herbs would trickle into us, and later we'd dump it all out and be clean as a whistle. Then we sit down and... It's clear we have no idea what to do with ourselves, our nostrils fluttering, bosoms heaving, nothing left but to powder our titties! To powder ourselves, to powder our titties! Gawd, we'll powder ourselves till we crumble into little bits! We'll powder our wigs till the fleas asphyxiate! And look how we perfume ourselves! But let me tell you, Paula: they didn't have atomisers back then. Instead, we took those heavy, dusky perfumes into our mouths, and the same way people mist their linens when they iron, we misted each other by spitting, spraying! Until you'd say: don't you get that in my eyes, you cunt! My mascara will run! And we'd twirl about in those crinolines of ours, twirl left and right until the whole thing keeled off. And we'd festoon ourselves with diamond collars and earrings, we'd stick sapphire-studded pins into our wigs, we'd adorn our fingers with rings, all of them! Beating each other black and blue over who got the biggest. And being the old queens that we are, decrepit, with withered scrags and double chins, we'd wear imitation necks made of plastic or whatever it was they made those imitation necks out of. That's right, imitation necks; didn't you ever read *The Coming Spring*, where those two aunties, Wiktoria and the other one, go off to the ball in Nawłoć wearing imitation necks, to enchant the world with their beauty one last time? And they'd wear artificial décolletages made of silicone... or, umm, they didn't have silicone back then, so they must have been made out of some other fake something or other, and on their necks they wore satin ribbons to cover the line where all that rubbish ended! That's right. Rich old bags decked out in tat, hands spotted with liverworts, dripping with diamonds... And the lads would be off bathing. And in the end I'd be sitting there on my throne, waiting for them. What's keeping them so long at the pond? Have they drowned?'

Further thunderclaps – it's raining cats and dogs. It's raining, it's raining and the sun is shining; in a moment a big gay rainbow will erupt over the beach – a sign that God has forgiven us! Perhaps we should hurl ourselves into the water like so many lemmings, so they can discover us later on the ecologically untainted beaches of Sweden? It's raining harder and harder, and we still have a ways to go, only at the green steps now, nothing up that way but woods and a lone Społem centre. I don't know if I've ever told you how obsessively afraid I am of lightning. I'm always certain I'll get struck by a flash of lightning. Basically we're all highly neurotic. That one's afraid of this, this one's afraid of that, and none of us can sleep a wink at night because of all our neuroses! Oh heavens, just listen to that noise, Paula, run, take to your heels! Shut up a second. Just shut your trap already! Look at them, a bunch of bedraggled witches, the way they're running off they'll lose their drawers, like the witches of Thessaly, or straight from the Sierra Morena! Look, but don't you stop running yourself! They forecast thunderstorms this morning, we should have returned to our rooms earlier! Of course they said we'd have fine weather, just not today. Oh my God, I've fucked up my foot! I can't run. Any more. Did I really need that last fag?

'And those lads would come back to us all fresh and clean, but just so they don't get too familiar, we won't receive them in that hall where Princess Lubomirska was, but in the inferior one, where the stewards go.'

'In the pipe-smoking room.'

'Yes, in the smoking room.'

'And we won't serve them with our good Baranówka family china. Maybe in something from Ćmielów.'

'What kind of twat would use the Ćmielów china?'

'Are you out of your fucking mind? What would you serve them with? Those clay pots from Cepelia? So they'll go down and tell the whole village that they eat like peasants in the palace of the Marquis de Merteuil?'

'Here!' – they locked horns – 'Now you have something to serve those lads with.'

'And they'll just sit there, too embarrassed to ask why they've been invited to dine at such an august table; it'll take vodka to loosen their lips, so that finally they pipe up:

"An invitation from a gentleman like you! But what reason do you have, sire, for inviting us?"

'And they'll still be wondering what it's all about until eventually they whisper slyly to each other:

"The gentlemen fear a peasant rebellion, the gentlemen mock us behind our backs!"

'And I'll answer mine, so he doesn't think we're just placating the peasants or that we're afraid of plebeian unrest in the villages:

"So Łukasz can give my back a good scrub, that's why." Then I'll lead him to the bath with my wrist as limp as a wet cravat.'

'They didn't have baths in the Baroque era, they simply powdered their spots, and when they began to stink they perfumed themselves, and when they got a spot they either painted over it or had it removed...'

'You know, we haven't been in the Baroque for quite some time. We've moved on. We have baths! So anyway, I infuse the bath with all those salts I brought back from Baden-Baden. He won't even know what they're for. Then I'll disrobe, placing my imitation neck next to the bath together with my ersatz bosom, and I'll enter the water wearing only my lace knickers, and he'll be standing there with his hands clasped behind his back...'

'And me?'

'What do you mean: you?'

'Well, what will I be doing all this time?'

'You?' Paula thinks. 'You'll be with yours in your room. You'll just have to make something up... I'll be busy saying things like this to mine:

'"You know, my dear, dear Łukasz, if you simply close your eyes, a fellow can imagine anything at all, even that he's with a woman..." And then I'll start to undress him like a commoner, ripping off all those simple, linen rags of his, and then I'll pull him into the water with me! He'll experience fellatio for the first time. Then later he'll question me, what and how and whether or not he needs to tell the parish priest about it, and I'll say:

'"Did the priest ever say anything in his sermons about doing it with other lads? If he didn't, that means it isn't a sin! But if you dare breathe a word about me to the priest, I'll smash your head in! Punch you right in your face, I will!" Anyway, even if he were to say something, it's a priest we're talking about... (stop winking, Paula). So it's like in the family... Everyone sitting round, playing cards together... Do you remember how in Gombrowicz's *Ferdydurke* he only had problems because he wanted to "fraternise"? But if all he had wanted was to have sex with a farmhand, it would have been written off as an aristocratic caprice.'

'He'll blab all about it.'

'No, he won't. In the morning he'll go home back to the family hovel and his mother, slicing bread in the countryside. One of those women who're wider than they are tall, like in *The Peasants*. A fire

331

burning in the hearth. She's furious, glaring out the corner of her eye, cutting an enormous loaf of bread, and says:

"'Where ye been, boy? At court all night?"

"'Aye, Ma, his lordship and another lord made me and Łukasz stay the whole night in the castle with them...'"

"'And what did you do there? Spit it out! On the hop from work were ye?!'"

"'Can't really talk about it now, Mother...'"

'She furrows her brows, her knitted brow, and can hardly control herself:

"'You spit it out now or I'll clobber you one, boy!"

"'Eh, I don't know if I...'"

"'Tell me now! Or I'll take this stick and...'"

"'His lordship called me to him like he was a woman, he wanted me to wash his back...'"

'Then she puts down her knife and runs over to him:

"'I'll thump ye, spawn! I'll thump ye, dunderhead, ye dunce, if ye ever dare say things like that about the squire! It's very well for ye to be thick as a ditch, but all of us is in his pocket, and it's a long time afore the harvest. If the old man loses his work hauling logs and the potatoes, we'll be turned out, all because of ye and your addled brains! How dare ye blather such things about our lordship, and before the harvest at that!"

'See? So take that, darling, and put that in one pan of the scales, and in the other put those gay bars of yours ...'

Heavens, look how it's pouring, Paula. Let's go, we'll take cover here, in the Społem Centre, with all those choice, luxury jellies straight out of the refrigerator, with all those locally bottled bevies. It's pouring, it's raining cats and dogs, but eventually it will rain itself out and then stop, and tomorrow the weather will be beautiful. Beautiful is what they said on Radio Zed. And that is that.

## UFO

But Paula, this is no normal storm, I'm serious… Those weird purple streaks of lightning look like… And what's that saucer thing that
landed on the dunes? What a bit of rubbish, Paula! Seriously, that
saucer has blinking lights on it! Like something dreamed up by a
crazy ufologist! Blinking in the ultraviolet light of lightning bolts
like a stroboscopic advisor to the department of planetary fellatio!
What rubbish, that is *too much*! *Le Gendarme et le UFO!* Help! The
hatch on top of the vehicle is opening and a little green man is coming out. With antennae on top of his head. And Prada moonboots
on. There, Wisława, there, Zdzisław, is your chance! Why are you
hesitating? Then Zdzisia walks up to him and starts fumbling
around the flies on his overalls. But that's no flies, and what's worse,
Zdzisia gets zapped by electricity! Eventually the little flap thing falls
off, but there's nothing inside, just that eerie ultraviolet light. Maybe
something will spring out, like the cuckoo in an old-fashioned
cuckoo clock: Here I am, blow me! But no, nothing. Like an empty
suit of armour. So now Wisława decides she's going to examine it
and compare versions. Find out the truth about their anatomy.
Maybe they have it somewhere else? Some elongated thing erupting

from under an armpit or something? Oh heavens! And round the back, what's that? A tail? But she gets zapped by electricity, too, when she attempts to put her mouth around it. Then laughter. Space laughter. As if it were coming from deep inside a tin.

It's another civilisation after all.

## Paula and Her Phone Calls (II)

Brring – brring – brring! It's Anna calling:

'Paula, what's going on? The whole country is in a flap!'

'What happened? But be quick, I'm on my way to see *Carmen* at the opera...'

'Your correspondence with Michalina was discovered by this bit of grunt who stole the letters and published them!'

'What?!'

'Everything, everything, all that fatuous twaddle – published! People know about everything now! About the blowjobs, everything, all of it! And just look what happened to Michalina! First they threw her out of every place they could, out of the university, and then they took all her money, but what's worse, she's contracted some kind of leprosy! She's lost an eye, half her face is covered in boils, she must be having a relapse... Michalina escaped back to Switzerland last night, to Zurich. She took the family silver and diamonds with her. She left behind a sea of debts – never settled her accounts, never paid her taxes... But on the road her diligence was overtaken by a band of Gypsies; they wanted to abduct her and take her to a harem, but the moment they unfurled the black veil the moon's light fell on what was left of her face, and, horrified by her hideousness they took her for a witch and decided to drown her in one of the Swiss lakes. Michalina told me all about it herself on her mobile! And she had some other misadventures there as well. Oh the things I could tell you. Reportedly she was spotted in the desert with some Arabs, there are these clans there, a load of bollocks, Kurps or something, Uzbeki Kashubs… She was abducted by this Uzbek Arab, the clan chieftain; they wanted to kill her, but she gave him her laptop as a peace offering, started up Windows Vista, and said it was Allah himself talking to them from the box! That desert turned out to be one big sex party, and she had so much sex she got this disease where you get sand up your arse. How true that is I have no idea, don't even ask, suffice it to say Michalina never made it to Zurich, she ended up going on foot to Roulettenburg, and now she's there playing pontoon on the slot machines, and roulette… She's saving her money for plastic surgery! She's never coming back, they say, and she's done with writing, too.'

'What?! We were supposed to be going to the opera, I was just wondering what was keeping her!'

'Michalina's in Roulettenburg, girl! Don't even bother going to the opera, because all of Wrocław is talking about one thing only, and they'll only heckle you! Go straightaway to Michalina, take only what you need, every moment counts! Quick, go to Chrobot Reisen, your car leaves at eight from the Hotel Wrocław, and off you go to Switzerland! Everything, all of it, all that arsing about, the people know about everything. Everything, Paula, everything!'

'Ha! Ha! Ha!'

# TRANSLATOR'S AFTERWORD

The first edition of *Lovetown* appeared in Polish bookstores, as *Lubiewo*, in early 2005, and its author was immediately acclaimed for his droll, sharp-witted, and inventive language and for bringing to light an unknown subculture of communist-era Poland. A second, revised edition of the book followed on the heels of the first, then an even more substantially revised third edition, and then a fourth... Within three years, six published editions had appeared. Most of this revising took place in Part II, where many of the stories are based on telephone interviews with relics of the pre-1989 Wrocław gay scene, who contacted Witkowski after the book was first published. In fact, much of the work is based on real people and their stories; but *Lovetown* nevertheless remains a work of the imagination, not of reportage – one index of this being the author's fictionalisation of himself in the narrative (the real Michał Witkowski, who was born in 1975, was hardly old enough to have trolled gay bars and cruising grounds in the 1980s).

It would be difficult to recreate among English-language readers the reception that *Lovetown* has had in Poland, where it was hailed, despite Witkowski's own reservations, as the first Polish queer novel. This is not because it is the first Polish book to represent homosexuality (it is not), but because, as critic Błażej Warkocki points out, after reading *Lovetown* it is no longer possible to overlook the queer sensibilities or situations present in earlier Polish literature. Witkowski refers to his predecessors throughout the book, above all Witold Gombrowicz and Miron Białoszewski. The opening words proposed by Lucretia at the beginning – 'The Countess left the house at half past nine in the evening' – are in fact a rewriting of the famous first line of Białoszewski's *Reports on Reality* (1973). More importantly, there are numerous passages in Witkowski's prose that invoke those two writers on the level of language, the implicit argument being that their queerness is as much a stylistic as a biographical category.

Readers in countries that have had gay-and-lesbian sections in bookstores and on publishers' lists, gays and lesbians openly and positively represented in the media, and officially licensed gay pride marches over the past three decades, may not grasp *Lovetown*'s watershed quality in its original context, nor the complexity of the position it represents. In the years since Poland's accession to the European Union in 2004, Polish gays and lesbians have been increasingly visible, but also increasingly subject to rancour and violence from conservative quarters; and their civil rights have been a primary testing ground for Poland's adoption of the secular civic values of the EU. One might then expect this so-called 'first Polish queer novel' to more closely resemble the book proposed by the volleyball-playing lad on the beach, the one about the gay couple who are thwarted in their ambitions to adopt a son (and must settle for a cat instead). But the author of *Lovetown* is less interested in calling for the emancipation of gays in Poland than in giving voice to a 'doubly marginalised' community, one whose subversiveness is, like that of the 'luminaries of affliction' in Genet's *Our Lady of the*

*Flowers* or the 'doomed queens' of Andrew Holleran's *Dancer From the Dance*, a matter of aestheticised behaviour and elocution rather than political action or discourse. In the long run, it is not necessary to be familiar with specifics of the book's Polish context; the worlds described in *Lovetown* are not limited geographically or historically, but exist wherever class and disenfranchisment are at issue and where language, gesture, and the imagination are deployed as means of survival.

Despite such universal qualities, Witkowski's own language presents certain challenges for translation. *Lovetown* is rife with words and phrases that are so culturally coded that they elicit immediate laughs of recognition from Polish readers, but for the same reason often fall flat when rendered literally into English. One such word is *emerytka*, which means 'lady pensioner' and evokes an image of the dour and ubiquitous women employees of communist-era shops, restaurants, post offices and workers' cultural centres, etc., who now constitute another 'doubly marginalised' group in capitalist Poland. But there is also something both quaint and campy about the word, especially when applied to men of a certain age (one imagines a communist-era shop staffed with drag queens); and that quality comes through quite well, I think, in the term 'old dear', which was recommended by Andrew Wille.

Another word, almost as difficult to translate, is *luj*, which is unfamiliar even to most gay Polish readers, and for that reason has been rendered not as 'trade', the usual English term for straight men who dally with homosexuals, but with 'grunt', an American idiom for a very low-level soldier, which, suggested by Philip Gwyn Jones, has been 'retooled' for this British context given its resonances with the Russian soldiers and with the noise itself. The Polish word *ciota*, a variant of the word for 'aunt', is used throughout the book to refer to a doubly marginalised homosexual, in contrast with the mainstream, westernised *gej* (gay man). I have generally translated it as 'queen'; but as it is somewhat more pejorative than that English word, it occasionally appears as 'poofter', 'poof', or 'queer' as well.

An expression that proved impossible to translate, but that is worth explicating since it illustrates how 'over the top' Witkowski's own writing can get, is the phrase *ciotowski bicz*, which I've rendered in the first instance, the title of Part II of the book, as 'the lewd beach' – a pun on 'nude beach' suggested by Antonia Lloyd-Jones – and in the second as 'lewd bitch', where it refers to the Apothecaress. The phrase plays on the antiquated epithet *dziadowski bicz*, which figuratively means 'spoilt brat', but literally means something like 'beggar's whip' or 'old man's whip', *dziadowski* deriving from *dziad* – a word for old man, beggar, or grandfather that resonates with Adam Mickiewicz's Romantic drama *Dziady* (Forefathers' Eve). The transformation here of *dziadowski* into *ciotowski* – which comes from *ciota* – thus literally involves a bit of linguistic cross-dressing. Adding to the complexity, the word *bicz*, which means 'whip', is an interlingual pun on the two English words 'beach' and 'bitch'. Clearly, this phrase was not going to make it out of Polish, but it is worth examining anyway because it illustrates in a nutshell Witkowski's poetics of exaggeratedly 'queering' language itself.

One last thing that might not be obvious to English-language readers is that with few exceptions the places mentioned in *Lovetown* are in the western part of Poland, that is, in an area that from the eighteenth century until the end of World War II had been part of Germany, and after the war, resettled by Poles from what is now the Ukraine, remained contested territory until the 1970s. Most of those cities and towns have a second, German name lurking in their past – for Wrocław it is Breslau, for Poznań Posen, for Lubiewo Lubau, for Legnica Liegnitz, etc. – just as Lucretia, Patricia, Jessica and the other queens all have masculine names in their papers. One might think of this double order of double names as an index for the inextricability and volatility of gender and nationality; at any rate, the real Lovetown, wherever one finds it, is a place where the order of things is quickly subverted and identity is never fixed.

Ryszard Kapuściński has written that reportage is the form of writing 'most reliant on the collective'; but I would argue that translation is even more so. In that respect, I have been extremely fortunate to have had help with this work from its editors and external readers. In addition to the huge debts of gratitude I owe to Andrew Wille, who localised the entire manuscript for British readers, and to Tasja Dorkofikis, *Lovetown*'s editor, for her patience and vision, I would also like to thank Antonia Lloyd-Jones and Jasper Tilbury, who were enormously helpful in vetting and offering suggestions for sections of the book; Agata Bielik-Robson, Jessie Labov, Joanna Niżyńska, Bożena Shallcross, Piotr Sommer and Błażej Warkocki, for their particular and general insights into it; Kinga Maciejewska, Witek Turopolski, Justyna Beinek, Agata Grenda and Marcin Pasek, who as native informants helped in answering specific queries; Susan Harris, Shaun Levin and Jeremy Davies, who commented on and published extracts of the translation (in *Words without Borders*, *Chroma Journal* and Dalkey Archive's *Best European Fiction 2010* anthology respectively); Stefan Ingvarsson, the book's Swedish translator, who provided helpful insights and support, and whose Swedish translation I consulted; Christina Marie Hauptmeier, whose German translation I also consulted; Ilay Halpern and Jan Jeništa, for discussing their translations of the book into Hebrew and Czech respectively; Zhenya Bershtein, for a useful account of Yuri Chainikov's Russian translation; the participants in the translation workshop led by Michael Henry Heim at the University of Chicago in April 2008; Moshe Shushan, Chris Pappas, Susan Bernofsky, Christian Hawkey and Uljana Wolf, Tomasz Markiewicz, Sunder Ganglani and especially Antonia Lloyd-Jones for their friendship and support; Izabela Kaluta of the Polish Book Institute, who initially drew my attention to the book; Michał Witkowski, for his patience and helpfulness in answering queries, and for permitting me to listen to the recorded telephone interviews he made with protoypical Old Queens; and Portobello publisher Philip Gwyn Jones and editor Christine Lo, for their commitment to this book and to literature in translation.

W. Martin

*For more background information about* Lovetown, *please see www.portobellobooks.com*